# GALAXY'S EDGE
## EDITED BY MIKE RESNICK

I0520627

ISSUE 25: MARCH 2017

Mike Resnick, Editor
Taylor Morris, Copyeditor
Shahid Mahmud, Publisher

Published by Arc Manor/Phoenix Pick
P.O. Box 10339
Rockville, MD 20849-0339

*Galaxy's Edge* is published in January, March, May, July, September, and November.

www.GalaxysEdge.com

*Galaxy's Edge* is an invitation-only magazine. We do not accept unsolicited manuscripts. Unsolicited manuscripts will be disposed of or mailed back to the sender (unopened) at our discretion.

Available by subscription (www.GalaxysEdge.com) or through your favorite online store (Amazon.com, BN.com, etc.).

ISBN: 978-1-61242-344-9

Advertising in the magazine is available. Quarter page (half column), $95 per issue. Half page (full column, vertical or two half columns, horizontal) $165 per issue. Full page (two full columns) $295 per issue. Back Cover (full color) $495 per issue. All interior advertising is in black and white.

Please write to advert@GalaxysEdge.com.

**FOREIGN LANGUAGE RIGHTS:** Please refer all inquiries pertaining to foreign language rights to Shahid Mahmud, Arc Manor, P.O. Box 10339, Rockville, MD 20849-0339. Tel: 1-240-645-2214. Fax 1-310-388-8440. Email admin@ArcManor.com.

## Contents

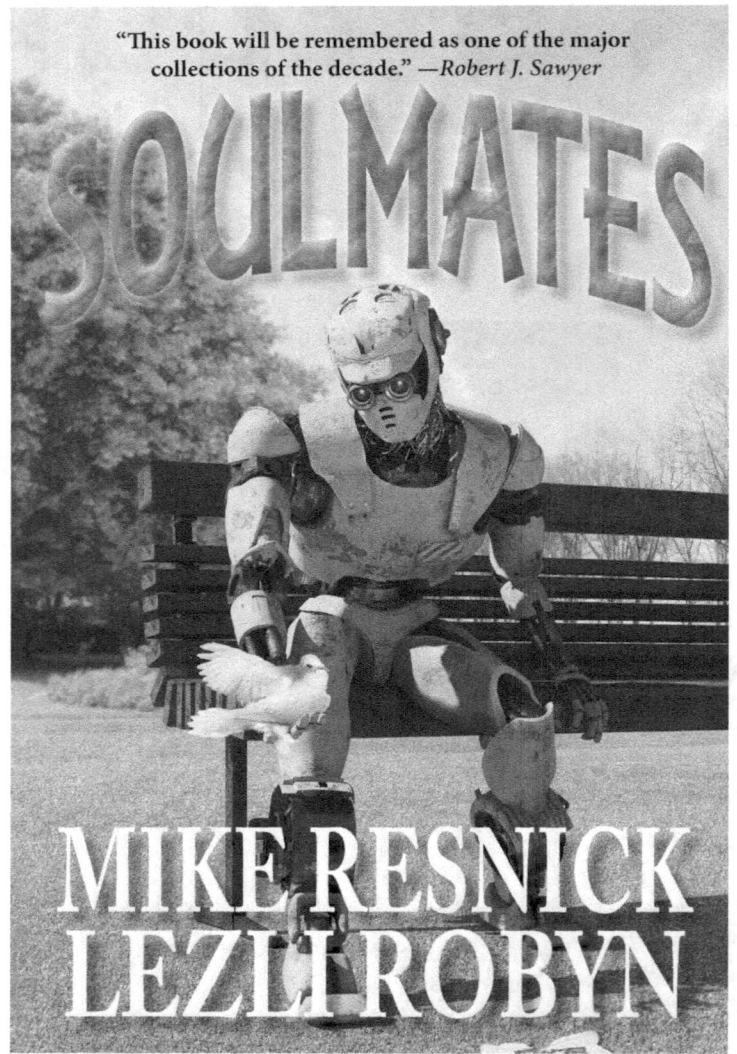

"This book will be remembered as one of the major collections of the decade." —*Robert J. Sawyer*

"…a satisfying sampler of solid stories from a team that rarely disappoints." —**Publishers Weekly**

"This book will be remembered as one of the major collections of the decade."—**Robert J. Sawyer**

"Standouts include…Mike Resnick and Lezli Robyn's beautifully sad "Benchwarmer," which takes us into the world of imaginary friends, and introduces us to one friend who simply can't let go of the boy who created him." (on "Soulmates")—*io9*

"In a classic example of cognitive estrangement, we learn the absurdity of our own cultural norms as seen by those on the outside…effectively played to humorous effect." (on "Report from the Field")—**SFSignal**

Multiple award-winning authors, Mike Resnick and Lezli Robyn, get to the heart of the matter in Soulmates, which showcases all the words they have penned together over their years as collaborators (with a bonus solo piece by each). Whether a robot, alien, some kind of supernatural being or human, rising above our prejudices and ignorance allows us to make emotional connections that can have a profound effect on our lives.

Each of these stories examine a facet of the simple, yet incredibly complex, concept of companionship. They will make you laugh; will make you cry…but most importantly they will make you look at the very basic notion of soul-mates in a different light.

# THE EDITOR'S WORD

## by Mike Resnick

Welcome to the twenty-fifth issue of *Galaxy's Edge*. We've got some fine stories by newcomers (and relative newcomers) Tina Gower, Samantha Murray, Alex Shvartsman, Andrea G. Stewart, Brennan Harvey, Sunil Patel, George Nikolopoulos, and Yaroslav Barsukov, as well as a few by old friends Robert Silverberg, Kay Kenyon, Kevin J. Anderson, and Kristine Kathryn Rusch. We've also got part two of the Robert A. Heinlein novel we're serializing, *Double Star,* plus our regulars: recommended books by Bill Fawcett & Jody Lynn Nye, science by Greg Benford, literary matters by Barry N. Malzberg, and Joy Ward's interview (this issue with Ye Editor).

There's lots to enjoy. Just dig in.

✧

Ever hear of Joe Esterhaus?

No reason why you should. He doesn't know that *Galaxy's Edge* exists. As far as I know, he's never read a word of science fiction.

I know about *him*, though. The reason I know is because he makes well over a million dollars a screenplay, often multiples of a million, and is one of the very few writers, even in an industry that seems to play with Monopoly money, to pull down that kind of fee.

Ever hear of Tom Cruise? Brad Pitt? George Clooney? Harrison Ford? Julia Roberts? Sandra Bullock?

Sure you have. They make ten million or more per film, plus a piece of the gross—and that, of course, has nothing to do with the quality of the film. Film bombs, film makes no sense, film has an IQ that would freeze water (and they've all made their share of them), they get their money anyway.

So what does this have to do with science fiction?

Bear with me while I explain.

Recently Carol and I rented some *Tales of Tomorrow* DVDs from Netflix. That's a show that was run from 1951 to 1953, starting when we were nine years old. It was in black and white, of course, always performed live (and you wouldn't believe how many professional actors, from Lee J. Cobb on down, muffed their lines), and boasted a series of young actors like Paul Newman who became household names.

About one in every seven episodes was pretty good, always allowing for the minimal budget and live performances by unprepared actors. About one in seven was acceptable. And about five in seven were unwatchable.

Moral: if the story is dumb, an actor, no matter how good he is, can't make it any smarter.

Then we tried *Suspense*, from 1949. Another nice batch of actors: kids like Newman and Charlton Heston, established stars like Lilli Palmer and Boris Karloff.

Not just bad, but embarrassingly, snicker-out-loud bad. Even those brilliant actors couldn't save it.

Finally, for her birthday, I got Carol a complete set of bootleg DVDs of the fondly-remembered but never-released two-year, seventy-eight episode run of *Science Fiction Theater* from 1955 to 1957, a time when most purported science fiction movies were actually anti-science and usually ended with lines such as "There are some things man was not meant to know." *Science Fiction Theater* was like a breath of fresh air, because it was clearly of the opinion that there is *nothing* man wasn't meant to know or learn. Each of these shows was introduced by Truman Bradley in a state-of-the-art lab (circa 1955) that I would kill to play in. He'd show a couple of related cutting-edge experiments, and then explain that the episode you were about to see extrapolated from the experiments he'd just demonstrated. No stars at all. Probably the biggest names were Warren Stevens and John Howard, a couple of journeyman B-movie actors.

And the shows were pretty damned good. Hell, for the time they were remarkably good.

And they were good for a simple reason: the producer understood that without a good script, all the stars in the world can't turn a sow's ear into a silk purse.

The principle still holds true today. Take a look at the latest Indiana Jones film. Got a huge superstar—Harrison Ford. Got the most powerful director in history—Stephen Spielberg. Got the most successful producer in history—George Lucas. Got a laughably bad script. End result: a laughably bad film. So bad it gave rise to a comment among screenwriters: "Nuke the fridge." Which is to say, when you run out of things to do, lock the hero in a refrigerator and nuke it.

It was true in 1949, and in 1955, and it's true today: every play and every movie starts with The Word. You ignore the words and you'd better be making a silent film or a ballet, or else you're in deep trouble from the get-go. Writers know that; television and movie executives still haven't figured it out.

Let me close with a wonderful (and true) story:

The great director Frank Capra was giving an interview to a few members of the press back in the 1940s, talking about how he put the famed "Capra Touch" on this scene and that…and finally his screenwriter could stand it no more. He walked over with a ream of blank paper, tossed it on the startled director's desk, and snapped: "Here! Put this Capra touch on *this!*"

A lesson worth remembering.

*Samantha Murray has appeared in* Escape Pod, Beneath Ceaseless Skies, Daily Science Fiction, Flash Fiction Online, *and elsewhere. This is her first appearance in* Galaxy's Edge.

## BRAGGING RITES

### by Samantha Murray

It was Tuesday and it was raining out and it was Carla's father's funeral. Carla sat up the back with her ankles crossed, and wished her gray dress didn't itch quite so much, and wished that she hadn't come.

She probably wouldn't have come if Paula hadn't pushed her. "Go," Paula had said. "Go. This can't be something you regret." Carla was in the habit of listening to Paula, who was usually right. Usually. And Paula had been all stern and forceful and Carla had loved her for the adamant little crease in her brow.

The only funeral Carla had been to before this was Aunt Janine's. Aunt Janine had regaled the mourners with the prizes she had won for her orchids, all nineteen awards, and the details of each, and who'd had to make do with runner up. She'd spent quite a lot of time describing how she'd perfected the art of making scones. She told everyone how she'd been quite the stunner in her youth with her hair up.

Carla scratched at her dress under her arm and shifted on her seat. Apart from a few murmurs the amassed crowd were growing silent, waiting.

Paula had said that she'd heard of one funeral where the deceased woman had shown up with nothing to say. That she'd sat there, and blinked for a while, then disappeared. But Carla didn't think her father would be the sort to . . .

There. A light at the front of the room, subdued as though it was being pulled back in on itself, but there. And then Carla saw that the light was actually a man and that the man was her father.

He looked young. Or rather, he didn't look any older than he had when she'd last seen him, which was twenty years ago.

He was handsome too, looking not at the crowd in front of him but up and out somewhere far away, his skin burnished with the glowing.

"I was always a clever lad," began her father, his voice rich with the timbre it'd had when he'd been living, "I knew how to find my feet no matter what life threw at me." He told tales of his childhood, painting himself as the lovable rogue who always won in the end. Clara could remember some of those stories.

Paula had been to more than her share of funerals. "They're making a narrative of their life," she'd said when Carla had asked her about it, asked why they left so much out. "They don't want to cast themselves as the villain, no matter what they've done. This is how they want to be remembered."

Clara's father wanted to be remembered, apparently, for his prowess on the cricket field, for his success in business; closing deals through the charisma of his personality alone, for the way the ladies had pursued him.

They probably had. He had cheated on Clara's mother after all.

*Paula was wrong,* thought Clara, *I shouldn't have come.* Yet she couldn't take her eyes from his face. Had his eyes always been that blue or was it the glow behind them?

Her father told the truth, Clara knew that was one thing the dead all did. They didn't lie. But his truth was not her truth.

In the pauses in her father's story Clara read her own subtext.

Her father told of his sense of adventure and discoveries; his *absence*.

His jokes and escapades; his *harshness*.

Being life of the party; his *drinking*.

The things her father didn't say fell like stones, sinking down into the river of her past without a splash.

Her father was quieter now, and harder to see. People were starting to fidget, ready to leave.

"I had a family once," said Clara's father, his voice only a murmur in the fading light. His outline blurred into the background, but by the tilt of his head he could have been looking straight at Clara. The dead couldn't see you, everyone said. Not properly.

He didn't say anything else for a long time, and Clara wasn't sure she could still see him, although she kept her gaze fixed on the spot where his eyes had been. The people to the side of her stood up and made their way out.

"I wish I'd done better," Clara's father said.

And Clara sat alone, right at the back as everyone else left, sitting still, very still, and thinking of her father, and one of his truths.

*Copyright © 2017 by Samantha Murray*

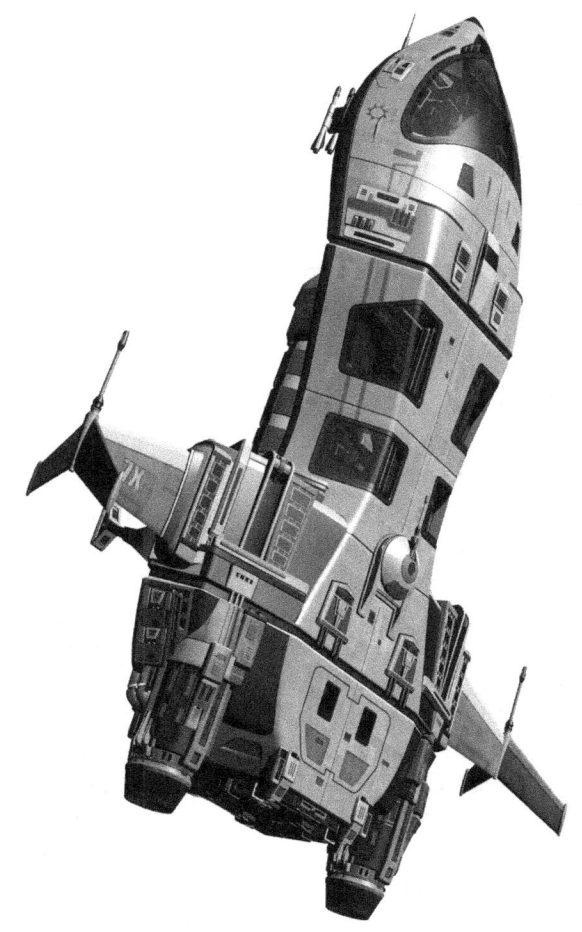

*Sunil Patel's work has appeared in* Asimov's Science Fiction, *Fantastic Stories of the Imagination, Clockwork Phoenix 5,* Flash Fiction Online, Genius Loci: Tales of the Spirit Place, *and elsewhere. This is his second appearance in* Galaxy's Edge.

# THE TRAGEDY OF THE DEAD IS THAT THEY CANNOT CRY

## by Sunil Patel

The tragedy of the dead is that they cannot cry. They may laugh, despite having no lungs. They may speak, despite having no vocal cords. They may do many things that should not be possible without physical bodies. But the creation, the excretion of tears is impossible in their non-corporeal form. Jonathan has been dead for fifteen years but he has never felt this dysfunction more acutely than at Rosita's funeral.

The shades gather by her grave at midnight to mourn her passing. The scent of memorial flowers reaches only Rosita, the single living person in the cemetery. Only she feels the chill of the wind like a welcome home. It has been three days since she passed, and she returns to allow them to pay their respects. Jonathan whispers into Troy's ear: "I don't remember the last thing I said to her."

"We were gonna go trick-or-treating next week," says Troy. "Just watch the kids, ya know? Our one night out a year."

"I guess she can go herself now," says Jonathan. He only knew her in passing, but she was a part of this community, this family of spirits who accepted him more than his own family. Those he thought of as friends in life were only acquaintances in comparison. Even the one friend who died, and Jonathan was able to cry for him. That is, after all, what one does at a funeral. Troy, a young man but an old soul, has been around almost as long as Rosita and has attended many funerals. He needs no tears to mourn his friend because he knows his grief to be real. He will be giving the eulogy in a moment.

"Never gets easier. Life, death, life again. Transitions, right? Always leavin' people behind."

Jonathan is surrounded by those who loved Rosita more than he, and their grief emanates like a strong perfume. This invisible miasma contains every story from every shade, every connection they made with her that he did not. It seeps into him, artificial, and he suddenly cannot understand all the things he will never get to do with Rosita. She will never direct him to the wrong gravestone, either on purpose or because she simply isn't paying attention. She will never describe to him in graphic detail the circumstances of her death, but with added puns. She will never say, "Hey, Jonathan, you know that star's been dead longer than me?" That is something she once told Troy.

Now she stands by her gravestone, the moonlight illuminating her light brown skin rather than passing through it. New flesh for a new life. He should be happy for her Second Chance. She's going to a better place, the others say, but deep down they fear a Second Chance of their own. To be pulled from one state of existence to another? Once is enough for a lifetime. Jonathan doesn't want to return, not after only fifteen years. You can't always get what you want, in life or in death.

Jonathan does not want this grief inside him. He has not earned it. But he cannot force it out through his tears, as he could when he was alive. He watched a movie whose name has faded from his memory, a movie that made him sob so strongly he couldn't read the credits. It felt good, that release, those false emotions. False emotions plague him once again, and he wants them to be real, or get out.

Yet neither of these options will truly resolve his conflict. Although he does not comprehend how much Rosita mattered—matters—to him, he cannot appropriate others' feelings. Nor can he be without his own. To have no feelings would be disrespectful to her.

Troy begins his eulogy, and he delivers it straight to Rosita, though she cannot hear him. Having crossed the border, she has severed their line of communication. She is no longer one of them, and even though it was not by her choice, Jonathan mildly resents her for it. For leaving them. The second chance he wants is to know her like Troy does. To have done the things he will never do. He misses most of what

Troy is saying as he struggles to find a memory to induce impossible tears.

But then Rosita speaks in the middle of Troy's eulogy. She cannot see or hear him so she has no idea.

"Guys, I think you can hear me. We could hear the living before, so if I…count now, hey." She scans the graveyard, unwittingly locking gazes with so many shades, including Jonathan. "I'm going to miss you guys. Really miss you. I'll come visit when I can, okay?" Rosita chokes on the last word, a feeling she has not experienced in over a hundred years.

Troy isn't sure whether she's finished. He wants to continue his remembrance, his futile praise of her that he should have given when she was dead.

"Troy, find me next week. I'll find us some kids to follow, somehow." Tears form in her eyes, and she wipes them away, looks at her damp fingers. "It shouldn't have been me. I didn't want this."

Rosita breaks.

Her face shimmers as a century of loss pours out. She cried coming into the world and she cries now as she returns to it. This time, however, she knows what she is leaving behind. Each tear is for one of them, thinks Jonathan. He chooses one, watches it roll down her nose, past her newly reddened lips, and fall to the earth. That is his tear. He traces its path down his own face, forging a new connection between him and his friend.

One day, if he ever gets his Second Chance, he will cry for Rosita, as she cried for him.

*Copyright © 2017 by Sunil Patel*

*Kay Kenyon is the author of more than a dozen novels, including The Entire and the Rose quartet. She is both a Campbell Award and a Philip K. Dick Award nominee.*

## THE LOYAL ORDER OF BEASTS

### by Kay Kenyon

*P*aco dreams. In sleep, the boy falls into the kingdom of enchantment where roam fantastical beasts, gatekeepers, dragons, and helpful allies. Where escape is always a wish away, as unicorns leap from their corrals, and maidens rappel from their turrets. And when a boy meets a hungry dragon, he will figure something out.

*When Paco wakes, the night visions evaporate like soap bubbles popping. That is a rule of the Realm. You cannot stand in both kingdoms at once.*

Grendel shifted in his chair, trying to get his old bones comfortable, waiting for his number to be called, trying to salvage another bad poker hand. Through magic, he could conjure a royal flush, but his poker buddies expected more of him. He was Grendel, monster of legend. A big deal once, and long ago. Did you have to live up to what you used to be? That was always the question for legends.

Most of the guys in the lodge were has-beens, sitting around playing cards instead of off on adventures. Unlike the self-important, inflated egos of the Realm who indulged in tedious replays of their quests, the Loyal Order of Beasts committed itself to good works, bringing a little magic into the Mundane World. In dreams.

Grendel glanced at the mirror on the wall, hoping to see his number appear, but so far, no such luck.

He and his poker buddies, Rudy and Polyphemus, had been lodge members so long they'd worn their chairs into the shape of their butts, a far cry from the glory days of heroism and epic meaning. These days *heroic* was out of favor, corny even. All that mattered to the new breed was box office on the latest movie, toy store tie-ins, and gross receipts. The fickle mantle of fame. Grendel could tell them how fickle, but who listened anymore?

He glanced at the table in the corner where some of those new characters were playing a high-stakes game of one-eyed jacks. Slouching, cards held close to the chest, they glared at the mirror, sneering at folks whose numbers got called—a sad commentary on the state of lodge civility. This was a fraternal order after all, not a biker bar. Not that it was strictly *fraternal* anymore, either.

Rudy glanced up at Grendel. "So. You goin' to visit the little kid again?"

"If my number comes up, I am."

Rudy rolled his unlit cigar to the other side of his mouth. "Won't do any good. Kid's autistic."

"That's why he could use a little magic."

Rudy shrugged, allowing Grendel his point. In truth, the World needed the Realm. The Mundane World was bound by all those picky rules of science—rules that left the place pitifully short in the imagination department. So Realmers sneaked it in—into that shared ground of dreams where it could inspire mere humans. The World created the myths, and the Realm housed the resulting immortals. A neat little feedback loop. The connecting path was the Isthmus, a bridge between worlds, traditionally managed by the Loyal Order of Beasts.

Problem was, the World wasn't creating decent legends anymore. These days the Big Mundane produced mostly those media types; over-wrought, empty characters that arrived pumped up with their own hype. They usually took up the fast life, stomping around castles and battle fields, forcing a bunch of yokels to play bit parts to their star power. Who was that one slob from some action movie? Jaba something. Came into the Realm lording it over folks, whining and demanding attention . . . .

Rudy dealt Grendel another lousy card. Polyphemus was staring at his own hand with that single-eyed intensity only a cyclops could muster.

Looking around the room at his fellow beasts, Grendel had a sudden and unwelcome view of how seedy the lodge had become. The folding chairs, the shabby flourescents, the lingering smell of disinfectant soap. It used to be nicer, didn't it? For one thing, they didn't use to let in women. Whoever heard of a female scaring the bejesus out of you? Well, there was Baba Yaga, the Russian witch, living in that creepy house with the chicken legs. You couldn't

take a myth like her and foist her off on the women's auxiliary. Besides, women had improved the lodge. Decent food. The number system instead of pitched battles to decide whose turn for dream duty. It was better. Sort of.

At thoughts like these, he felt a familiar weight settle on his chest. The old ticker wasn't what it once was. The apothecary had given Grendel a potion, and he took it faithfully, immortal or not. Having a vial of medicine made him feel proactive. Because, all around him, the world was taking on dark little spots. In his peripheral vision, shadows gathered, but when he looked dead on—nothing. Disconcerting. What was it they said about not being able to identify a threat? It caused *anxiety*. Not a problem you'd ever have had in the old days. But it seemed to fit now.

"Gren," Rudy said, raising the ante, "you don't look so good."

"Yeah? And your mother was a troll." Grendel threw down a few coins, staying in the game.

Rudy put on a hurt face. "*I'm* a troll."

"Still."

Polyphemus rolled his eye. "Play cards."

Rudy tapped his unlit cigar on the table edge shaking off imaginary ash. Grendel had to admit the hall was better since the women banned smoking, second hand smoke being bad for the heart. Old guys like him had to be careful. Take those smells he was subject to lately for example. Spore-ridden, bloated smells like tuna sandwiches on the turn. They said weird smells could be a precursor thingy—an aura—before a seizure. Removing the vial from his pocket, he took a little nip.

"Your problem, Gren?" Rudy said, reading his mind. "You worry too much."

Rudy had a point. When had Grendel become such a downbeat? Immortals didn't have to worry about heart attacks and the like. And females in the lodge were nothing to get all bothered about, the way they played bridge and bet quarters. Kind of sweet.

No, if you wanted a real problem, it was those other guys. The new boys on the block, always lurking at that corner table. Their type was nothing more than slasher-hackers, getting story impact from gore and body counts. You take death, with its implications of sacrifice and transformation, and turn it into a bloodbath. Scary, yes. Uplifting, no. Grendel campaigned against them, but the twinks got their memberships. Rudy argued that the lodge needed new blood, and Polyphemus caved in too, despite the fact that the candidates hadn't even read *The Odyssey*.

Or *Beowulf*, for that matter.

The mirror on the wall lit up with a new number: eighty-one.

"That's me." Grendel folded his cards and pushed back his chair. As he stood, his heart clenched, like it just got an over-friendly handshake. He paused, getting steady.

Rudy waved the cigar at his friend. "Have a good one."

As Grendel passed the table of punks, one of them reached for a new card, knife-hands glinting. The rotten tuna smell was stronger here. These creeps could really use a bath.

Snip snip, came the sound in his wake. One of the morons waved his slasher hands at Grendel's big ass.

No respect.

☼

A silvery downpour ran over Grendel's scales as he entered the enchanted forest. That was strange, since it never rained in the Realm unless it was a trumped-up storm for, say, King Lear, who was so big on reenactments.

In front of the cave entrance, Grendel shook himself, scattering raindrops from his back. Looking around, he was surprised to find the cave unguarded. Bluebeard was usually the gatekeeper on duty. The fellow didn't have much else to do these days, now that it was mythically incorrect to menace young women—and now that those same damsels were as likely to burn his beard as take any crap from him.

Grendel conjured up a note, pinning it to the side of the cave: *What, you guys taking coffee breaks these days? Geez. Grendel.* Stunts like that made the Order look bad. In the old days . . .

Aw, the hell with the old days. He was eager to dream up a good one for Paco. That was one thing that never changed for the worse: kids—at least the little ones. Paco needed good dreams, if anyone did. Couldn't even recognize his parents' faces. Yeah, dream world was about all that kid had.

He hesitated before plunging into the abysmally dark entrance. Without Bluebeard's chattiness and shrewd pointers on Isthmus conditions, Grendel felt like a trespasser. Also, and annoyingly, he became acutely aware of his heart beating, and the thought occurred that if you paid attention to it, you'd throw it off stride, so to speak, causing little…what did they call thems—arrhythmias. He reached in his doublet for the vial and took a swig. Then he strode into the cave.

The Isthmus jumped into being, fanning out before him, about six spans wide, arcing into the smoky void of nowhereland. The bright surface of the bridge was quilted as though Here must be stitched to There every step of the way.

Grendel could see maybe a hundred yards down the Isthmus. When he got to the limit of his vision, as always, he would see another hundred. What was different these days was how his feet sank into the way-fabric and left impressions, like skin that has lost its elasticity. The Isthmus was growing weaker. And smaller. Every time you touched the sides—if you got tired and staggered, for example—the Isthmus got a little smaller. That's why the lodge needed the numbering system. Only room for a few crossings at a time.

In the glory days, the Realm and the World had freely mixed. He'd heard it said that the worlds began by overlapping, and had been separating ever since. Some expanding universe theory, or such like. These days, the Realms didn't touch, except in dreams. But over the millennia, the Isthmus suffered from too much traffic, such as from hoards of orcs and swarms of fairies, that sort of thing. All these picky rules for how the Real and the True could mix. Yeah, *Real* and *True*. The Mundane World was Real, all right. But the Realm was True, and if you didn't get it the first time you heard it, you never would.

Here before him were the footprints of Baba Yaga, her stiletto-heeled boots making a track like a zipper. It formed a rut, and not springing back, either, like it would have even a few dreams back.

"Grendel?"

He jumped, chest thudding.

A shadow on the side of the road wavered, then snapped into the form of a beefy white guy. He looked familiar.

Grendel staggered against the wall—he hadn't realized he'd strayed so far that way—and jerked his hand back from the forbidden contact.

"That you, Gren?" the man asked.

"Bluebeard?" Grendel approached the fellow. It was him, all right. But no beard. "What the hell happened to you?"

Bluebeard rubbed his chin, perhaps discovering for the first time that he had one. "He challenged me, this guy did. So what could I do, I just played along, you know how folks are about their little myth deals. He says, 'Gatekeeper, I come to slay you,' or some such, and I said, 'Well, have at it, asshole,' expecting the usual mock combat, and then the fucker ripped my beard off." His voice wavered as he patted his unfortunately receding chin. "That wasn't supposed to happen."

"Shit," Grendel said, feeling stupid that he couldn't think of something more empathetic.

"You're telling me?" Bluebeard looked incensed at Grendel's remark. "No skin off your nose if I lose the one thing I ever loved."

"Who was it that did it?"

"That punk. That guy with the mean manicure. We never should of let in somebody that couldn't even do the handshake. You know? And now here he is, taking your role, the stuff *you're* supposed to do."

"Tell me about it. I was against it from the start." Underneath his calm words, Grendel was thinking that nothing like this had ever happened before, and that the dark spots he'd been seeing were massing into a storm.

Meanwhile, Bluebeard was still dealing with his loss. His eyes pleaded with Grendel as he said, "I look just like a beefy white guy."

Grendel shook his head, denying it, though it was horribly true.

"What kind of person would *do* this?"

The words came to Grendel: "Someone who enjoys pain."

Confusion spread over Bluebeard's face. "The pain of personal growth? The pain of the betrayal of human love? What?"

"No. Pain for the sake of pain." Bluebeard was living a fairy tale. And that punk wasn't.

"Son of a bitch." Bluebeard pursued his lips. "I'd better get back to the entrance. I don't even know how I got here, but I'm on duty. None of the rest of those new guys are getting in."

"Good man," Grendel said. "But one thing? I need that book of yours." Despite the beard fracas, the gatekeeper still had the huge tome tucked under his arm. "You wrote down who's gone in and what their assignments were?"

Bluebeard nodded, handing the book over. "Going after the asshole, huh?"

Grendel looked down the length of the Isthmus, in the direction of the World. "A scary dream is one thing, but the scare has to *mean* something. If these guys are just into nightmares, I'm going to drum 'em out of the Order."

He took a little nip from the vial to steady himself. Brave talk. But now that he'd said it, he had to do it. Unlike in the Real, in the True you always kept your word.

☼

The longer he walked, the madder Grendel got. The Order had been slipping from its high standards for eons. Little lapses, small compromises. Then big ones, like letting in the movie monsters, ending with the nadir of popular taste: slashers and hackers. In that slow decline, you never got your Big Test or Final Battle. It was honor lost in increments. Like the science-types said, entropy prevails. To keep a state of order, effort must be applied. Without work, a hero dissipated into commonality, even in the Realm.

He was forced to admit that this dissipation described himself, too. And, worse, he'd known it, all these years. That ticker problem? It was nothing but his immortal body wincing in disgust.

Sweat dripped from his brow as he stopped to check the book. He was nearing the end of the bridge, and would have to make his insertion accurately. His claw traced down the page, *Laing, Zlotnick, Le Sueur, Castillo, Dowling, Lopez. . .* this guy had been busy.

Grendel would begin at the top of the list, with Laing. He hazed his vision, altering his focus for that dimensional catapult into the kingdom of dreams. Then he moped his brow and, filled with the energy that comes from a good dose of indignation, made the jump.

Laing, Laing: looking for a dreaming Laing . . . . Through the haze of the dream state, Grendel could see Laing's back porch where the man had been sleeping to escape the South Carolina heat. But there was no dreaming Laing, only a pervasive smell of wrongness. The porch screens held back one hundred and eleven mosquitoes, their feet picking across the mesh in a delicate longing for blood. But the punk had gotten there first.

Laing's fine dark skin had once held this mundane man together—but now all that remained was a red debris and the smell of death. Grendel had to sit down. Sweat pouring, heart swelling like it collected that sweat and could expand no more.

The slasher had moved beyond dreams.

There had been rumors of this new generation of Beasts. Unholy mixtures of magic and science that could actually touch the other realm. He had thought it was all made up. Not everything you could think of came true, thank the gods. But a new, more cynical era had bred—straight from the human mind—monsters able to feed the new appetites for shock and mayhem. And the Loyal Order of Beasts had them in its fraternal embrace.

He staggered to his feet and opened the book again, hands shaking.

*Zlotnick, Le Sueur*—if the slasher had gone in order, those would be Grendel's next stops. Then his nail traced down to the last name in the registry. *Lopez.*

A shadow fell on Grendel's heart like dew on a cool glass.

*Taking* your *role*, Bluebeard had said. *The stuff you're supposed to do.* Paco was Grendel's assignment. And his last name was Lopez.

The bridge elongated just then, extending another hundred yards. Grendel plodded on, afraid to run because of his sagging heart, but lugging his huge body along as best he could. His feet hurt under his weight, and as though in response to that thought, the bridge jumped again, adding on yardage. *Knock it off*, Grendel whispered. That old dream stunt, how you kept going and never got anywhere, such a cliché. He needed a good oath to sharpen his purpose, and uttered, *As God is my witness*. Less than inspiring, that old movie line, with

Scarlett kneeling in the Georgia mud, spoiled and selfish to the bitter end.

This time with feeling, he whispered, "By all that's True," and dragged his scales and bones down the damn expanding Isthmus.

He didn't have a plan. He didn't know how a Realm monster got Real and he didn't know how he could save Paco but nothing was going to get saved if he didn't arrive there in time. The first rule of the heroic quest was to show up.

At last the bridge settled down, and he got within range of Paco's dreaming head. The boy's visions welled up from the other side, making bulges in the Isthmus, marking the insertion point. Tossing the book down to get his hands free, Grendel blurred his vision and jumped. Behind him he left a divot on the way-fabric, a cleft that remembered his leaping hind feet for a very long time.

Paco lay sleeping. As usual, he slept in the little shed in back that he preferred to the company of his five brothers and sisters.

Relief washed over Grendel. The boy, his hair a damp tangle on the pillow, clutched a favorite blanket, sleeping soundly. Grendel could see these details from his position under the boy's bed—a metaphorical position under the bed, from which spot a Realmer could cast up a decent dream by lying on his back and feeding off a youngster's sense that there *was* something under the bed.

But that smell.

For a second Grendel thought he'd trailed it with him from Laing's screened porch.

A noise at the door, where a blanket covered the opening. It was just the faintest skritch of claws on wool but Grendel knew the slasher had arrived.

Grendel crawled out from under the bed and stood beside Paco, forming a dreamland scrim between the boy and the monster.

The slasher had the face of a human, but knives for hands. "I thought I smelled a wet dog," he said. "Get caught in my diversionary rainstorm?" He squinted to bring the phantom that was Grendel into clearer focus.

"Yes I did. A nice touch, that rainstorm. Foreshadowing the ugliness to come."

The slasher shook his head in pity. "It's a mistake to think figuratively about real things, Grendel. You're used to chasing metaphors, but it's a poor substitute for experience—you know, the crunch and muck of real life."

"Real death, you mean."

The slasher leaned against the adobe wall, seemingly at ease, perhaps open to reason. "Can't have one without the other. Once you get past your horror of death you realize that it adds intensity to life, gives it its meaning. Not that I expect you to see."

"Whose death are we talking about here," Grendel spat out, "this little kid's, or yours?"

The slasher paused. "Well. Bear with me here." He took a few quick steps over to the foot of the bed and peeked at the boy. "Fine, he's still in alpha." He glanced up at Grendel. "I like to give them a premonition before I take them. I signed on for dreams, and I keep my word."

At this reference to the Order, Grendel's outrage swelled.

The slasher continued, "Once I manifest in the World—as now, for example—then I automatically incur death. Here today, gone tomorrow. Much too temporal for my tastes. So, I make up the gap by letting the kid die for me." He frowned. "Is that a metaphor? I was never good in lit class."

"No, it's not a metaphor. It's a crime."

"Nicely said. A good feel for dialogue, Gren. But what is the topic here, exactly? I have work to do."

He reached past Grendel—actually through Grendel—and picked away Paco's blanket to gaze on the boy's bare shins, glowing faintly in the spill of moonlight from a crack in the ceiling. "Kids look so sweet while they're asleep, don't you think?"

While they'd been talking, it occurred to Grendel that this Big Test he was in right now might take a sharp turn for the worse. Might, in fact, be fatal. After all, to be heroic, something had to be at stake. Usually something big. His chest filled with a draught of calming air.

Grendel wasn't sure how to manifest himself so he winged it. Gathering his thoughts, he released the Realm with all his strength. While his heart scrambled like a cat brought too near a swimming pool, he untethered from the Isthmus and fell into the Mundane World—all of him, heavily and finally.

A plume of nausea moved through him and vanished. He was Real.

The slasher cocked his head. "Bold," he murmured, impressed in spite of himself. "Yes, indeed. But I fear you're not Real material. The boys won't accept you. You're too old, too limited in your thinking." He squinted as though trying to imagine Grendel as a slasher. "Sorry."

Grendel steadied himself, reeling from the transition, but braced by the slap of cool, Real air. "Not your fault if you're a little slow to catch on here," Grendel said. "Perhaps we should step outside where we can talk without waking the kid."

"Lead the way," the slasher said, pointing his knives at the door flap.

"After you," Grendel said.

The fellow took a parting look at Paco. He was making little scissors noises with what passed for his fingers. Snip snip. Then he strode over to the door, ducking past the blanket.

Sage smells and cricket songs lent an earthly charm to the night, but such delights must be short-lived for Grendel.

"Time's a wastin'," the slasher said. "Don't you love these Mundane sayings? Anyway, cough it up, I'm busy tonight."

Here in the World, Grendel towered over the slasher. He could kill the fellow, and he was up to the deed. But on the other hand, he wasn't the Being he once was. The old ticker, once a metaphor for his lack of life purpose, was now in fact a defective heart. He might not stand up to old-style hand-to-hand combat. If he lost, Paco was the sacrifice.

"Take me in his place," Grendel said. "I'm Real now, my death is as good as the boy's." Doubt passed over the slasher's face. "Maybe better. Think of it, the glory of taking Grendel down. It'll add to your mystique—Grendel is still a big literary name."

"That was the St. George deal, right?"

"No, but you've got the general idea. Kill a legend, become one yourself."

But the slasher was shaking his head. "No, you missed a piece here. I like to shed a little blood, sure. But frankly I get off on, you know—the fear."

"Oh, don't worry about that. I'm afraid." Those shivers weren't his scales drying in the hot night breeze.

"Yeah?" The punk came closer, his nostrils flaring.

Grendel's mouth went dry as he smelled death under the slasher's armpits. "Yeah."

Again, the little snip snip noises, as the slasher-hacker came to a decision. "OK, deal."

"Your word is still worth something, even in the Real? You'll leave Paco alone?"

The slasher raised his eyes dramatically to the night sky. "As God is my witness."

Grendel winced. "Could you make another oath than that one? My dignity, I still have a little left."

"Oh." The slasher pursed his lips. "OK, I swear by . . . by the Loyal Order of Beasts."

The final insult. But maybe Bluebeard had been right. The Order had brought this upon itself.

Now the time had come for Grendel to think of a worthy last utterance. In the Realm it would have been a cinch. But here, Grendel had heard, the usual last utterance of a heroic airline pilot about to crash was, *shit*.

Grendel crouched down and exposed his neck. "I'm ready." In a way, he'd always been ready.

It must have been that the slasher took pity, or that a moment of decency unaccountably took hold, because when he snapped out his knives, he drew them quickly over Grendel's neck, not lingering, and finally, not mutilating either. But Grendel's blood spilled from his neck in shuddering pulses.

The slasher moved off, toward his next nightmare. He paused at the edge of the courtyard. "Puff? You know, the magic dragon?"

"No," Grendel whispered, "wrong again." The guy was hopelessly illiterate.

Then he was alone, lying in the Lopez backyard, his heart emptying itself in the dirt, forming a shallow red pond. His irrelevant thought was, how was the world going to explain the body of a monster lying here?

He stared up at the night stars, those wondrous natural pearls, thinking how much he would have liked to spend more time in the Real. In one thing, at least, the slasher had been right—about the intensity thing. These last moments were vivid, more than some eons had been in the Realm.

Hearing a noise at his side, he opened his eyes. Paco. The boy wrapped his shirt around Grendel's throat.

Grendel tried to pull away. "No. Leave me be."

But Paco kept on, unafraid of Grendel's monster shape. Paco had laid his blanket atop Grendel like a postage stamp on a hippo.

Helpless before the boy's ministrations, Grendel lay staring at the night sky as the stars left tracks on his vision.

Sometime during that long night he told Paco about his life. He thought the boy would get bored and fall asleep, but instead he sat cross-legged in front of Grendel, and it encouraged the old Beast to talk. He told about his beginnings, the *Beowulf* story, and then about the Realm and the creatures there, both heroic and craven. He mentioned Rudy and Polyphemus and even the media stars who, in retrospect, seemed more deserving than Grendel had once thought. He told of all the Beasts that had touched his life, those who had risen to the status of myth, and those who merely kept the old stories alive.

Paco brought him water in a dog dish, and Grendel was not too proud to sip from it.

As morning came on, Grendel found that a little strength had returned. He believed that he might have time for one last thing.

"Sorry about all the blood," Grendel told Paco. "You're not afraid, are you? Because monsters aren't going to be bothering you anymore."

Paco watched him with full, round eyes.

"On my honor," Grendel said.

Then he heaved himself up, and testing his legs for a moment, side-stepped into the Realm.

On the Isthmus he noticed how dreadfully he stank. No help for it. He found the book where he had dropped it, and managed to magic up a pencil to write down what had happened—the Final Test of an aging hero and the last adventure of the Loyal Order of Beasts. Then, winding up, he threw the book with a mighty cast, skittering it along the Isthmus like a flat stone on a pond. He hoped it reached the Realm but with stories there was no guarantee of forever.

Then he went to the Isthmus wall nearest him and began beating on it. He hammered with his fists and when they became too weak he lay on his back and kicked with his strong back feet, using his mortal body to hammer at the walls that brooked no mixing of the realms. Under the assault the bridge darkened, and as it did, Grendel's body began sinking into the deep folds. The Isthmus was dying, along with him. Those old dark spots at the corners of his eyes had always been death waiting, in a figurative premonition of what must be. It was sad to think that, as the Isthmus passed away, the Realm, too, would gradually atrophy. He was sweeping it all away, for the sake of all the dreamers who counted on their dreams not to slay them. For the sake of never letting another slasher go over to the World. It was true that now the World had one real bad ass. But he could be killed. It was the price he paid for being Real. Even in the World there were a few heroes who would relish such a task.

With his strength finally spent, Grendel rested, laying his head on the quilted pillow of the bridge.

Then the path that Baba Yaga had tread along the Isthmus opened up like a zipper and let in the dark.

In the Realm, Rudy stood with the Book in his hands, his troll's heart moved in spite of himself. Polyphemus put a hand on his shoulder, steadying him.

"It wasn't supposed to be like this," Rudy said.

Grendel's words spoke to him from the page: *There are some good things about temporality, Rudy. The stakes, for one thing. They're higher. You got to take a stand. You got a few good years left. Make them count.*

"But what about our poker group?"

*Baba Yaga. You need an anchor legend.*

Rudy allowed as how that might be true. "But how about the World? How will the Mundane get by without us?"

*They'll think of something. They usually do.*

*Paco lies dreaming. He dreams of unicorns and beasts, half-man, half-monster. He conjures fire-belching dragons and fairy queens in gossamer carriages, as well as beings never seen in any realm at any time. He remembers tales told at the lake of blood, where a voice had spoken to him all night long, a voice that had often soothed his terrors and painted his imaginings. He dreams some of these beasts, as well as new ones.*

*And as he dreams, an Isthmus begins to form . . . .*

*This may very well be the shortest science fiction story on record. It is George Nikolopoulos's second appearance in* Galaxy's Edge.

## YOU CAN ALWAYS CHANGE THE PAST

### by George Nikolopoulos

Adrenaline rushes through my body like a mad sprinter and I still can't believe I did it. He lies face down in the mud, my rifle's bayonet still buried in his neck. I pull it off, absently wiping it on my soldier's uniform trousers. Who would have thought? I, Charles Ecclestone, have killed the monster, succeeding where so many time travelers had failed before.

I try hard to calm down. There's still the First World War going on around me, and here's a young soldier lying on his back, coughing and shivering. I take his hand and help him up.

He's still trembling. "He would have killed me," he says. "Thank you." He hesitates for a moment. "I'd like to know my savior's name."

"I'm Charles," I say. "Charles Ecclestone." *It doesn't matter. You don't know my name. But in your future, everyone will.*

I've made the world a better place. I've killed the greatest villain of all time—Jacques Leroux, the mad mass murderer; saving this nice young man was just an added bonus. I can't wait to go back and read the revised history books.

The soldier extends his hand. "I'm Adolf Hitler," he says, rousing me from my reverie.

I smile and shake his hand. "Nice to meet you, Adolf."

*Andrea G. Stewart was a Writers of the Future finalist. Her first novel was published last year, and she is hard at work on the next one. This is her fourth appearance* in Galaxy's Edge.

# IT TAKES A SPECIAL-SPECIAL PERSON

## by Andrea G. Stewart

The carpet stinks of plastic and cheese, and Gloria's got her knee digging into my back in her version of a therapeutic hold. I can feel the heat from her skin. My lips mash into the spot—I'm sure it's the exact spot—where Tim-Tom barfed last week. Gloria had forgotten to lock the medicine cabinet, and Tim-Tom drank all the cough syrup in a pathetic attempt to get high.

Who'm I kidding. I'd have done the same if I'd gotten there first.

"I'll let you go when you can remain calm," Gloria drones on above me.

I can't help myself; I try to zap her even though I know it won't work. The crackle rushes through me, lifting the hairs on my arms. But when it gets to where Gloria's holding my wrists, it just fizzles. They've got a dampener over the whole house, locked up tight in a fireproof safe. I should be thankful for the dampener, my social worker says—otherwise we'd be caged like animals.

Can't find the gratitude in me right now.

"Tim-Tom puked here," I say. I wriggle and squirm, but she's got my arms secured, and I can only kick uselessly.

"I'll let you go when you can remain calm."

"You're a bitch. A fucking bitch-whale." The knee in my back digs a little harder.

"I'll let you go when you can remain calm."

For a second I try the thing my therapist told me to—three deep breaths. I get past the first one before I stop. Man, *fuck* that shit. I kick and scream as loud as I can. I hope I disturb the neighbors. I hope my voice shatters the windows. I hope I put a hole in this ugly-ass carpet or a hole in ugly-ass Gloria.

Twenty or so minutes later, Gloria gets off of me and goes to the office. I just lie there, my throat aching and my toes sore, my face pressed into Tim-

Tom's puke spot. Therapeutic hold means back down to level zero—no privileges which means no Net. I keep thinking I'm close to getting out of this place, and then I screw up all over again. I can't even remember how I got on the floor—what it was that made me lose my cool. The sun has started to set, sending pink beams of light through the shades.

"Jeff. Jeffrey. Jeff. Jeff." Birdy walks into the living room and crouches next to me, head cocked to the side. I scoot to the side, but he follows. He wraps his skinny little arms around his knees. Birdy's not his real name, but we call him that and he never seemed to mind. The kid creeps me out. I don't know what kind of special-special he is, but he rarely goes out of the house, and when he does, someone has to cart along another dampener behind him.

He reaches out, one cold finger tracing across my forehead. He smiles. "Jeffrey."

I jerk away from him without a word. The rest of us try not to talk to him unless one of the staff makes us. We may be freaks, but Birdy's in a category of his own.

He curls his fingers to his chest. "Jeff." It's halfway to a whine. "Jeff Jeff."

Kinda feel bad, even though Birdy's no use to me. He doesn't ever get Net access. I push myself to my feet, wipe my mouth with the back of my hand. I keep my voice low, so the kids in the family room can't hear me talking to him. "Yeah well, whatever."

Birdy's smile widens, as if I've apologized. He follows me into the family room and perches next to me on the couch, pale toes and fingers curled around the edge of the cushion. An infomercial about a push-up bra blares from the television. The other on-duty staff, Mike, makes dinner in the adjoining kitchen. Mac 'n cheese, by the smell. Yay.

"Yeah," Tim-Tom says from his spot in the recliner. "Yeah, lemme see the front again, girl." He's leaning forward, blinking like he's saving each flickering image for later use. Probably is. We don't get regular Net access unless we're on level three, and even then the good sites are blocked. The light from the television shines off his pimply face, his limp brown hair.

"You could do your homework, you know," Mike calls.

All three of us ignore him. Birdy, 'cause he's, well, Birdy, and Tim-Tom and I 'cause it's Saturday, and everybody knows you don't do homework until Sunday. Roland would ignore him too, if he was here. He's visiting his mom in Bellford. He tells all the other residents how they're transitioning him back to living at home, dampener-free. Most parents of specials don't use dampeners—they teach their kids control when they're young. It's special-specials like me, ones with labels like "conduct disorder" or "schizoaffective disorder" who get dumped in group homes when they can't behave, and cut off from their abilities. And besides, dampeners are expensive.

Birdy makes a happy little noise when the oven timer goes off, rocking until he swings off the edge of the couch and onto the floor.

Birdy and me are the only ones who don't get to visit family. I've been kicked from foster home to foster home until three years ago, when I lost my temper and took out the electricity on an entire block. Never could keep my temper, but I guess that was the last straw.

I'm not like Roland; I don't know who my mom is. All I know is she's probably living out there in a house without a dampener, without constant supervision. I need the Net so I can find her, get her to take me in and get out of this shit hole, no matter how I feel about her.

She's the reason I'm special-special, and living in this goddamned house.

✿

Gloria drops me off at school just after second bell. I'm on a modified schedule, on account of my status. Roland and Tim-Tom slide out of the van before me. Roland's nearly as fat as Gloria, but I never call him names. He's special-special with a nasty side—he can open wounds with a glare. The dampener at school is huge—a metal whirring box as big as a person and locked up behind steel bars in the office. They say it's mostly to keep crazies from using their abilities on school grounds, but I think we all know it's there to keep the special kids from dicking off in class. It doesn't run on lunch breaks, or at P.E., but I zapped somebody once and got suspended for a week. Gave him enough of a jolt to sit him on his ass and make his hair stand on end. I thought it was pretty funny, but the only thing more boring than school is not being in school while everyone else is.

While Roland and Tim-Tom head toward where the older kids like to sneak a smoke, I find Phil.

He spots me heading for him and tries to lose himself in the crowd, but his height does him no favors. The guy is built like a giraffe. I snag his backpack. "Hey," I say as I pull him closer, "I need to ask you a favor."

His hand goes immediately to the transmitter stuck to the right side of his face. "No," he says.

"C'mon, I just need to borrow it for a few minutes, before third period. Twenty bucks. Five minutes." I wouldn't push Phil so hard if I didn't know that he's a wimp. He's special—can jump higher than the basketball hoop—but his mom didn't use her abilities while she was preggers with him, so Phil doesn't have any mental problems. He doesn't get another "special" tagged on. Follows the rules just like his mom. Won't hit me or jump on me or whatever, no matter how much I bother him.

He pulls off the sticky tube, tugs free the earbud. "Fine." He clicks a button on the bottom of the tube. "Just don't unlock my settings. Whenever it starts to adjust to you, it gives me a screaming headache when I get it back."

"Sure, sure." I stick the transmitter on my face, hook on the earbud, and then I'm connected to the Net.

It's an assault on my senses. Phil's got things lined up in color-coded categories, with sub-categories beneath those. I focus and blink to access e-mail. The transmitter scans my retina and then my messages pop up.

There's one from the postmaster—message undeliverable—and another from someone I thought might be my mom. She's around the right age, and the bio on her webpage mentions an ability to zap things.

Her message only has two words. "No" and "sorry" with a comma in between, no period, as if she couldn't even be bothered to finish the goddamned sentence.

I click the button on the transmitter to "unlock" and scatter Phil's stupid color-coded categories across the view screen. I just can't give a fuck about what Phil wants right now, and at least his settings don't give *me* a headache anymore. Before the bell rings, I hop over to ConGlom and start a new post.

*I know ur out there. may 18 2001. thats the day u left me at the fire station in oakland. i no u dont wanna be found cause I ben looking 4 u 4 ever. u made me this way. Special special. Ive got a right 2 a real home.*

Phil grabs for the transmitter. "Time's up."

I wrestle with him for a minute, struggle to add the name of my group home and get the thing posted before he sees what I was doing. Makes me look like a real pussy, crying about my mom. Done. I let him take the transmitter, slap twenty bucks in his hand and walk away before he sees what I did to his settings.

Maybe, if I'm lucky, she goes on ConGlom, or she probably knows somebody who does—somebody who can say, "Hey, what happened to that baby you dumped sixteen years ago?"

'Cause he's a grown-ass man now.

Some weirdo's prodding Birdy with a machine when I get home. Happens a lot, like Birdy's a car someone can fix. Kid's got this look on his face, like it hurts, but he's smiling through it 'cause he doesn't want to say "no." Or maybe he just doesn't know how. The machine sits on the dining room table, and the guy's got this metal rod stuck in Birdy's ear.

"Hey," I say to him.

The guy looks up. He's wearing a lab coat. His lapel covers most of the name on the tag, but I can see the company logo—a globe with a lightning bolt down the center.

I wave a hand at the machine. "Whatever you're doing with that rod? He doesn't like it."

Weirdo pulls out the rod and opens his floppy mouth to respond, but then Mike calls from the kitchen. "Jeffrey, someone's on the phone for you."

A tingle runs through me. Nobody calls for me. Not ever.

When I get to the kitchen, Mike's holding the phone out to me. I take it and turn away. "Hello?"

Whoever's on the other line's a mouth-breather. I just hear that: in-out, crackle. "Hello?" I try again. Nothing. "You called and asked for me for a reason. You got something to say, say it." I cover the mouthpiece and look at Mike. "Did they say who they were?"

He only shrugs. "She said she was one of your friends."

She.

I slide my hand off the mouthpiece. "It's you, isn't it?" I don't even know what to say; I've played out so many different scenarios but none of them started with a silent phone call.

On her end, someone whines in the background. "Mooom, you said you would come see…!"

And just like that, *click.*

Takes me a few minutes to lower the phone from my ear. Whoever my mom is, she's got another kid.

"Ow! Goddammit!" Weirdo shouts from the dining room.

I flip the phone onto the counter and dash around the wall, Mike on my heels. Birdy's sitting at the dining room table, a goofy sort of grin on his face.

Lab-coat man is rubbing the back of his head. A book lies on the floor at his feet—a hardcover.

"Stupid thing fell off the shelf," he says, waving a hand at the bookshelf against the wall behind him. "Do these kids not know how to put a book on a shelf?"

I'm formulating a reply, something with "your mom" in it, but Mike gets there first.

"You okay?"

"Fine." The man grimaces. "Can't you bring him into my lab next time?"

Mike shrugs. "You'll have to take that up with his social worker. Be glad you're allowed to see him at all."

I exchange glances with Birdy. Soon as our eyes meet, I know he did it. The dampener's downstairs, in a safe in Gloria's study. It runs on batteries and it's always on. The dampener should cover the entire house and some of the yard, but somehow—some way—Birdy got through. Just tipped a book off the shelf is all, but if he can do that with the dampener on, what can he do without it?

I always have trouble sleeping but tonight is worse than most. After Birdy's little outburst, I tried to track the call and didn't get anywhere. Private number, blocked. I'm so close, and all I can do is squirm around in bed, trying to get comfortable.

Just as I start to doze off, I feel a cold finger on my forehead.

"Eight three eight five five five two three eight seven."

I open my eyes and stare into Birdy's smiling face, my heart knocking at my ribs. "The hell, Birdy? You always sneak up on people when they're sleeping?"

"Eight three eight five five five two three eight seven. Jeffrey Jeff." He prods at my forehead one more time, and then slinks away, quiet as a cat.

It takes me a moment longer to fully awaken and when I do it hits me: Birdy, little shit that he is, just gave me my mom's telephone number.

☼

I try the number in the morning and get voicemail. "Hi, you've reached Jocelyn Mulvaney. I can't answer the phone right now, but leave your name and number, and I'll call you right back." I don't leave a name or number, just hang up and think about trying again, but I don't.

At school, I look for Phil again. I've got a name now, and I wanna know more about the woman it belongs to. Does she have space in her home for me? I try to sling an arm around his shoulders, but he's way too tall for that, and he shrugs me off easily.

"Hey Phil, do you think I could—"

"No." He crosses his arms and tilts his head, and suddenly he looks like a wall. "You're an asshole, you know that, Jeffrey? It took me almost an hour last night to get my settings back to the way I like them."

I shrug. "Sorry, man. You're right, it was a dick thing to do."

He shakes his head. "You only apologize when you want something." Deliberately, he peels the transmitter from his face, puts it into his messenger bag, and snaps the metal buckle shut. "You want a favor? Ask someone else." He turns and walks away.

I've been waiting sixteen fucking years to find out who my mom is, to get out of the system. The energy gathers behind my eyes and I put out a hand to zap him. But it doesn't even slide down my arm; it fizzles, leaving my head fuzzy and irritated, like I've just licked a battery and then stuck it between my ears. Goddamn school dampener—it doesn't even let me hope, not for a second. "You're such a pussy, Phil!" I shout. "A six-foot-two, giant, limp-dick pussy!"

A few kids turn their heads to stare at me, but Phil doesn't even look back.

☼

School is torture. It's like death by waterboarding. I skip out on fifth period to carve curse words into the boys' restroom stalls. Anything's better than listening to Mr. Nichols talk about history. There's something calming about the scratch of metal against metal, the peeling paint. I put my cheek against the partition, and the coolness of it seems to leach into my brain. I just need to get through the day.

When lunch hits and the dampener gets switched off, I entertain myself by running a small current through the stall walls so that anyone trying to open a door gets a little static shock.

By the time eighth period rolls around, I want to shoot myself in the face just to put myself out of my misery. My head hurts, and anytime I think of Jocelyn Mulvaney, my pulse starts racing. Pretty sure my pits stink, with all the sweating I'm doing.

Gloria picks us up after ninth period. Roland and Tim-Tom shove one another in the back seat and I just want to scream at them to shut the hell up.

I make a beeline for the phone as soon as we get in the door.

"Hey," Gloria says. "Hey!"

I stop and turn, 'cause I know she's talking to me.

She huffs and puffs from the dining room to the kitchen. "You're on level zero, Jeffrey. Mike marked down a phone call this morning. You get one a day, ten minutes tops."

Gloria is such a bitch. I clench my hands into fists. And then what my therapist said pops into my head again. Stupid deep breaths. I try it, faster than he probably intended.

Feels like the heat in my chest dies down a little, gives me room to think. "I just got an answering machine this morning. C'mon, Gloria, I didn't even get to talk to anyone."

Tim-Tom, behind her, makes kissy noises. I flip the finger at him.

She shakes her head. "One phone call. The rules are the rules."

All day. I've been waiting all day. Deep breaths. How the hell Birdy stays calm with people poking at him all the time, I've got no idea. "I think I found my mom. Her name's Jocelyn Mulvaney." I grit my teeth. "Please."

Gloria purses her lips, and she looks like a puffer fish with beady little eyes. "Fine. Ten minutes."

I grab the phone off the counter before she can change her mind. This time, when I call, someone picks up after the third ring.

"Hello?" For a second, I think it might be her, but it's just a little girl voice.

"Can I speak to your mom? Jocelyn Mulvaney?"

The girl sniffles. And then she takes a deep breath. "Mooom!"

I've got to hold the phone a few inches from my ear just so her voice doesn't kill my eardrums. Definitely the same kid as yesterday. Birdy pointed me true. Could be my kid sister I just finished talking to. A sister. It's like I woke up on another planet.

A shuffling sound, and then a different voice. "Hello?" Deeper, more mature.

"Hi," I say, "my name's Jeffrey." I stop there, my mouth drier than a camel's balls.

"Hi…Jeffrey." A quick tapping sound, like she's flicking the end of a pen against a table. "Is there a reason you called?"

"Did you leave a baby at a fire station in Oakland sixteen years ago? 'Cause I think you might be my mom."

Silence, not even the crackle of breath.

"Jeffrey," she says it in a half-whisper, her breathing almost covering the sound of my name. "How did you get this number?"

Not exactly the first thing you want to hear from your long-lost mom. "A friend." Is Birdy my friend? I don't know, but it sounds cool to say. I want to ask her all the important questions, but a lifetime of hurt bubbles to the surface. "Why didn't you ever want to see me?"

On the couch, Roland mimes a crying baby. I turn my back before I do something stupid, like chuck the phone at his head.

"I'm not…I'm not a hero, Jeffrey." She sounds like she's about to cry. "I know what happens to a baby if you use your gifts when you're pregnant. I'm not cut out for that. I can't handle a kid with special needs."

"I'm in a group home." Thought I'd feel angry, but I just feel cold. *Get me out get me out.*

She chokes back a sob. "I've got a little girl to think about now, too."

I hear the implication. I'm irrational, wild, dangerous. I want to peel my own skin off—that's how

dirty I feel. Instead, I start bargaining. "You could just have lunch with me on weekends—Tim-Tom's dad does that. I didn't mean I had to live with you. Jesus!" I try to scoff, like it's a joke, but my throat's all tight. "Least tell me where my dad is." Maybe he can get me out of here.

"I'm so sorry," she says, and my heart sinks to the soles of my feet. "He's incarcerated. He tried to rob a bank, and shot someone on his way out. His name's Edward Bent, if you ever wanted to look him up."

It feels like she's shoveling crumbs off a plate that once held caviar. She's sorry, just as I imagined, but it's my kind of sorry—it changes nothing. "Come see me in person. That's all I'm asking for." She can't say no if she sees me, I know it.

She takes a long, shaky breath. "I just wanted to hear your voice, once, to know that you're living a decent life."

"You think this is a decent life?" Having to ask permission just to breathe, living with a bunch of boys just as messed up as me, being watched like a hawk—it's a group prison, not a group home. "You've got some balls on you."

She swallows, and her voice is steady when she speaks. "I don't think you should call this number again."

My hand starts shaking, the phone wobbling by my ear. I dig my fingers into the plastic until my nails ache. "Fuuuuuuuuck!" I scream into the phone so loudly I never even hear it click on the other end, but I know it does. She's putting down the phone, shaking off the tears, turning back to her normal, perfect life with her normal, perfect child.

I chuck the phone, hard as I can, at Roland's head. He deflects it with an elbow, and it crashes into the wall, leaving an ugly black streak. "The fuck, man?"

Next thing I know, I'm on the floor, my cheek pressed into the linoleum, Gloria's knee at my back. I don't even hear her; I scream and sob as a little voice in the back of my head says, again and again: "It's over."

✿

I wear myself out in Gloria's therapeutic hold, and when she finally gets off of me, I go to my room and shut the door. I don't want dinner, don't want anything except to lie in bed and stare at the ceiling. My mom's a bitch and my dad's a criminal and I'm stuck in this home until I'm eighteen.

Gloria knocks a while after dinner. "Jeffrey? Are you okay? Did you want to talk about it?"

I'd usually cuss her out, but I can't even muster up a response.

She slides something under the door and then her footsteps fade.

It's almost dark by the time I turn over to see what she shoved under my door. Looks like a few sheets of paper. I get just enough curiosity to roll out of bed and crawl over to them.

A headline in stark letters catches my attention. "Local Hero Saves Fifty." Next to the article is a picture of a solemn-looking young woman, the flash catching the whites of her eyes. I see my chin in hers, and we've got the same eyebrows and dark, curly hair. The caption underneath reads "Jocelyn Mulvaney," but I knew it would after looking at her.

The article lays out the scene: a storm that started near the end of a basketball game. A crowded parking lot rife with puddles. A fallen tree, a snapped power line.

And there was Jocelyn, catching it before the line could fall, absorbing its power into her own body. "I didn't think about it," her quote says. "I just did it. I'm not a hero."

I don't know why Gloria gave this to me—maybe she's trying to tell me that even specials make mistakes. Jocelyn must have known already, at the time the article was written, what was happening in her belly. I can see it in her face, even if no one else did. She did a good thing; she did a terrible thing.

But she moved on.

I'm the one that's stuck in the same place.

Early morning squirms its way in through my blinds, highlighting everything in orange. I check the clock. Five forty-three, way too early to get ready for school. Besides, what's the point? I've got no future, no matter how hard I try. But my stomach rumbles, so I haul myself out of bed, still wearing yesterday's clothes. My own odor surrounds me, a personal stink-cloud.

Birdy waits for me on the other side of the door. He crouches on the floor, knees to chest, pale fingers blending with pale toes. I want to smack him out of the way I'm so upset, but he did me a solid.

"Thanks," I tell him, "for that number the other day." Lot of good it did me.

He just stares up at me as if I haven't said a word. No one else is around, so I reach out and pat his head, like I would a little kid. "You did good," I say. Birdy sucks in his lower lip and smiles, his whole face going bright.

Funny thing is, it makes me smile too. He's kind of dopey, Birdy is, if I don't think about what he can do with a dampener on. Then he's all sorts of creepy.

When I go downstairs Kevin, the night staff guy, is sitting on the couch with a book. "You're supposed to be in your room," he says as I step foot on the first floor.

"I'm hungry. Didn't get dinner."

Kevin's gaze follows me as I raid the fridge for leftovers, and I wonder if he can tell I've been crying. "Gloria told me about your outburst," he says.

I pull out a plastic container with pork and rice in it and pop it in the microwave. "Yeah, so what?"

"You keep that sort of thing up—for instance, not listening when people tell you where you're supposed to be—you're going to end up in a locked facility."

I shrug, like I don't care, but my stomach turns. In a locked facility, all the schooling takes place on the grounds, all the counseling. You don't leave. If I think I'm stuck now, a locked facility is even worse. I didn't think I was being that bad, but maybe this last therapeutic hold's got Gloria thinking she doesn't want to deal with me anymore. And she'll get a call from school about my class skipping, maybe even the vandalism in the bathroom if they put two and two together.

I shut the microwave door with more force than necessary. "It's done. Did you want me to eat it down here or in my room?" Either way is a rules violation, but I'm starving and not scared enough to put the whole thing back in the fridge.

"You can eat it down here."

Whatever. I scarf it down past my aching throat and throw the container in the dishwasher.

"You can come back down at six thirty." Kevin turns the page.

I flip off his back with both hands as I head back up the stairs. It's six oh three. What a dick.

I don't wake up again until nine. Gloria lets me stay home. I don't like that she feels sorry for me, but I sit on my bed, feeling too sorry for myself to care. Never gonna get out of the group home. It's still hitting me.

Birdy's tutor arrives mid-morning. I hear her downstairs, reading letters and animals off a chart. Birdy never says a word. I can picture him perched on the edge of a chair, rocking a bit, that silly grin on his face. I think he likes being talked to.

Sometime in the afternoon, Gloria knocks on my door. This time, she comes in when I don't reply. I look back, just to make sure it's her, but turn my attention back to the window. Quiet day in the neighborhood. Some old guy's planting flowers by his front door.

"We need to talk."

I get that tingle again, and I really don't like it. "What's there to say?"

She comes nearer and sits on the edge of my bed. The whole thing tilts, like the mattress is a ship about to sink into the sea. "I got a call from the school this morning." Gloria rattles off the things I've been caught doing lately, and why the school administration is unhappy I've been doing them.

A white van pulls onto our street, puttering down the road like the driver's not sure he's got the right place. "It's just this stuff with my mom. I'll do better." I put my elbow on the windowsill and my head in my hand.

"That might not be good enough."

The white van slows and then *pulls into our fucking driveway*. The tingle bursts, white-hot, at the base of my neck. All the hairs on my body stand on end. They're here for me. They're gonna take me away to a locked facility, and I'm gonna be there 'til I'm eighteen. I glance back and forth between Gloria and the van. "I'll change, I promise. I can do more chores, my homework. Just gimme another chance." Before she can answer, the van door rolls open and two guys get out.

Shit shit shit. I spring from the mattress and dash out the door. If I run, I might be able to get a head start, if I go out the backyard, stay off the roads. I take the stairs down two at a time, and I can barely feel the soles of my feet.

I run face-first into Birdy on the landing. I think we smacked our foreheads together 'cause my vision gets wobbly. He turns in circles, hands outstretched, eyes wide. "Jeffrey. Jeff Jeff. Jeff."

Gloria emerges from my bedroom, hands on her hips. "They're not here for you, Jeffrey. For God's sake. You're not hopeless." A knock sounds at the door, heavy and insistent, and Gloria sighs as she waddles to the staircase.

Birdy grabs my hands. "Jeffrey."

They're here for Birdy. Gloria passes us on the stairs and I'm still trying to figure out what's going on. I pull my fingers free from Birdy's clammy grip. "Birdy? They gonna run more tests?"

She turns on the bottom step. "He's been breaking through the dampener. Don't think I haven't noticed. I don't have the funding for anything more powerful, so he's got to go."

"But he's never hurt anyone," I call after her.

She's already around the corner, answering the door. I get it. She can't take a chance. Still doesn't seem fair. Birdy practically grovels at my feet. "Please. Jeffrey Jeff."

I can't even help myself, don't know why he thinks I can help him.

The two guys appear at the bottom of the stairs. They're wearing navy blue pants, and short-sleeved, light blue polo shirts. Embroidered on each shirt is the same logo I saw on the guy's lab coat—the globe with the lightning bolt through the middle. "They're taking him to a *lab*?"

Gloria shows up behind them, her fat face peeking between the guys' shoulders. "It's just temporary, until his social worker can find a permanent placement for him. Their facilities have a better dampener."

God, I thought *my* life was pathetic—Birdy's parents never visit him either, people barely talk to him, and now he's getting taken away to a lab where they're going to poke and prod him for the weeks it takes for his social worker to find a place with a stronger dampener. A place where he won't know anyone, probably out-of-state. Kid's alone enough as it is.

One of the guys, the one with the buzz-cut, places a foot on the first step. "Look, we're not going to hurt him. Just back away, okay?"

I'm standing in front of Birdy, between him and the two guys. I don't even remember doing it. I may not have a mom or dad, but Birdy's got nobody. At least I've got school, and even Gloria seems to give a damn about me. "What if I don't? You gonna make me?"

The two guys glance at one another and then start up the stairs. Birdy crouches behind my legs and rocks back and forth. "Jeffrey, no. Please, no."

That's when I notice that all the shit on the kitchen counters is hovering above the tiles. The broom by the back door levitates too, and all the books on the coffee table. "Gloria," I hiss to her and point at all the flying shit. She glances back just as the guys reach the landing. I try to wave them off. "Guys, you might not want to—"

Ah, fuck. Too late. One of them reaches around me and grabs for Birdy's skinny-ass arm.

Something in the downstairs office explodes. It rattles the pictures on the walls, makes my hearing go dim. Nobody makes a sound except Birdy and his rocking, and I know we're all thinking the same thing.

The dampener.

Everything's quiet for a second—and then the world implodes. The roof cracks, sending plaster raining from the ceiling. It all crumbles. It's like a giant's digging his fingers into the roof and just peeling it all away. The staircase is the only thing that doesn't get touched. Gloria still stands at the bottom, and she screams.

Doesn't stop Birdy. Dishes fly out of the cupboards, crashing onto the tiles. Pictures fall, glass shattering. It's all dust and shards and creaking pieces of lumber.

One of the guys tries to grab Birdy's arm again. He gets flung back, and he staggers into Gloria at the bottom of the steps, both of them falling to the floor. The other guy's just pissing his pants as the walls break down around us. Something metal falls from the second floor to the first—I think it's my bed frame. The ceiling is gone now, just daylight above us. My heart's going so fast I think I'm gonna die.

I can see the house next door through the crumbling walls. Its windows shatter, the glass glittering as it tumbles.

Birdy rocks, and moans, and no one does a goddamned thing. He's gonna take out the whole neighborhood. There are people in those houses, like the old guy planting his flowers across the street.

I crouch next to Birdy, my palms sweating. His hands are over his ears, his eyes squeezed shut.

*I'm not a hero.*

"Birdy, c'mon, you've got to stop this." I talk low and quiet; can barely hear myself over the racket. "Take a few deep breaths," I tell Birdy. Oh man, it sounds so stupid—like a few deep breaths is gonna stop Birdy from ripping the world apart.

He peeks at me, still rocking, his fingers digging into his hair.

"I'll do it with you, c'mon." I take in a deep breath, trying to ignore the way the top of the staircase crumbles. His gaze focuses on me, and I see him take a breath too.

He tries, I think he really does. And then he shakes his head and shuts his eyes and I've got nothing to work with.

A crackle runs through me, and I remember: the dampener is gone.

Something in the house groans; a spray of water hits my face from a busted pipe. I put a hand on Birdy's shoulder, and I don't get flung away like the other guy. The kid trusts me. Takes me only a second to think things through. "Sorry, buddy."

I zap him, real good.

The house stops shuddering. Birdy's eyes flicker open, and for a moment, he gives me that dopey grin of his. And then his eyeballs roll back in his head, and he collapses onto the carpet.

Nobody moves.

☼

Local hero—that's what they call me. Flip off enough interviewers, though, and people start to leave you alone. Even so, I get a gajillion offers from families wanting to adopt me. Idiots. They don't know what they'd be getting into. Everyone wants to know about me, and nobody seems to give a damn about Birdy.

I do.

I didn't give him enough voltage to stop his heart, just enough to knock him out for a while. He's recovering at the hospital.

People who never cared about our special-special group home start donating money to rebuild it. Gloria comes to see me at the Children's Home a week after the incident. There's no dampener here, but I'm the local hero, so nobody cares anymore.

She sits on the couch across from me and hands me a paper covered in numbers. "It's a tally sheet," she tells me. "All the donations."

"So?" I try to hand it back, but she doesn't take it. "What's that got to do with me?"

"You saved my life," she says quietly.

This is awkward as shit. "Whatever." What do I say now: you would have done the same? It was no big deal? Anytime?

"It's more than enough to rebuild the house," she says. "I'm putting the rest into a college fund for you."

I bark out a laugh and pick at the fraying cloth on the sofa armrest. "That's a joke."

She leans forward, clasps her hands together. "It's not. I know you say you don't want to get adopted, but there are a lot of families interested in at least fostering you, and you're going to click with one of them. You can do more with your life, Jeffrey." Yeah, I can, but it won't be college. I make a split-second decision I'll probably regret later, but I'm used to that. I make mistakes and then I gotta live with them. "Keep your stupid money. Buy a stronger dampener. Let Birdy stay." I may not know what the hell I want to do with my life, but I know what I don't want to do with it. Don't wanna be like my mom.

I'm not gonna just move on and pretend this never happened.

She stares at me for a while, and then just says, "Okay."

And you know what? I feel like a fucking hero.

*Copyright © 2017 by Andrea G. Stewart*

❖

❖❖

❖❖❖

*Kevin J. Anderson is a Hugo nominee, the author of more than fifty national or international bestsellers, and has recently become a publisher as WordFire Press. This is his third appearance in* Galaxy's Edge, *and the first featuring his popular detective Dan Shamble, Zombie P.I.*

## LOCKED ROOM
### A Dan Shamble, Zombie P.I. Adventure

### by Kevin J. Anderson

### 1

When a harpy tells you to do something, there's no room for discussion.

As a zombie private detective, as well as a regular customer at the Ghoul's Diner, I had plenty of experience with Esther the harpy waitress. She had been a client of mine, seeking to get rid of a bad luck charm that a customer had left her as a tip for the awful service Esther usually provided (if "service" is a word that even applies in that situation.)

Esther had a hawkish face, a raptorlike demeanor, and a vulturelike personality. Her curled iridescent feathers looked like straight razors that had been mangled in a mail-sorting machine. With her glittering eyes, she could shoot a sharp glare at anyone who looked at her the wrong way, and Esther considered almost any way "the wrong way." Her mood swings were best measured on the Richter scale.

Nevertheless, she was a client of Chambeaux & Deyer Investigations, and a paying one. In the Unnatural Quarter, where monsters tried to make quiet, normal lives for themselves, I'd had far worse cases before.

Late this afternoon, Esther had called our offices demanding—because Esther was incapable of making a mere request—that my ghost girlfriend Sheyenne and I meet her out in the Greenlawn Cemetery for the grand opening of a very special new crypt.

"It's imperative that you're both there," Esther said in a voice that made fingernails on chalkboards sound like sweet music.

As our office administrator, Sheyenne already knew about the case. "I'm surprised you want me along too. Dan is our private investigator. I often help out on cases but—"

The harpy cut her off. "Stop arguing with me! I need a zombie and a ghost. Be there."

We'd had a quiet day wrapping up cases and waiting for new ones to walk through the door. Robin Deyer, my human lawyer partner, had left town to visit her parents for their anniversary celebration, so it was only Sheyenne and me in the offices. I wouldn't normally leave the place unattended, but I had my phone and I didn't expect this would take long.

Besides, who was going to tell Esther she couldn't have what she wanted?

The Greenlawn Cemetery was a nice place, as far as cemeteries went, with well-tended lots, midrange tombstones, and used crypts for rent or for sale. The flowers were replenished regularly, and a park and recreation area for new tenants had been added as part of an urban beautification project. After being killed during one of my cases as a human detective, I had been buried here, and then I clawed my way back out of the earth, cleaned myself up, put on a change of clothes, and got back to work. Yes, this place held fond memories....

As Sheyenne and I arrived at the cemetery, I wore my usual sport jacket with its stitched-up bullet holes and my traditional fedora that didn't quite go low enough to cover the exit wound in the center of my forehead. I looked fairly decent—maybe even handsome enough to accompany my vivacious blonde, blue-eyed ghost girlfriend. Sheyenne drifted along beside me through the lanes of tombstones, ectoplasmic and glowing, too beautiful to touch (which was a good thing: since she was a ghost, I couldn't touch her anyway).

We found the harpy standing next to the impressive new crypt, which looked like a private fortress with thick granite walls and massive columns that conveyed an ornate but unwelcoming appearance. I wasn't surprised to see a broad-shouldered and barechested Minotaur standing next to Esther. Yes, the classical architect would want to be there for the grand opening of his special new tomb.

With a loud snort, Percy Minotaur, Sr. adjusted the golden ring through his blocky nose. "Thank you both for coming."

The door to the crypt was wide open to show an austere, cold interior, dimly lit by high narrow windows.

"Where is everyone else for the celebration?" Sheyenne asked.

"We only need you two," Esther snapped, and gestured with a feathered arm. The harpy had an odd and unsettling feminine appearance, a sexiness that at first attracted men, then made them ill as they realized exactly *what* they'd been attracted to. "You're here to test Elspeth's tomb. There's no time to waste."

"How is your sister's condition?" I asked. "Any change?"

"No, still terminal." Esther sounded disappointed. "And still no closer to it."

The Minotaur invited us through the open door of the tomb. "Allow me to show you the finer points of the new construction. It is magnificent, as usual."

Sheyenne and I entered the tomb, though there wasn't much to see—an open empty vault with stone walls, stone floor, stone ceiling. The narrow slit windows at the top of the wall were thickly barricaded. The harpy's hard face curled in a smile as she saw me looking at them. "Those are so my undead sister can look out like a sad kid on a rainy day ... if she ever dies, that is."

The tomb walls glistened as if coated with some kind of thick varnish ... or maybe saliva. "A special anti-ectoplasmic preventive coating," said the Minotaur architect. "One of the special upgrades Esther requested."

In the center sat a raised slab on which the resident's body would lie in repose. "Is this where you'll place your sister's coffin?" I asked Esther.

"Coffin? Hell, no! Why buy a fancy coffin? Who's going to see her in here anyway? She can just lie on the slab."

"I take it that's why you didn't waste money on interior decorating, either?" Sheyenne asked.

"Why would I waste money like that on Elspeth? This damned crypt is already costing enough arms and legs to make a body-repair shop happy! And it's all his fault." She snorted at Percy, who snorted right back.

"Great work doesn't come cheap," said the Minotaur. "This crypt is my finest creation so far. It is beyond a masterpiece, because I've already produced a masterpiece, and that's just a beginning. Elspeth's tomb will be—"

Esther cut him off, "Will be *serviceable*, I hope."

"It looks secure," I said. "Impressive."

"We'll see about that," said Esther.

She and the Minotaur slipped back outside the crypt, and before Sheyenne and I could ask any questions, the Minotaur flexed his muscles and swung shut the massive door.

The harpy had just enough time to say, in her shrieking voice (which could cut through stone blocks), "I sincerely hope you never get out. Ever!"

After the slab sealed, we heard the loud clang of the massive bolt slamming into place.

# 2

When the harpy had first contacted us about her sister's ailment, I couldn't be sure if she was angling for sympathy or something else. She preened herself in front of Sheyenne's desk. "Elspeth is dying, and she's been doing so for a very long time—an unconscionably long time!"

"Oh dear," Sheyenne said. "I'm sorry to hear that."

"Don't be sorry for her—be sorry for me! I've had to put up with all this."

Esther's sister suffered from a debilitating mange—a lingering illness that made her linger … and linger … and linger, like something out of a heart-wrenching movie of the week but not at all poignant. Esther had been tending her, reluctantly, for some time.

"Elspeth was obnoxious even on her good days—I got all the charm in the family." Esther clacked her teeth together and curled her fingers so that metallic black talons extended from the tips. The harpy family must not have gotten a large share of charm to start with.

"Elspeth won't let anyone see her because the mange makes her revolting. I told her no one would notice because she was revolting before she caught the disease—but she doesn't believe me."

"You certainly have a bedside manner," Sheyenne said.

Esther fluttered her feathers. "I always wanted to be a doctor, except that I can't stand sick people. They're so needy."

I wished Robin were here, because she was always good at handling difficult clients. "Is the mange contagious?" I asked.

"Always thinking of yourself, Mr. Chambeaux!" Esther snapped. "You have nothing to worry about—zombies can't catch it."

"Actually, I was thinking about you," I said.

Esther flapped her arms, extended her plumage, inspected the small pinfeathers in her underarms. "What, do you see any symptoms? I douse Elspeth with bleach every day, as therapy—but if she's infected me, I'll pluck her naked, then tar and feather her all over again!"

I tried to calm her. "Just asking a question. I didn't notice anything in particular."

Sheyenne turned on the charm, which I knew hid her acid annoyance. "And how can we help you at Chambeaux and Deyer Investigations, ma'am?"

"I'm having a new tomb constructed for my sister, a special monument with many added features, designed to my exact specifications. I've got to make sure it's done on time—and properly. There's no room for error."

She withdrew blueprints and spread them on Sheyenne's desk, unceremoniously knocking aside the other papers and folders for our pending cases. As far as Esther was concerned, no other pending cases were as important.

"I've hired the greatest architect to build thick walls, reinforced windows, and an unbreakable door, with a few external decorative flourishes that will make the tomb fit in with the other ones in the cemetery. They have covenants for landscaping and exterior design."

Looking at the blueprints, I was impressed. This massive structure would certainly stand out among the ostentatious crypts and memorial markers at Greenlawn Cemetery. I understood what she was thinking. "It'll be like the great pyramids of Egypt."

Esther snorted. "No—more like Alcatraz. Once I'm finally rid of my sister, I'll seal her up inside there. If she stays dead, then fine—but a lot of people don't stay dead anymore."

Since I had come back as a zombie and Sheyenne came back as a ghost, I said, "Yes, we're well aware of that."

The harpy strutted about our offices. "Elspeth is just too mean to stay dead. Once she goes, I don't want to deal with her anymore. If and when my sister comes back, whether as a zombie or a ghost, I want her sealed up where she can't bother anyone again. *Ever*. So, I have to be sure that tomb is undead proof." Her eyes glittered at me and Sheyenne. "That's where you two come in."

# 3

A private investigation agency has to take cases of all kinds, but some are more unpleasant than others.

We were sealed inside Elspeth's fortress-like crypt, but I had no intention of staying there. As Sheyenne drifted in front of me, her faint glow illuminated the austere vault. Her blue eyes sparkled, and so did her smile. "It's not so bad, Beaux—we're getting paid to be alone together in a very private place."

"I'd rather take you to a coffin-and-breakfast of our choosing." I walked to the solid stone door, pressing my hands against it, tentatively using my strength. I knew it wouldn't be easy to break out of the tomb, but I had to start somewhere. I pressed hard, felt no movement—the old immovable object and irresistible zombie conundrum. I felt around the crack with numb fingers but couldn't find any latch or self-release button on the door.

Partly due to Robin's recent legal efforts, laws had been passed requiring all crypts to have emergency-release locks since you never could tell when someone might wake up and need to get out. But Percy the Minotaur had not built this tomb to code.

I pounded on the door, hard, but that did no good. My cold flesh didn't even make a satisfying thump. I wondered if Esther and Percy were still waiting out there, amused, trying to see how quickly we could escape from this trap.

"If you're that anxious, I'll just slip through the wall, undo the latch, and open the door," Sheyenne said. "It's handy to have a ghost around."

She drifted in front of me, gave me an air kiss. As a traditional ghost, she could flit through any solid object, and her poltergeist abilities allowed her to manipulate inanimate objects.

She gathered speed as she headed toward the stone wall. Normally she would've melted right

through without a sound; instead, I heard an alarming wet *smack*, and Sheyenne's beautiful form flattened out as she pushed and pushed against the stones. It was a very strange sight. I heard a thrumming as she continued to push, growing more and more flustered. Her form was distorted into a strange blob-like female outline plastered against the impenetrable wall. Finally she withdrew, recomposed herself, and hovered in front of me, shaken.

"That's not what I expected," I said.

Sheyenne ran her ghostly fingers on the surface. The glistening coating sparkled faintly with an afterwash of her spectral impact, and I remembered the protective film that the Minotaur architect had applied throughout the interior of the tomb.

She sighed. "Maybe this case is going to be more difficult than we thought."

If Esther's sister came back from the dead, she would return as a zombie or a ghost; therefore, Esther had instructed the architect to design a tomb that was proof against either one. A ghost harpy sounded even more unpleasant than an everyday harpy. And a *zombie harpy* … well, I didn't even want to go there.

Zombies were strong and persistent, but it wouldn't be hard to build thick enough barricades to contain a shambler, even a well-preserved one like me. A ghost was more difficult to contain permanently, but this new anti-ectoplasmic film seemed quite durable and effective.

"Esther must really be worried about her sister harassing her from beyond the grave," I said.

With increasing persistence, then frustration, Sheyenne flung herself against different walls of the crypt, then the ceiling, even the floor, but she couldn't get through. She drifted up to the narrow windows, hoping to find some chink there, but the reinforced panes remained sturdy. The anti-ecto coating was everywhere.

When hiring us to break out of this unbreakable crypt, we hadn't established any kind of time limit. That was my fault for not thinking through the parameters. Robin always chastised me for entering into agreements without my lawyer partner vetting them first. Live and learn … or, live, die, come back from the dead, and still miss the point.

I yanked on the raised stone coffin slab, and Sheyenne stood on the other side using her poltergeist powers, hoping we could uproot it, topple it, find a loose floor tile or something. No good. The slab and its base remained as sturdy as a redwood tree.

I removed my .38 from its holster, and Sheyenne looked at me, puzzled. If I fired the pistol, any bullets would just ricochet around the walls, but I had something else in mind.

I use the butt of the weapon to hammer the saliva-like varnish, pounding and pounding, but the film remained smooth, unscratched. "I was hoping to make a dent, chip away enough so that you could work your way through a chink in the armor."

She pressed her ghostly hand where I had been hammering but couldn't find the tiniest nick. That stuff was tough!

Thinking the windows might be more vulnerable, I pressed up against the wall, reached as high as I could, and grasped the narrow sill. Pulling myself up, I raised my other hand and pounded on the glass with the .38. Again, the glass was armored, and the anti-ecto coating too thick. I didn't make a dent.

Back on the floor again, I tried to think the problem through. The cases don't solve themselves, but even with a hole in my head I can usually figure out a puzzle.

"Ah, of course!" I reached into the pocket of my sport jacket, removing my phone. "I'll just call somebody to get us out of here."

"That's probably cheating," Sheyenne said.

"The case agreement didn't preclude it."

Robin was far away and wouldn't be back in the Unnatural Quarter for days, but I had plenty of other friends in the Quarter I could call—particularly, Officer Toby McGoohan from the UQPD, my best human friend. I just needed to get him on the phone and we'd be all done here tonight.

The phone said No Service. Of course. Esther and Percy would've thought of that and put in shielding. These days, almost everyone elected to be buried with a phone handy.

I sat down on the stone slab. "I hate to admit it, Spooky, but I think we're stuck."

## 4

Early in the case, Esther insisted that we meet her architect, as if we were challengers in a grudge match.

Percy Minotaur, Sr. was well respected in his field, not just in tomb design, but he had also studied with a man who claimed to be Houdini's ghost, working on a contract job for the Unnatural Quarter's prison system. Houdini's ghost and Percy developed specialized unbreakable prisons and holding cells for various unnaturals, demons, specters, and the like. Eventually Houdini's ghost was exposed as a fraud, that he was actually *Jim* Houdini, no relation whatsoever to the legendary magician. Jim Houdini was arrested, but before he could be brought up on charges he had miraculously escaped and still remained at large.

Percy the Minotaur's work, however, was quite remarkable. He had accepted Esther's commission to build an inescapable, unbreakable tomb for her sister, just in case. He seemed to relish the challenge.

Upon first meeting the bare-chested Percy, I asked him why he insisted on remaining shirtless all the time. Sure, he had a broad chest and decent biceps, but he wasn't going to win any Mr. Unnatural America contests, especially with a paunch showing over what should have been washboard abs.

The Minotaur reached up to touch his big blocky head and his wide set of curved bullhorns. "Because of these. I can't ever pull a shirt over my head."

That made perfect sense, I supposed.

"How about something that buttons down the front?" Sheyenne suggested. "Maybe a nice Hawaiian shirt?"

Percy seemed embarrassed. "I never thought of that."

Esther stood in the architectural offices, impatient. "On with it. Just show them your portfolio." The Minotaur displayed and explained photos of other buildings he had done, the façade of the Metropolitan Museum, several impressive tombs.

"My aim is to become the most respected, most widely known Minotaur architect in the entire Quarter. I'm very bullish on my career."

He had spent a summer sabbatical at Notre Dame, considering how to create a fusion of Gothic cathedral architecture with typical Unnatural Quarter buildings.

"A developer wanted me to design tract homes in a new subdivision but I would never stoop that low. A gated community is the minimum I would consider." With a fist he pounded his unspectacular chest. "My great works will endure the test of time. They'll last for millennia, like the pyramids."

"As long as they can endure a pissed-off undead harpy," Esther said. "That's all I care about. Better hurry up and finish the building."

"How long do you think your sister has left?" Sheyenne asked.

Esther made a disgusted sound. "She's been at death's doorway for years and years but she just stands there on the welcome mat. How I hate it when she lingers. I wish she'd get on with her death so I can get on with my life." She pointed a talon at me. "Your case, Mr. Chambeaux, is to test out the new crypt. My architect is confident but I don't believe anyone. I wasn't hatched yesterday."

"What exactly do you want us to do?"

"You'll be locked inside. If you can escape, then you get paid. If you stay trapped in there until Elspeth dies—and that could be years and years—then the Minotaur gets paid."

# 5

I had heard grim stories of trapped undead who were left to tolerate an eternity of unending boredom: vampires given the Jimmy Hoffa treatment, sealed in a coffin wrapped with silver chains and then sunk at the bottom of a deep cold lake where the poor bloodsucker had to lie there without even a book to read or a digest of Sudoku puzzles. Or zombies that rotted and fell apart, unable to move … but if the brain remained alive, did the inanimate decomposing pile of tissue just while away the hours pondering the meaning of life?

Now Sheyenne and I were stuck inside a sealed crypt. Nobody knew where we were, and the harpy certainly had no intention of letting us out.

Through the narrow windows, we watched night set in, then daylight again … and now night had fallen once more. Sheyenne's frustrated spectral glow was the only illumination to keep me company.

We'd been stuck in the tomb for more than a full day. After we had exhausted the first round of escape

possibilities, neither Sheyenne nor I had any idea what to try next. Robin wouldn't come back to the office for another week. As soon as she found us missing, she would immediately know something was wrong but she'd have no clue where to look for us.

Officer McGoohan would be concerned much sooner than that but he wouldn't know where to look either. He'd file a missing monsters report and he'd worry about me far more than he would like to admit—but that didn't mean Sheyenne and I were getting out of there any time soon.

For a while, Sheyenne let herself enjoy the quiet solace of the two of us together. We had all the makings of a romance to last throughout eternity, though I had never pictured our epic romance would all take place in a single room.

"Somehow I thought I'd have a more spectacular end than this, Spooky," I said as we sat together on the slab. "My first death was kind of embarrassing, getting shot in the back of the head in a dark alley while trying to solve your murder." I had no reason to wear a fedora inside a sealed tomb, so I took it off, set it in my lap. "Now here we are, stuck, with no place to go, not even solving a case."

"You'll figure out something, Beaux."

"I suppose we can hope that Elspeth gives up the ghost soon so they'll have to open up the crypt. But that's not the way I'd like to wrap up a case. After all my detective work, I never thought I'd be stumped by a locked-room mystery."

Sheyenne snuggled close to me so that her ectoplasmic body blended into mine. I wished I could feel something solid, but we took comfort in each other's presence nevertheless. Although death was no piece of cake, her afterlife hadn't been too bad. We had a good thing.

We reminisced about the times we had together, but I could tell she was growing agitated. Finally, Sheyenne flung herself at the film-coated walls and ceiling, again and again, becoming panicked. She smashed against the barrier, distorted her spectral body, then flew off to strike a different wall, trying to find some weakness in the protective film. She was like a moth, battering herself against a lamp.

I lurched to my feet and tried to catch her, but of course she slipped right through my grasp. I tried to calm her. "Hey, Spooky—let me think. I know you have faith in me, so let's work this through. Calm down."

"I don't want to be stuck in here anymore! I just want to get back to normal." Sheyenne slumped back on the slab and sat shuddering.

"Normal?" I said, cocking my eyebrow. "We have to break out of a sealed tomb that was built for a harpy by a Minotaur, and then go back to work for a detective agency in a city full of monsters. Yes, let's get back to normal."

I worked my way around the sealed door again, looking at the corners, looking at the wall. Maybe I would notice a clue after all.

Sheyenne said in a depressed voice, "Looks like this tomb will stand the test of time, like the pyramids—just like that arrogant Minotaur said."

"He's talented, I'll give Percy that. He did exactly what Esther hired him to do," I said. "But I didn't really see him as arrogant—just proud of his work. He intended for this crypt to be his masterpiece." Which was saying something, I realized, because we had looked at his architectural portfolio, all the great works he had already created. His masterpiece …

I sat up straighter, turned slowly around. An architect like Percy the Minotaur took so much pride in his work—he would never leave a masterpiece unsigned. Esther wouldn't have let him make a big flourish since she owned the crypt, had commissioned it for her own purposes. But Percy … I was sure he would have found some way.

"Let's look for initials," I said. "Comb every block. If that architect is the artist I think he is …"

Sheyenne didn't let herself show too much hope, not yet, but she flitted to the ceiling and scrutinized the stone crown molding while I methodically—or as is fitting for a zombie, *relentlessly*—went from block to stone block, studying each one, looking for a signature or initials, hoping I'd find what I needed.

Finally, on a floor tile in the corner, back behind the coffin slab designed to hold the harpy's body, I discovered it. "Found it!"

The ghost swooped over, hovering next to me so that her lambent glow illuminated the initials: PMS.

"Percy Minotaur, Senior," I said.

"PMS," Sheyenne said, "could well be Esther's initials. But what good does that do us?"

I ran my fingers over the initials and felt the roughness. If my heart had been beating much, my pulse would've sped up. "Percy chiseled his initials in here at the last minute. He must have slipped in, pounded the letters, and then left before Esther could spot him."

With a fingernail, I tapped the chiseled letters, found a noticeable nick. "And he carved them right through the ectoplasmic protective film. The barrier is broken here, a chink in the armor." I smiled up at Sheyenne. "I've seen you slip through a keyhole when you needed to. Can you get through this crack now?"

She brightened—literally. "Even if there's only a little slit, I'll make it work."

Sheyenne bent over, concentrated, and extended her finger, sliding it through the tiny chisel mark of PMS. The rest of the crypt was sealed to her with the anti-ecto film, but she managed to push her spectral form into that tiny crack.

Her finger went first, elongating, then her entire hand plunged after it. She was gathering speed. "I can do this, Beaux." She flashed me one of those beautiful grins until she spun down and dove entirely into the chiseled letters. She disappeared through the floor tile with a faint *pop*, and her spectral light went out in the crypt, leaving me all alone in darkness.

Until she used her poltergeist powers to throw open the heavy bolt that sealed the door, cracking open the entrance to the crypt. I pushed as hard as I could, shoving open the stone barricade. I worked my way out into the humid miasma of the cemetery night.

Sheyenne was there waiting for me, smiling in triumph. I inhaled a deep breath, and it smelled like roses.

## 6

Proud and satisfied, Sheyenne accompanied me as we presented our bill to Esther the harpy for services rendered. Sheyenne insisted on carrying the paperwork herself. Somehow, I don't think she liked the harpy much.…

Esther was meeting with Percy the Minotaur inside his offices, going over landscaping concepts and shrubbery arrangements for the exterior of Elspeth's tomb. Esther was never in a good mood but right now she was particularly unhappy to see us. Instead of welcoming us back, instead of graciously accepting defeat, her bird-bright eyes flashed like black lasers. She whirled to the Minotaur, shrieking. "You miserable failure!"

"Now there's no need for that, Esther," I said. "You hired us to test the tomb. I'm sure he can make modifications." I wasn't sure I wanted to suggest improvements, though; no matter how awful Elspeth was—and harpies had their own separate category for "awful"—no one deserved to be sealed away like that for eternity.

"No! I want him to start from scratch and do it right next time—and I'm not paying you until it's perfect."

Percy snorted so loudly that the gold ring in his nose flapped and jangled. "This is bull!"

Sheyenne slapped our bill down in front of the harpy. "We, however, expect to get paid. We did exactly what we were contracted to do."

Esther shrieked, "You'll get paid when—"

"We'll get paid *now*, thank you," Sheyenne said. "You can take it out of your tips at the Ghoul's Diner."

Esther always provided abominably bad service, but she was so intimidating that customers were afraid *not* to leave a tip.

With a huff and a squawk, the harpy found a purse somewhere among her plumage and paid us. "This has been a lousy day. My sister suffered a relapse."

"Sorry to hear that," I said. "Is she getting worse?"

"No, a relapse of *health*! Looks like she might last after all.... This is the worst day of my life. And they keep getting worse and worse."

"There's always tomorrow," Sheyenne said in a flippant voice, and she drifted out of the Minotaur architect's offices, with me following her.

As I closed the door, the harpy was launching into a long succession of nagging instructions, but this was no longer my case. "We should make it a general practice not to take harpies as clients."

"Sure, there were problems, Beaux," Sheyenne said as we headed through the bustling, colorful, and unnatural streets of the Quarter, "but I did get to spend time with you, and I like cases like that."

I stuck out my elbow, and she slipped her ghostly arm through mine. It was a charade, but we were

good at it now. As we strolled along, other naturals and unnaturals saw how we were both positively glowing. They smiled at us, and we smiled back.

It was a good day to be alive but, barring that, it was a good day for us to be together.

*Copyright © 2014 by Kevin J. Anderson*

*Alex Shvartsman is a writer, translator, and anthologist from Brooklyn, NY. He's the winner of the 2014 WSFA Award. Over ninety of his short stories have been published to date, including seven at* Galaxy's Edge.

# GOLF TO THE DEATH

## by Alex Shvartsman

"Golf, eh?" the shuttle pilot asked without turning away from his controls. "That's the one with the little white ball that isn't ping pong?"

"That's not a very flattering comparison," said Randy Moreno. "Golf is a noble sport with a long and storied history. I'll have you know it's been called the sport of kings."

"And now it's extinct, just like the kings," said the pilot. "No one plays it where I'm from."

"Oh yeah?" Randy tried his best to look down his nose at the pilot, which wasn't particularly effective as the man faced away from him. "And what backward colony world is that?"

"I'm from Earth, born and bred," said the pilot. "Chicago."

"I think that's horse racing," said Ferrett.

Randy turned to his diplomatic corps handler. He never quite figured out whether Ferrett was his name or a nickname, and the diplomat wasn't forthcoming on the subject. "What's that?"

Ferrett scratched his chin. "Horse racing is the sport of kings. I'm pretty sure."

"Aren't you supposed to be on my side?" asked Randy. "If golf wasn't important, you wouldn't be flying me god-knows-where to play it against god-knows-who."

"That may be." Ferrett held up an index finger. "But I feel compelled to correct you when you're wrong. For your own good, of course. And, in that spirit, it's 'god-knows-whom'."

"Nitpicker," said Randy.

"So, why golf?" asked the pilot. "And why *him*?"

Two weeks out of basic training, Randy was petty officer third class, the lowest of the low on the navy totem pole. He was summoned to the captain's office and asked to volunteer for a diplomatic mission that would involve playing golf against aliens. Even a freshly-minted navy recruit knew better than to volunteer for anything, ever, but the prospect of playing his favorite sport seemed infinitely better than the alternative. It was only a matter of time until his ship was sent to the front lines. Randy would rather play golf with the Devil himself, using hot pokers for clubs, than be thrown into that meat grinder.

"We need someone to play against a Taneer, and Grouchy here happens to be the best golf player we could find on short notice," said Ferrett.

Randy was an excellent player. He might have gone pro if he hadn't been conscripted. But he hadn't expected that skill set to pay off in the navy.

"I've never heard of an alien playing golf before. Even though they totally *should*," Randy added, mostly for the pilot's benefit.

"We're trying to get the Taneers to join our side in the war," said Ferrett, "but we hit a snag. Theirs is a rigid and ritual-based warrior society. Happens a lot with the species evolved from carnivores, rather than omnivores like us." Ferrett's face lit up. Alien cultures must've been as exciting to him as playing eighteen holes was to Randy. "There's a ritual when it comes to opening any sort of negotiations. The parties must designate champions to compete in a pair of one-on-one sporting events, with one challenge chosen by each side.

"If the entreating side wins both contests, it has a huge edge in the negotiations. The other side will pretty much assent to any reasonable requests. If, on the other hand, they lose both times, the talks are over before they begin.

"The most common result is a draw. Everyone's happy, no one's pride is wounded, and the negotiations can proceed in earnest."

Randy thought it over. "And so, our side chose golf."

"Yup."

"Don't take this the wrong way," said the pilot, "but it seems to me the diplomatic corps are a bunch of idiots."

"Is that your professional opinion as a glorified cab driver?" asked Ferrett cloyingly.

The pilot bristled, but Randy cut him off. "Far be it from me to agree with this guy, but seriously, why golf?"

"Neither of you has seen a Taneer before, have you?" asked Ferrett.

They hadn't.

"They look like shaved gorillas, except they're eight feet tall, can bench press four hundred pounds, and have great reflexes. Basically, they're a mix of Spartans and Klingons, with a healthy dose of bulldog thrown in for good measure."

"What's a klee-gon?" asked the pilot.

"An obscure cultural reference," said Ferrett. "Point is, they're stronger, faster, and better coordinated than our top athletes. We needed a sport where physical prowess doesn't provide an overwhelming advantage, and where an experienced player is likely to defeat a stronger, faster opponent."

"Sounds like you should have gone with curling," said the pilot.

"They still play curling in Chicago?" asked Randy.

The pilot shrugged. "They don't play curling anywhere. Just like golf, it's become obsolete since someone invented the superior sport of watching paint dry."

"We'd considered a variety of sports," said Ferrett. "It had to be a one-on-one competition, so no curling. Taneers wouldn't call chess a sport, no matter how much we'd like that. And we had to come up with something quickly, which meant using an athlete from a diplomatic mission or a ship within a few hours' traveling distance of their planet."

"An athlete. Ha!" said the pilot.

"Shut up and drive," said Randy.

☼

The steppe where they landed was covered with sparse, dry grass. Randy nodded to himself; this region of the planet seemed like a fine place to play golf. The air smelled a little funny, and the sky was of a strange, purplish hue, but the temperature and winds were mild, and the gravity felt close to Earth standard. He could work with this.

As soon as the bay doors opened, Ferrett grabbed his bag and got out, without saying goodbye to the pilot.

"Thanks, buddy," said Randy as he picked up his own hastily packed duffel.

"Hey, man," said the pilot. Randy braced himself for another insult, but the older man's lips stretched into a thin smile. "Good luck, all right?"

Randy smiled back and exited the shuttle. A car with extra-large wheels for off-road driving was waiting outside.

Ferrett waved him over. "Come on. There's the unarmed combat bout the Taneers chose as their sport, and then you tee off."

"What, today? I was hoping to play the course a few times, rest up… I'm not even dressed for a game!"

"You can change in the car and rest your eyes until we get there. Sorry if you aren't used to doing things on the fly, but extra prep time is a luxury rarely found in the diplomatic corps."

Ferrett took the seat next to the driver, and Randy climbed into the back. On the seat next to him were two sets of golf clubs. Randy recognized the brand. They weren't top-of-the-line, but they would do.

Randy rummaged through his duffel for the change of clothes. "Two sets of clubs?"

"One for you, one for your opponent," the driver said. "We had to move heaven and earth to find golf equipment in this sector. If you're the superstitious kind and want to chant any sort of voodoo stuff over your set—or the other guy's—now is the time."

"I'm not superstitious," said Randy as he pulled his navy-issue T-shirt over his head and replaced it with a comfortable, loose cotton shirt. He eyed the clubs. "Do I have time to take a few practice swings, at least?"

"Sorry," said Ferrett. "But look at it this way: neither does your opponent. The alien will have never seen a club before the game; that's one of the reasons we rushed everything. They're arrogant enough to accept these terms, and we figured we'd give you every advantage possible."

Randy buttoned his shirt and dug through his bag for pants and sneakers. "This doesn't seem sporting," he said.

Ferrett and the driver both guffawed. "Welcome to politics," said Ferrett.

The car drove past mud huts. Exotic-looking birds and animals grazed behind low wooden fences. There were no signs of electricity or machinery of any kind.

"Just how primitive are these guys?" asked Randy.

"They'll make fine ground troops," said Ferrett.

"And they come cheap," said the driver. "If we can get past their idiotic ritual, we're talking the buying-Manhattan-from-the-Indians sort of bargain."

Ferrett nodded. "Well worth the trouble of bringing you and Mr. Wozinsky here. That's the fighter."

Randy noted the empty huts and abandoned roads. "Where are the natives?"

"At the arena," said Ferrett. "It's not every day they get to see a challenge, and a challenge against extraterrestrials, at that." He pointed ahead. "Speaking of which."

As the car raced forward, the black dot Ferrett was pointing at resolved into a large crowd of aliens. The car parked and the crowd parted to let them through.

A succession of human diplomats shook Randy's hand and introduced themselves. "You're just in time," he was told. "They're about to begin." And, "Thank you for volunteering. You're a brave soul to take on one of these brutes." He promptly forgot everyone's names; he wasn't good with names anyway, and he couldn't help focusing on the aliens standing only a few feet away.

The adult Taneers were seven to eight feet tall, their children almost as big as Randy's five-foot-nine frame. Ferrett's description of them as hairless apes seemed rather astute. Their skin was gray, and they wore gray clothing, making the crowd appear monotone.

Suddenly the background noise among the Taneers spiked. Randy looked around and spotted a Taneer-sized human. He was nearly seven feet tall and twice as wide as Randy. His arms and legs were thick with muscle.

"That's Brad Wozinsky," said Ferrett. "Navy MMA league regional champion, two years running."

Wozinsky and a Taneer faced each other in the center of the arena, waiting for the signal to begin.

The fight lasted all of ten seconds. The Taneer landed three lightning-fast blows in a row, aiming for Wozinsky's face and neck. On the fourth punch the MMA champion collapsed onto the ground.

The Taneer picked up his human opponent. Wozinsky struggled weakly in the alien's grip. The alien said something, the sound lost in the howls of the crowd. Then he grabbed hold of Wozinsky's head with both hands, twisted and released. Wozinsky's lifeless body crumpled, his neck broken, his head turned at an impossible angle.

Randy gasped. Some of the humans around him turned away. They appeared disturbed and revolted, but not surprised.

"What is this?" Randy grabbed Ferrett by the shirt collars. "It was over, the alien had already won. Why did he have to murder him?"

Ferrett spoke, his voice barely audible over the noise. "It's how things are done here. Every Taneeri challenge is to the death."

Randy stared at Ferrett, then at the lifeless body of the marine, then at Ferrett again, fighting the nausea in the pit of his stomach the entire time. When he finally managed to form words, he said, "Hell no," and walked toward the car.

Ferrett caught up to him, grabbed him by the shoulders and spun him around. "Where do you think you're going?"

"I didn't sign up for this," said Randy.

"You literally did," said Ferrett. "You signed waivers."

"I volunteered to play a game. Not to have my neck snapped by a brute."

Ferrett folded his arms. "You listen to me, Randy. You're part of the diplomatic corps now. You'll do what you're told, or be court martialed for treason and executed by firing squad. We tell you to play golf, you play. We tell you to walk barefoot into a fire, you salute and march right in." Ferrett relaxed slightly. "Besides, it's not like you're going to *lose*. It will be one of the bogeys getting their neck snapped. Go get them, man. For Wozinsky."

Randy pictured himself trying to snap a Taneer's neck at the eighteenth hole and the nausea returned in earnest.

✧

The grass on the Taneer-built golf course was yellow, sickly and sun parched—not like the genetically enhanced and well-kept grounds back home. Randy thought he could make it work. No sense worrying about some turf variance when he was playing an unfamiliar course, with never-before-used clubs, on a world with slightly higher gravity than he was accustomed to.

And he was playing for his life.

"No golf cart, sorry." Ferrett pulled the bag of clubs out of the back seat. "No caddies, either. Goes against their idea of one-on-one competition. Hope you're in shape." He handed the bag to Randy.

Randy hefted the bag. He guessed thirty to thirty-five pounds, give or take. Carrying that around for four hours could be strenuous, but he had carried more for longer in basic training.

"Come," said Ferrett. He carried the second golf bag. The crowd parted and let them through to the teeing ground.

The Taneer waiting for them was dressed in the same gray garb as the rest, except his lower legs were bare and the cloth covering his upper legs featured a checkered pattern. He accepted the golf bag from Ferrett.

"Is that… a *kilt*?" asked Randy.

Ferrett stared at the alien with a bemused expression and turned to make sure they were out of earshot of the other humans. "Seems so. I don't know what our diplomats have been telling the natives about golf, but one thing is for sure: the corps didn't assign their best and brightest to this dirtball." He nudged Randy forward.

Reluctantly, Randy approached the alien. He was a little shorter than the others, but his muscular frame still towered over Randy. The alien tilted his head slightly and gave Randy a long, evaluating look.

"Umm, hi," said Randy, realizing that his opponent would likely not understand him. "I'm Randy. I'd wish you luck, but under the circumstances…" He shrugged.

"No luck. Skill. Best warrior wins." The Taneer spoke in a strange, grating but intelligible voice. "Call me Ishmael."

Randy blinked. "Seriously?"

"Learn words when study human speech. Like how words sound. Like name. Use name when speak human."

Randy wondered at how well the Taneer could understand his language, despite the basic sentence structure he used. *Moby Dick* wasn't exactly an early reader book.

"You play first," said Ishmael.

Randy looked ahead to the first hole in the distance. It seemed awfully far away—definitely a par five course. He withdrew the driver from the bag and set up the ball in the tee box. Ishmael watched carefully as he took a few practice swings, then hit

the ball, sending it half way toward the green. Randy smiled. The shot was about as good as he could expect. The crowd howled in what he thought was approval, but quickly realized it was because Ishamel's turn was up next.

The alien had paid careful attention. He copied Randy's stance, and also swung the club several times. Then he sent the ball soaring, all the way across what must have been five hundred yards, landing it near the edge of the green.

Randy winced. The shot was way better than an amateur—let alone someone who had never held a club before—should have been able to muster. He tried to tell himself that the alien's natural ability wouldn't be enough to trump his skill and experience, but all he could think of was Wozinsky's corpse back in the arena.

Randy's next shot placed the ball firmly on the green. The Taneer observed and again imitated his stance and swing. He made the mistake of using the three wood just as Randy had, however, instead of choosing a putter, and overshot by a good amount.

Randy smiled. Despite the physical advantages, his opponent was still a beginner.

As expected, the alien's real difficulty was with the precision putting. It took Randy eight strokes to complete the first hole. Three over par would have been embarrassing back home, but not unreasonable considering his lack of recent practice and the unusual conditions.

Ishmael fared far worse. When the ball rolled past its target on his eleventh stroke, the Taneer roared in frustration and flung his putter toward the little white flag that mocked him as it flapped in the breeze.

He may not have the skill, thought Randy, but he sure has a golfer's temper.

This was when most amateur golfers went on tilt. Their play deteriorated further until there was hardly any point to continue. But those golfers weren't playing for their lives. Instead of tilting, Ishmael sat down cross-legged on the grass, closed his eyes, and remained still for close to a minute. Randy didn't know whether he was meditating, praying, or merely resting, but tension drained from Ishmael's face and his oversized muscles relaxed. Ishmael rose looking like he was in total control, and studied the path between the ball and the hole.

It took him two more strokes to sink the ball.

Randy widened the lead on the second hole, but he gained fewer strokes on his opponent that he had previously. Ishmael was a quick learner and fierce competitor. While Randy managed to play the hole at par this time, Ishmael only went over by two.

Randy rounded the bend, saw the third hole and said, "What the hell?"

The hole was encased by a basket-like fence woven from twigs. There was an opening the size of a melon cut out from the side of the basket. In front of it hung a contraption made from wooden planks which looked suspiciously like four windmill blades. They rotated at a steady pace, hand-cranked via a lever manned by a Taneer.

"What the actual hell?" repeated Ferrett when he saw what Randy saw. "Hang on." He retreated and got into an animated discussion with some of the other diplomats.

After a couple of minutes, he approached Randy with the look of a surgeon who had amputated the wrong leg.

"You do know the difference between golf and mini-golf, right?" said Randy.

"I do," said Ferrett. He pointed at the diplomats clustered behind him. "They don't. Those idiots decided the vague notions they had about the sport based on pop culture references were sufficient because, and I quote, 'The bogeys won't know any better'. When I file my report, heads are going to roll." He caught the look in Randy's eye. "Sorry. Too soon."

"So what do we do about it?"

"We don't want to mess with the game in progress, especially since you're winning. Can you make this work?"

"Yeah. But I don't like it."

"You don't have to like it, Randy. You just have to win."

✧

On the ninth hole, Randy managed to land the ball in one of the hazards. It rested in the bunker. He took several careful steps down the gentle slope of bluish-white sand and tried to work out his best strategy for the next swing.

He was far enough ahead where losing a stroke to a hazard wasn't a huge concern. The alien sun was pleasantly warm against his skin and a gentle breeze caressed his hair. Despite the high stakes, Randy found himself enjoying the game.

He planted his feet firmly and took aim, but before he could take a swing tentacles shot out from under the sand, wound themselves around his right foot, and pulled. He fell backward, and pushed away with his arms and feet, but the tentacles held firm. Each was as thick as a baby's arm. The sand in front of him twisted and shook as something large rose toward the surface.

Randy screamed.

The beast that emerged from the sand looked like a giant worm. Its thick tube-like body towered over Randy for a moment, its eyeless face focused on him like a venomous snake about to strike. The worm opened a circular mouth and its head moved toward Randy in what looked like a slow-motion lunge.

Ishmael rushed past him with a three iron. Wielding it like a great sword he swung mightily at the worm's head. He swung again and again, beating the head back.

The creature growled and its tentacles released Randy, who crawled off the sand on all fours. From the safety of the grass he watched the tentacles re-emerge and try to grab at Ishmael's feet, but the alien was ready. He jumped over them, delivered another blow to the worm's head, then retreated onto the grass next to Randy.

Sensing that there was no more prey on the sand the worm slithered underground.

"Are you well?" Ishmael asked. He was calm, as though he didn't just nearly recreate the scene of Laocoön fighting the snakes. He wasn't even breathing hard.

"Fine." Randy panted. "Thanks."

Ishmael offered his hand and helped the human up.

"Why did you do that?" asked Randy.

Ishmael said nothing, but looked quizzically at his opponent.

"Why did you help me? You're losing the game. And, given the stakes…" Randy trailed off.

Ishmael contemplated this, or tried to find the right words. "Unfair victory is an unfilled victory," he said.

Randy blinked. "You mean hollow. *An unfair victory is hollow.*"

Ishmael nodded, a gesture that left Randy wondering whether similar body language for assent existed among the Taneers or if Ishmael was an even more perceptive student of the humans than he previously suspected.

"Thank you," Randy said again.

☼

Ferrett had nothing but meaningless apologies and excuses to offer. "Taneers are savages," he told Randy. "No wonder they interpreted the term 'hazards' literally. You're doing great. Just stay on the fairway from now on, okay?"

Randy wondered who the savages were. Was it Taneers like Ishmael who, despite his primitive ways, could read Melville months after encountering humans and was capable of doing the honorable thing even if it would likely cost him his life? Or was it the humans who had no qualms with doing everything they could to rig the contest and drag the Taneers into a bloody interstellar war?

Yes, they'd killed Wozinsky. But Randy, a ringer, was condemning Ishmael to death as well.

"I quit," said Randy. "I won't be party to this any longer."

Ferrett's ever-present smile vanished.

"You don't get to quit, Private. Do you want to die instead of him?" He pointed at Ishmael, who waited patiently to resume the game, his face a picture of serenity. "I don't like what we're doing any more than you do, but we've got no choice. The way the war's going we need every bit of help we can find, and if that means sending an occasional good man—or good alien—to their death, we will grit our teeth and learn to live with it, for the sake of humanity."

Randy was sure Ferrett meant business. He liked Ishmael, but wasn't brave like him. Wasn't prepared to give up his own life in order to save his opponent's. And he had his duty. How many human soldiers might die if this treaty wasn't negotiated?

His shoulders slumped, Randy returned to the golf course. He continued to play, even as Ishmael's words stayed with him: An unfair victory is hollow.

☼

It was a landslide. Ishmael was a fast learner and given a few months of rigorous training he might have had a chance against Randy but when he finally putted the ball into the eighteenth hole, he was behind by twenty-three strokes.

Ishmael saluted Randy with the extended fist gesture. "Good game," he said.

Randy swallowed the knot in his throat. "Good game," he managed.

Ishmael kneeled on one knee in front another Taneer, and presented his neck.

"Wait!" Randy shouted.

Everyone looked at him.

"What about the scorecards?"

"What?" asked Ferrett.

"A scorecard must be signed after every round of the tournament, or the player is disqualified," said Randy.

"The scorecards aren't necessary," said Ferrett through his teeth, shooting a venomous glare at Randy. "There were only two of you playing, and the representatives of both species observed and kept score."

"Rules are rules," said Randy. "Both of us should have been disqualified after the first round." He was fairly certain no one present, including Ferrett, would know the difference between a round and a hole. "As such, there will have to be a rematch."

"Unacceptable," said Ferrett. "You've clearly won, regardless of technicality."

"Golf is full of technicalities," said Randy. "What's the point of competing if you don't abide by all of the sport's rules?"

The Taneers huddled. "A rematch is acceptable," said one of them.

Ferrett groaned.

"Not so fast," said Randy. "According to the Augusta National rules, my victory stands until there's a rematch." He was making up rules as he went along, pressing for the desired outcome. "However, Ishmael and I are suspended from competitive play for continuing the game after being disqualified. Seventeen unauthorized holes, at a year each. It will be some time until either of us is permitted to play again."

"This means the negotiations may proceed in the meantime," said Ferrett.

"Absolutely," said Randy.

"This is unusual," said one of the Taneers. "We must discuss this." They walked away.

Ferrett frowned at Randy again and ran after them.

☼

"We negotiated a treaty," said Ferrett. "And I should add you're very, very lucky. If the stunt you pulled to save your playmate had backfired, you'd be charged with treason."

"I just couldn't have his death on my conscience," said Randy. "Glad everything worked out."

"I wouldn't say *everything*." Ferrett grinned in a way that made Randy very uncomfortable.

"What do you mean?"

"The Taneers weren't happy about the Schrödinger's victory bullcrap you made up, so we had to sweeten the deal."

Randy waited for the axe to drop.

"They seem to actually like golf," said Ferrett. "So we traded you to them."

"You *what*?"

"Technically, you're assigned to the diplomatic mission here, long-term. But your actual assignment is to be the bogeys' golf instructor."

Randy relaxed a little. Teaching super-strong, possibly violent aliens to play golf was a hazardous occupation, but not as hazardous as fighting the war.

"For how long?"

Ferrett's grin widened. "For seventeen years, of course. Then you get to have your rematch."

Randy knew the diplomat thought he was punishing him, but seventeen years was a long time. Hopefully, the war would be over long before then.

"Fine." He pondered the legions of Taneer students taking their frustrations out on their equipment. "We're going to need golf clubs. Lots and lots of golf clubs."

*Copyright © 2017 by Alex Shvartsman*

*Brennan Harvey is a quarterly winner of Writers of the Future. His work has appeared in* Golden Visions Magazine, The Spirit of St. Louis, *and* Animism Flash Fiction Anthology. *This is his second appearance in* Galaxy's Edge.

## MY MONSTER CAN BEAT UP YOUR MONSTER

### by Brennan Harvey

I considered remaining in the closet when my kid, Patricia, stomped into her room after school and slammed the door. Lately, she wore a bad mood like no other eight-year-old could, and I understood her emotional wardrobe only too well. This afternoon, she chose anger—a garment she'd chosen more and more these days.

She hadn't always been like this; only for the last year, and I prayed for the day when she'd return to normal. I couldn't bear it if our remaining four-plus years together would be clouded with such dreadful conduct.

My dread turned real when she yelled, "Gell! Come out, now!"

The safety of my dark closet beckoned me to remain in its embrace, and I desired nothing more, but she called me again. I slunk out and approached her, bending low so we were eye-to-eye. Her normally pale cheeks were crimson with fury, and a swash of her hair cut a blonde slash across her face, almost obscuring her wrath-filled, blue eyes. "Me here," I said.

"Good. You're fighting Ogg tomorrow."

"What are you talking ab—" What she wanted struck me with such disbelief I'd forgotten our orders to appear less intelligent in front of our charges. Patricia looked confused by my utterance. I played it off by shaking my head. "Ogg friend."

"Tough. I hate Cal, so you hate Ogg."

Patricia's classmate, Cal, was a good kid. Ogg was Cal Preston's monster, and my comrade. He and Cal played for hours at a time, making up adventures where they would banish evil kingdoms, decimate hordes of skeletons, slaughter legions of malicious wizards, and rescue thousands of oppressed serfs. Ogg loved Cal as much as I loved Patricia.

She and I used to spend hours together sipping make-believe pink tea, playing dress-up, creating adventures with her Barbies, and playing in the backyard. Lately, though, she just made me answer her every irate whim—cleaning her room, sneaking snacks from the kitchen, doing her school work, and entertaining her when she was bored, or worse, when she was being ignored by her parents.

"What Ogg do?" I asked, careful not to stoke the fire of her ire.

"He's Cal's monster. Cal's a stupid head."

"Me no understand. What Cal do?"

"He wouldn't let me play in his stupid kickball game. He said I was too bossy. Bossy! I'm not bossy, right?"

Before I could say anything, she continued, "So, I told Cal that my monster could beat up his monster. Tomorrow."

I shook my head again. "Me can't—"

Patricia stomped her right foot hard enough that I felt the floor shake. "Gell, you *have* to do this. Tomorrow, after school. You're fighting Ogg." She left, and slammed the door upon her exit.

I lumbered back to my closet, shut the door, and sank into my comfortable corner under Patricia's winter wardrobe. Fight Ogg? It was the worst thing she'd ever demanded of me. Worse than using me as a target while she threw shoes. Worse than demanding I rummage through the disgusting trash to retrieve the doll she'd thrown out in anger, and then had to have back. Worse than making me let the air out of her dad's tire after he'd grounded her for pinching her baby brother, Michael.

That was when her behavior turned—the day her mother gave birth to her new baby brother. He was four weeks premature, and the family spent much of their time with him at the hospital. Patricia was mandated to stay in the waiting room. When the baby did come home, her parents felt Patricia was too young and didn't have a delicate-enough touch, so they isolated him from her. They spent all their time with him, in his room or carrying him around the house. She complained they hugged him more than they hugged her, kissed him more that they kissed her, played with him more than they played

with her. She believed they loved him more than they loved her.

Rather than bonding with her new brother, Patricia learned to hate Michael. I tried to council her, teach her, reason with her, but every time I did, she discarded my advice with the flick of her wrist. "What does a stupid old monster know?" she'd ask.

*Over a thousand years of experience*, I thought. I'd mentored hundreds of children in the past, and I reminded myself I'd get through this crisis with Patricia as well. I just needed the time.

Consequently, Patricia did anything to get her parent's attention—any attention, good or bad. She tested their every boundary; not getting up for school, cutting her own hair, running away from home, revolting against her bedtime, and defying every rule, be it at school or at home. Her self-fulfilling rebelliousness got her into more trouble, and reinforced those feelings of jealousy, hatred, and her own insecurity.

In less than a year, she'd turned horrid to everyone. She even started taking out her frustrations on me. Now it seemed Cal—and by association Ogg—provided the focus for her retribution.

"I can't fight Ogg," I whispered to myself in the darkness. The Great Council forbade monster-on-monster fights. Besides, Ogg and I were friends since ages ago. We'd grown up in the same tiny academy, the same troupe, even the same bunk bed—me on the top (at Ogg's insistence,) him on the bottom. We studied Latin, philosophy, chemistry, and mathematics together, ate breakfasts and dinners together, and took vacations and school holidays together. Centuries later, when Patricia became my kid and Cal became his, it was the first time we'd seen each other in almost a hundred years. It was like we'd never been separated. It was refreshing to—

Patricia interrupted my recollections with, "Gell, get out here!" I'd been so wrapped up in reminiscing, I hadn't heard her come in. I stepped out and bowed low. "Me here."

She plopped down on her bed, and a whooshing wave traveled out under her pink bedspread. She lay on her back with her arms spread wide. "Mom and Dad are in Michael's room." She let out a long, loud sigh.

I didn't know how to reply without hurting her feelings, a situation I'd found myself in more and more frequently. Silence was often the best action around Patricia these days, so I nodded and sat on the floor next to her bed.

She sat up, faced away from me, and said, "Braid my hair." It wasn't a command, but a simple request from a friend. She sounded like she used to, before her brother arrived and upset her comfortable world. I pulled the brush off her chest of drawers and, pinching it between my thumb and forefinger, gently smoothed out her luxurious hair, parted it into three tresses, and started plaiting it together.

"Me like your hair," I said.

"Thanks."

I felt warm and comfortable deep in my chest. Just like that, my Patricia was back—my Patricia from last year, my wonderful little girl who I'd spent the last five years with. I finished braiding as we sat in relaxed silence. She inspected my work in a hand mirror, gave me big hug, and said, "I love you, Gell."

A lump formed in my throat. I placed my mammoth hand on her tiny back and said, "Me love you." And I did. My Patricia, my kid, my charge, my world. My friend had returned, and joy filled my bosom.

The moment shattered when her mother called her down for dinner. Patricia's mood turned in an instant. "Okay!" she yelled, and whispered "God!" She stormed out of the room.

I lumbered back to my closet. For a wonderful, but fleeting moment, I'd had my Patricia back. I smiled in the darkness. She was returning. I'd seen a glimpse of it.

I couldn't have been happier.

✿

Late that night, Ogg knocked on my closet door. I invited my associate in, pleased to see him, yet concerned at his unscheduled visit. We monsters usually ventured out to visit one another after our kids were slumbering, but I knew this wasn't a routine social call from my old friend.

I hugged him. The sharp scales of his shoulders brought back fond memories of our crèche days. "Well met, my old friend," I said. "Might I assume your reason for this evening's congress?"

"This altercation between us, scheduled on the morrow. If the Great Council discovers Cal and Patricia's plan . . . ."

He didn't finish his sentence; he didn't have to. There were few circumstances that merited the separation of kid from monster—we called it cleaving—other than the kid finishing her twelfth year. But, if they learned of the fracas scheduled between Ogg and me, they'd cleave both of us from our kids.

I swallowed. "I understand, but the Great Council won't find out. They have more important matters to attend to than a couple of misguided kids." I'd kept Patricia's foul treatment towards me from the Council.

Ogg's glowing eyes narrowed into two slits of fiery red. "I'm not willing to risk the cleaving! Cal still has much to learn during our next four years."

I shook my head. "Patricia does as well. She stands at a crossroads. After her brother's birth, she became *the sister* instead of *the daughter*—the older child, rather than the only child. Her bewildered ego is fighting to reestablish its importance. Her confidence is in peril. If I refuse her request—"

Ogg tapped his finger in his palm, and his nail made a tick-tick sound on his scales. "You're worried about how she'll turn out. I share the same concerns about Cal. But think. What outcome would befall your Patricia if you are taken from her right now, when she is the most susceptible? You'd lose the opportunity to teach her, and he'd learn nothing more from you. She wouldn't receive a subsequent monster. She'd forget all about you. She'd remain as sullen as she is right now. You can't want that for her, and Cal surely doesn't deserve it."

Ogg, as usual, clarified my dilemma perfectly. If I refused her now, I had a guaranteed, four-year timeframe to council her, guide her, make it up to her. If I acquiesced to her demands, there was a probability that I could lose her tomorrow. I said, "Curse you," and embraced Ogg again. "Per usual, your persuasion is beyond rebuke."

✿

The next morning, Patricia was in cheerful spirits. That made it hard to tell her, "Me no fight Ogg."

She rolled her eyes. "What?"

I took a deep breath and stared at her. "Me no fight Ogg."

"Don't be such a big baby," she scolded me. "You have to do what I tell you to."

She turned toward the bedroom door, and I grabbed her arm. She wouldn't run out on this conversation. I pulled her back to me and put my hands on her shoulders, forcing her to look me in the eyes. "I will *not* fight Ogg," I said.

Her gaze fell to the floor. Her cheeks reddened. The only part of her topsy-turvy world where she felt she had an iota of control had just been snatched from her. She ducked away from my grasp and took a step backward, her expression a mask of rage. "I hate you," she said, and stormed out of her room.

I returned to my closet, realizing I'd have four hard years of grueling work ahead of me. But at least Patricia and I would confront those four years together.

☼

Patricia had changed on the day I refused to fight Ogg. In the weeks that followed, she never, not once, played with me. She rarely even talked to me or summoned me from my closet. Every time she did call me out, she was horrid. Her ire had poisoned our relationship. My charge to make her a kind, caring little girl was failing terribly. I spent many a night contemplating whether I'd made a mistake by not fighting Ogg. Patricia was so much better before I'd disobeyed her.

On her ninth birthday, only a fraction of the friends attended that were present a year ago. Her parents had set up the party in dining room, and I could observe it through the upstairs banister.

This year, Patricia wasn't the bubbly playmate she used to be. She was more like a dictatorial tyrant. It was a make-your-own-pizza party, and I cringed at the atrocious manner in which she treated her guests. Instead of staying in her seat and asking for toppings, she ran around the table, shoving her guests aside to get what she wanted. She hogged all the cheese, and even stole toppings off the other kids' creations.

When the cooked pizzas were served, Patricia insisted that Cynthia had stolen hers. I'd recognized Cynthia's flower-shaped pepperoni artwork, and thought it was quite artistic. Apparently, so did my kid, because she screamed that it was hers. During the argument, Patricia threw the pizza on the floor,

and Cynthia left the party in tears. Two other guests followed, leaving only two others, who left immediately after Patricia's father dragged her into the kitchen to chastise her for her behavior.

I slunk back to her room and returned to my closet. It was clear that I'd made an enormous blunder not agreeing to fight Ogg. Regardless of the risks, my kid needed some reassurance, some support, some accord.

And I knew how I could do that for her.

☼

The next morning, I stepped out of my closet just after Patricia's mom woke her. My kid was still in bed, and rolled over, turning away from me. "What do you what?" she demanded. Depression dripped from her every word.

I swallowed. "Me fight Ogg."

She sat up in bed and turned toward me. "What?"

Hope returned to her eyes. It gave me added courage. I pushed back Ogg's warnings of cleaving, pushed back the possibility that I might never see her again. Pushed it all away and focused on what she needed from me, right now. I closed my eyes and said, "Me fight Ogg." I paused a moment, looked at her, then added, "If you want."

Patricia smiled in delight, an expression I hadn't seen since I'd refused her request. She threw off her covers, scampered across the bed, and hugged me tightly. "Oh, Gell, thank you."

I put my arms around her and held her gently, relieved at her newfound joy. We stayed that way for a good minute before she broke our embrace. "This will teach stupid old Cal," she said. "This will teach him good. He'll have to let me on his kickball team now. And then he'll see that I'm just as good as him and his dumb boy friends."

She went on and on, just like the joyous chatterbox she used to be. She formulated excited plans, with nary a shred of anger or depression. I nodded at her declarations, smiled at her hopes, and applauded her plans right along with her. When her mother finally called her down for breakfast, she answered with a cheerful, "Coming" instead of the "Okay!" she'd recently started barking with annoyance.

She hugged me again, said, "I love you," and rushed downstairs.

My merriment vanished with a shard of panic that stabbed me in the gut. I'd lose Patricia forever if this didn't go exactly right. I swallowed and focused instead on the glee Patricia expressed. It'd been an excruciatingly long time since I'd seen her so elated. If I could battle Ogg without the Great Council discovering, it'd be a milestone in recovering the Patricia of old, the Patricia who, until the birth of her brother, was a fun-loving, wonderful kid. I'd see my dreams of Patricia growing into a loving, graceful teenager full of caring, charisma, and confidence come true.

I returned to my closet, confident that my plans would be triumphant.

Two days later, on a cold February afternoon, after Patricia's school was dismissed, I stood in the center of a circle of chanting children, face-to-face against best friend, Ogg. No other monsters were present. They must have been afraid what would happen if the Council found out. I was almost surprised that Ogg was there.

The snow on the playground had already been trampled into a gray mess by the children's recess, lunch, and after-school footprints. It was so battered that even the monster-on-monster skirmish would leave few traces, thankfully.

Ogg stood three yards away from me. His eyes betrayed his thoughts—he didn't want to be here, didn't want to fight me, didn't want the consequences he believed were inevitable. I understood, but ignored my nagging conscious and focused on Patricia's rekindled jubilation during the past few days. Ever since I'd agreed to her plan, she hadn't had one angry outburst, hadn't had one cross word for her parents, hadn't had one bout of depression. She was improving, and I focused on that. It was all that mattered.

I stared Ogg down, pushing aside the memories of our years in the academy, pushing aside his warnings of cleaving, pushing aside my fear of the Great Council. I focused on Patricia's improved behavior. When she said, "Get him," I charged Ogg, determined to give her the victory she needed.

Ogg sidestepped at the last moment and I shot past him at full speed. I reached out, and my fingers brushed his scaly skin, but I couldn't get any purchase. It was then that I realized my momentum carried me toward the circle of cheering children. I jumped just in time and cleared them, thank goodness. Skidding to a stop, I stared at Ogg, then at Patricia.

Her grin was infectious as she cheered me on. I walked back into the circlet of kids, closing the distance to Ogg. He said, "Me no fight!"

I roared at him. Bare-leafed trees shook and window panes rattled at my anger. My guttural reverberation bounced off the buildings and refocused on the circle of kids, transforming their cheers into an eerie silence. A towheaded, crew-cut lad whimpered and stepped back. On the front of his pants, a stain formed. Other kids backed away as well.

My stomach collapsed. The children were terrified. I looked to Patricia. Her former glee was now a mask of horror. Cal ran forward and hugged Ogg around the leg, staring at me with contempt. He choked out, "Y-You leave him alone." Ogg used his huge, protective arm to move the boy behind him.

There was a blinding flash and, in an instant, Ogg and I were no longer in a slush-covered playground surrounded by terrified children, but stood on a smoothly polished, obsidian floor in front of the Great Council.

Ogg snarled, "I hope you're satisfied."

Grand Council Monster Bly said, "Silence!" Her voice resonated throughout the chamber.

A trickle of dread ran down my back. I'd gambled, bet on the pass line, and it had all come up craps. My thoughts weren't focused on Ogg, anymore. They weren't focused on the council or Bly. My thoughts weren't focused on my predicament at all, but on one thing, and only one thing.

Patricia.

She and I would be cleaved from one another. I'd get joined with another kid eventually, but what consequences would Patricia suffer? Her memory of me would be erased without fully coming out of the sulk she was in. She'd remain a mean girl forever because of my poor decisions.

Before I could pull my thoughts back to the Council and my situation, Ogg caught me around the waist and tackled me to the ground. The hammer-falls of his fists pummeled my head and face.

Fighting him now served no purpose, so I covered my head and let him exercise his furor. The vehemence in his eyes hurt more than his pounding, and I deserved his frenzied indignation.

Two guards pulled him off me, subduing him some five yards away. Ogg's breathing came in frenzied gasps as he struggled against the guards who restrained him.

Grand Council Monster Bly raised her slime-covered arm and said, "Remove these hooligans from our presence!"

✿

For half an hour I'd waited in an anteroom lined with purple drapes and drank mud coffee. Eventually, two guards arrived and escorted me to Grand Council Monster Bly's chambers. It was the first time I'd ever been summoned by a Council member, let alone the *leading* member. My stomach should have churned the whole trip there, but it remained idle. Even when standing on the opposite side of her desk, I felt no anxiousness, nor fear for myself. My only unease came from thoughts of Patricia; how I'd failed her, how'd we be cleaved, and how she might metamorphose in her solitude. I shivered at the real probability that she'd grow up to be horrid.

Ms. Bly cleared her throat, refocusing my attention toward her and my predicament. I endured her gaze, prepared for her wrath. I'd heard how her serene voice could transform in an instant and strike terror into any monster's soul. "Gell, I understand your charge initiated this altercation between you and Ogg."

Cal had agreed to the fight as well, but I didn't want to destroy Ogg's future. I said, "It's true, Ma'am."

"And that you initially balked at the proposal."

"Ogg convinced me that the risk of cleaving was too great." I shook my head. Why hadn't I listened to my old friend? "I initially agreed, but . . . ."

"You and Ogg grew up together, attended school together, even petitioned for assignments a mile apart from each other on eight separate occasions. And yet, you agreed to this mêlée, endangering both of your assignments."

And now Ogg would be cleaved from Cal. I didn't know if our friendship could withstand what I'd done. My emotions closed off my throat, constricting

any speech. I could only nod in confession of Grand Council Monster Bly's accusations.

Bly's voice dropped an octave. "Explain yourself."

"Patricia," I choked out.

"No," she answered back, standing and leaning over her desk. "She manipulated you into this. Your charge hadn't abandoned the idea of a monster battle, she manipulated you into it."

I cleared my throat. "No, Ma'am. She had given up on the fight. But she hadn't just given up on that. She'd given up on me. She'd given up on everything. She'd become a depressed, angry, mean girl."

"You violated our rules to help your charge? You don't expect me to believe—"

"It's true, Ma'am." I heard the elevated tone of my own voice, took a breath, and lowered it to a more respectable level. "Grand Council Monster Bly, Patricia has changed so much in the last year. Her prematurely born sibling, coming in her formidable eighth year, was like gigantic boulder dropped onto her self-esteem. Her parents, obsessed with their frail child, isolated Patricia's from her brother. The mother and father simply didn't have the time or the skills to reassure her. Her life shifted around her, more than she could handle."

Bly nodded. "Inferiority complex."

"Exactly! Her parents switched much of their attention to her new, helpless baby brother, and she suffered in their absence. She no longer felt wanted. She started openly disrespecting everyone; authority figures like parents and teachers, even her friends. She started misbehaving, acting malicious, and treating her peers unkindly. I'd felt I'd failed her. By agreeing to her foolhardy demand, I was sure I could turn her around."

"But, Gell, you understand our non-combative policies."

I lowered my head. "Yes, Ma'am."

"Monster-on-monster altercations are not allowed, period."

"I understand." This was going as gravely as I'd imagined, other than the lack of shouting. "I'm sorry, ma'am. I'd hoped the Council wouldn't—"

"Wouldn't discover your clandestine plan? The Council knows everything about the monster world, both in our realm, and in the human's. Nothing escapes our notice."

"Sorry, Ma'am. I only wanted to help my kid. To fulfill my charge."

"How does cleaving help your charge?"

I sighed. "It doesn't. Not one iota. But when I agreed to her demands for a battle, it returned her confidence, made her feel competent, valued. By doing the impermissible, she'd stepped back from the abyss she was heading toward before her world summersaulted."

Ms. Bly just stared at me, her face an indecipherable mask.

"I only wanted to help Patricia," I said.

Bly rose from her desk, and asked, "Would you do it again?"

Of course I wouldn't. Being cleaved was the most scandalous act that could befall a monster, and by fighting Ogg, I'd discredited myself and Ogg as well. I'd not only lost my kid and my reputation, I'd probably lost my best friend as well. It was the most miscalculated mistake of my long career.

And yet, I'd witnessed a transformation in Patricia's demeanor when I finally agreed to her wishes. I witnessed the success in her eyes, the triumph in her smile, and the achievement in her posture.

"I want to say no," I confessed, "but that would be a falsehood. Agreeing to the fight had worked. It had helped Patricia, and I'd do anything to help Patricia. She had a sense of importance again.

"I'd suffer any dishonor, defamation, and disgrace over and over and over again, if it would help her." And with that admission, I knew I'd never get another kid again. I knew her memories of me would be deleted. I knew she'd never get another monster. I knew she'd grow up to be just another mean girl, despite all my efforts. My heart beat in my throat, and I swallowed it down.

Ms. Bly turned away from me. "You are dismissed."

I turned and slogged out of her chambers, resigned to my child-less fate. I'd no more than closed the door when another brilliant flash consumed me. I'd been teleported again, into darkness this time. The smell was a familiar one, and my exhilaration swelled with every breath. I was back in my closet again. I reached forward, felt Patricia's clothes, and accidently banged my hand against the wall.

Patricia's voice came from the adjoining room. "Gell?"

Grand Council Monster Bly had returned me to my kid. I felt for my closet door, turned the knob, and stepped into her room. Patricia smiled broadly, resonating her delight throughout the room. She ran toward me and wrapped her arms around my leg. "Where did you disappear to?"

"It no matter." Warmth spread throughout my soul. I put my arm around her shoulders and hugged her. "Me here."

*Copyright © 2017 by Brennan Harvey*

*Kristine Kathryn Rusch has won the Hugo as both a writer and an editor, and has won several reader's choice awards. This is her seventh appearance in* Galaxy's Edge.

# THE OBSERVER

## by Kristine Kathryn Rusch

And so we went in.

Combat formation, all five of us, me first, face masks on so tight that the edges of our eyes pulled, suits like a second skin. Weapons in both hands, back-ups attached to the wrists and forearms, flash-bangs on our hips.

No shielding, no vehicles, no nothing. Just us, dosed, altered, ready to go.

I wanted to rip something's head off, and I did, the fury burning in me like lust. The weapons became tools—I wanted up close and I got it, fingers in eyes, fists around tentacles, poking, pulling, yanking—

They bled brown, like soda. Like coffee. Like weak tea.

And they screamed—or at least I think they did.

Or maybe that was just me.

The commanders pulled us out before we could turn on each other, gave us calming drugs, put us back in our chambers for sleep. But we couldn't sleep.

The adrenaline didn't stop.

Neither did the fury.

Monica banged her head against the wall until she crushed her own skull.

LaTrice shot up her entire chamber with a back-up she'd hidden between her legs. She took out two MPs and both team members in the chambers beside her before the commander filled the air with some kind of narcotic to wipe her out.

And me. I kept ripping and gouging and pulling and yanking until my fingertips were bone. By then, I hit the circuits inside the door and fried myself.

And woke up here, strapped down against a cold metal bed with no bedclothes. The walls are some kind of brushed steel. I can see my own reflection, blurry, pale skinned, wild eyed.

I don't look like a woman, and I certainly don't look like me.

And you well know, Doc, that if you unstrap me, I'll kill the thing reflected in that brushed metal wall.

After I finish with you.

You ask how it feels, and you know you'll get an answer because of that chip you put in my head.

I can feel it, you know, itching. If I close my eyes, I can picture it, like a gnat, floating in gray matter.

Free my hands and I'll get it out myself.

Free my hands, and I'll get us all out of here.

*How does it feel?*

By it, I assume you mean me. I assume you mean whatever's left of me.

Here's how it feels:

There are three parts to me now. The old, remembered part, which doesn't have a voice. It stands back and watches, appalled, at everything that happens, everything I do.

I can see her too—that remembered part—gangly young woman with athletic prowess and no money. She stands behind the rest of us wearing the same clothes she wore to the recruiter's that day—pants with a permanent crease, her best blouse, long hair pulled away from her horsy face.

There are dreams in her eyes—or there were then. Now they're cloudy, disillusioned, lost.

If you'd just given her the money, let her get the education first, she'd be an officer or an engineer or a goddamn tech soldier.

But you gave her that test—biological predisposition, aggression, sensitivity to certain hormones. You gave her the test and found it wasn't just the physical that had made her a good athlete.

It wasn't just the physical.

It was the aggression, and the way that minute alterations enhanced it.

Aggression, a strong predisposition, and extreme sensitivity.

Which, after injections and genetic manipulation, turned her into us.

I'm the articulate one. I'm an observer too, someone who stores information and can process it faster than the fastest computer. I'm supposed to govern the reflexes, but they gave me a blocker for that the minute I arrived back on ship, then made it permanent when they got me to base.

I can see, Doc; I can hear; I can even tell you what's going on, and why.

I just can't stop it, any more than you can.

✧

I know I said three, and yet I didn't mention the third. I couldn't think of her and not think of the Remembered One at the same time.

I'm not supposed to feel, Doc, yet the Remembered One, she makes me sad.

The third. Oh, yeah. The third.

She's got control of the physical, but you know that. You see her every day. She's the one who raises the arms, who clenches the bandaged and useless fingers, who kicks at the restraints holding the feet.

She's the one who growls and makes it impossible for me to talk to you.

You know that, or you wouldn't have used the chip.

An animal?

She's not an animal. Animals create small societies. They have customs and instinctual habits. They live in prides or pods or tribes.

She's a thing. Inarticulate. Violent. Useless.

And by giving her control of the physical, you made the rest of us useless, trapped inside, destined to watch until she works herself free.

If she decides to bash her head against the wall until she crushes her own skull or to rip through the steel, breaking every single bone she has, if she decides to impale herself on the bedframe, I'll cheer her on.

Not just for me.

But for the Remembered One, the one with hopes and dreams and a future she squandered when she reached for the stars.

The one who got us here, and who can't ever get us out.

✧

So you say I'm unusual. How nice for me. The ones who separate usually kill themselves before the MPs ever get into the chamber. The others, the ones who integrate with their thing, get reused.

You think that the women I trained with—the ones not in my unit, the ones who didn't die when we got back—you think they're still out there, fighting an enemy we don't entirely understand.

I think you're naïve.

But you're preparing a study, something for the government so that they'll know this experiment is failing. Not the chip-in-the-brain thing that allows you to communicate with me, but the girl soldiers, the footsoldiers, the grunts on the ground.

And if they listen (ha!) they'll listen because of people like me.

Okay. I'll buy into your pipe dreams.

Here's what everyone on Earth believes:

We don't even know their names. We call them The Others but that's only for clarity purposes. There are names—Squids, ETs—but none of them seem to stick.

They have ships in much of the solar system, so we're told, but we're going to prevent them from getting the Moon. The Moon is the last bastion before they reach Earth.

That's about it. No one cares, unless they have a kid up there, and even then, they don't really care unless the kid is a grunt, like I was.

Only they don't know the kid's a grunt. Not until the kid comes home from a tour, if the kid comes home.

Here's what I learned in our ship: Most of the guys never came home. That's when the commanders started the hormonal/genetic thing, the thing that tapped into the maternal instinct. Apparently the female of the species has a ferocious need to protect her young.

It can be—it is—tapped, and in some of us it's powerful, and we become strong.

Mostly, though, no one gets near the ground. The battle is engaged in the blackness of space. It's like the video games our grandparents used—which some say (and I never believed until now)—were used to train the kids for some kind of future war.

The kind we're fighting now.

What I learned after a few tours, before I ever had to go to ground, was that ground troops, footsoldiers, rarely returned. They have specific missions, mostly clearing an area, and they do it, and they mostly die.

A lot of us died that day—what I can remember of it.

Mostly I remember the fingers and the eyes and the tentacles (yes, they're real) and the pull of the face mask against my skin.

What I suspect is this: the troops the Others have on the ground aren't the enemy. They're some kind of captured race, footsoldiers just like us, fodder for the war machine. I think, if I concentrate real hard, I remember them working, putting chips places, implanting stuff in the ground—growing things?—I'm not entirely clear.

And I wonder if the talk of an invasion force is just that, talk, and if this isn't something else, some kind of experiment in case we get into a real situation, something that'll become bigger.

Because I don't ever remember the Others fighting back.

If Squids can look surprised, these did.

All of them.

☼

So that's my theory for what good it'll do.

There's still girls dying up there. Women, I guess, creatures, footsoldiers, whatever they want to create.

Then we come back, and we become *this*: Things.

Because we can't ever be the Remembered Ones. Not again.

But you know that.

You're studying as many of us as you can. That's clear too.

I'm not even sure you are a doc. Maybe you're a machine, getting these thoughts, processing them, using some modulated voice to ask the right questions, the ones that provoke these memories.

Since I've never seen you.

I never see anyone.

Except the ghosts of myself.

☼

So what are you going to do with me? Reintegration isn't possible; that's been tried. (You think I don't remember? How do you think the Remembered One and I split off in the first place? Once there was just her and the thing. Now there's three of us, trapped in here—well, two trapped, and one growling, but you know what I mean.)

Sending us back won't work. We might turn on our comrades. Or ourself. (Probably ourself.)

Sending us home is out of the question, even if we had a home. The Remembered One does, but she's so far away she'll never reintegrate.

Let me tell you what I think you should do. I think you should remove the chip. Move me to a new location. Pretend you've never interviewed me.

Then you'd just be faced with the Thing.

And the Thing should be put out of its misery.

We should be put out of its misery.

Monica and LaTrice weren't wrong, Doc. They were just crude. They used what methods they had at their disposal.

They were proactive.

I can't be. You've got all three of us bound up here.

Let us go.

Send us back, all by ourselves. No team, no combat formation. Hell, not even any weapons.

Let us die.

It's the only humane thing to do.

*Copyright © 2017 by Kristine Kathryn Rusch*

*Yaroslav Barsukov is relatively new upon the scene. His work has previously been published in* Nature: Futures *and* The Sockdolager. *This is his first appearance in* Galaxy's Edge.

# YOUR GRIEF IS IMPORTANT TO US

### by Yaroslav Barsukov

"I'm in no need of your services, never have been," Mr. Franke said to the pale-faced young man behind the reception desk. "Don't you understand?"

When he'd received the invitation to the family planning center on the official yellow paper, Mr. Franke's first impulse had been to call Catherine and say, "Imagine that, the government is trying to set me up on a date..." For some reason, he never understood why, she loved such absurd situations. He even took out the phone before realizing what he was about to do, that her name wasn't on the contact list anymore, that there was nobody on the other side to answer.

"You're not single, then?" the receptionist asked.

"What do you mean by that?"

The man leaned forward and said slowly, as though addressing a child, "Do you have a new partner?"

"No, but you need to understand, it's been only two months—"

"If you don't require our services, why didn't you call to cancel?"

"I tried. I spent four hours on the phone."

"Well, yes." The receptionist looked down and started writing something Mr. Franke couldn't see. "Our operators can be quite busy. But you should've kept trying."

Mr. Franke wanted to ask him if he knew what it was like to wait on the phone in a hollow room.

If there was one thing Mr. Franke hadn't been prepared for in the wake of Catherine's death, it was how different the house felt without her—like a hotel he'd checked into. In the back of his mind, this thought lingered, that he needed to stay a little longer, and could then return to his real home. To her.

"Well I'm afraid you'll have to explain yourself to the metal head then," the receptionist said. Mr. Franke stared at him, and the man sighed. "To the android. Haven't you seen our new tagline?"

Mr. Franke looked down where the receptionist was pointing. At the desk's front side stood, in red block letters, '2021: YOUR GENES ARE IMPORTANT TO US.'

"Increased funding since January," said the receptionist. "We're employing androids for interviews now, for setting up your profile and all. Experts say people are more upfront with them." The lamp on the desk blinked, dimmed, and lit up again. "And, as you can see, we're still experiencing power issues whenever they recharge."

"Could it all be a mistake?" Mr. Franke said. "I've never been invited here before—"

"What's your IQ?"

"Hundred forty-one."

"Limit used to be hundred fifty and higher." The receptionist shrugged. "Same reason really: more funds, lower cut-off point for the program."

Mr. Franke glanced at the glass cage that was Lincoln's Family Planning Center, at the benches and office plants washed of color by the bleak daylight.

"Have you brought a photo of yourself?" the receptionist said. "It's for the records."

Mr. Franke closed his eyes. "Have you brought me that photo?" Catherine had asked him.

"No," he said to the receptionist, and his past self, at the hospital, repeated the word.

✧

The door hissed open into a small green room with no windows. In the center, a middle-aged man with a crew cut and a hint of bristle sat at a table; there was another chair, and as soon as Mr. Franke settled into it, the man smiled.

"Good day, my designation is AH-56-C. It's a pleasure to meet you. We have one hour."

"The android interviewer."

"Yes, Mr. Franke."

"Then I'd like to tell you, so that we both don't lose valuable time: I don't need this, my wife died two months ago—"

The fluorescent light fixtures under the ceiling blinked and faded. For a moment, Mr. Franke found himself in absolute darkness; then, in silence, a portion of light returned, a bowl-like lamp that glowed dimly on the wall.

He swallowed and, unable to look anywhere else, stared at the android's eyes: in the scant illumination, the backlight from some invisible mechanism bled into the irises.

"What happened?" Mr. Franke said.

"The building has switched to backup generators." The android stared back at him. "On cloudy days, this sometimes happens. The Center's still trying to work out the power issues. Are you straight, gay, or bisexual?"

"I've told you already—I don't want this interview." Mr. Franke stood. "There's been a mistake, I'm not single, I'm a recent widower."

"I sympathize, but the appointment has been fixed. An hour has been allotted, and utilizing my technology costs money."

"How much for me to cancel?" he asked, and when the android answered, Mr. Franke nodded. "I can afford that."

He walked to the door and stopped one pace short of bumping into it: the two panels remained squeezed together.

"We need to wait until the main power comes back online," the android said. "Meanwhile, I suggest we use our time productively and, despite your concerns, conduct the interview."

Mr. Franke ran his hand across the door's frame and slapped the panels—the sound was dull, as though there were something solid behind.

"Have you brought me that photo, darling?" she had said to him on their last day together.

He returned to his chair and, after a short hesitation, sat down. As he leaned forward to prop his elbows on the table, something in his shirt's pocket pressed against his belly, something which felt like a piece of cardboard.

"Are you straight, gay, or bisexual, Mr. Franke?"

"What do you mean? I was married to a woman—"

"Many people remain in denial of their sexuality."

"I'm straight."

"What is your age preference?"

"Same age as myself."

"Height preference?"

"I beg your pardon?" Mr. Franke said.

The android tilted his head. "Do you prefer tall women?"

"What kind of interview is this? And, for that matter, what the hell is wrong with this whole program? Gene preservation—really?"

"Too many migrants," the android said. "The government feels that the national gene pool gets diluted."

"And they plan to fix this with those horrible one-sided questionnaires?"

"The *queries* are only one part of the procedure, Mr. Franke. I'm also running twenty complex heuristics to analyze your behavior during the interview—this data forms the bulk of your profile. The only thing impossible for me to determine are your own preferences. And don't worry, your potential spouse will answer the same questions." The android paused. "Do you prefer tall women?"

Mr. Franke tried to distract himself from the two glimmering irises, and that proved to be a mistake. Tall women. Uninvited, memories surfaced of Catherine on the beach, in a yellow swimsuit, a picture he'd taken while she was staring into the distance. Long legs, that look of casual beauty—she could've been a model if she'd wanted to.

"Mr. Franke?"

He closed his eyes. "Please," he said, "Please. Could we skip this question?"

"We can return to it later. Hair—blondes or brunettes?"

The waves rolled in and washed the beach into nothingness. The lamp on the wall sizzled, and Mr. Franke thought back to all those times Catherine would put a tea kettle on fire and leave the little thing to melt.

"I need to write down your preferred hair color," the android said.

"Brunettes." The room seemed to shrivel around Mr. Franke, bringing the walls and the android closer.

He comes into the bedroom where she sits at the night table, brushing her hair. How was your day, she asks. Fine, how was yours. Brushing her hair, a brown wave upon her shoulders.

There's a mail from the agency; want to open it together? Catherine has tender skin, tender arms. He keeps silent, and her hands pick up an envelope from the table and tear off the edge.

"Eye color, Mr. Franke?"

She takes something from the envelope, a photo, looks at it for a second and smiles. Don't you think he has my eyes? He walks up to her. A picture of a boy, bronze cheeks, sad stare, and the eyes ...

"Gray. She had gray eyes."

The android leaned forward. "By 'her' you mean your prospective spouse?"

"Spouse?" Mr. Franke said. "Oh, yes, of course. Spouse."

She wished a house full of children. He won't be my son, he says. She shakes her head: that little one wants a home too. They all want a home and a mother and a father so badly. Not my responsibility, someone else's, not my seed, someone else's, someone else's. Give me that photo.

I should've agreed to adoption, Mr. Franke thought and said, "Why didn't I say yes?"

Two glimmering splinters blinked from the shadow. "You mean to one of my questions?"

"Pardon ... I'm sorry."

"What type of music should your prospective spouse prefer?"

The room shriveled further. No, Mr. Franke thought, not that memory, not that one.

At the hospital, he had brought her a recording of a violin concerto, and she smiled at him from behind the wrinkles the disease had carved on her face. Cancer took her away from him, bit by bit, over a year.

At the edge of the overbed table lay a half-eaten croissant. "Where's that photo, of the sad-eyed boy we wanted to adopt?" she said.

"I couldn't find it, I couldn't, maybe I'd thrown it into the bin with other papers," he said. "I'm so sorry."

"Mr. Franke? Are you talking to me?"

An expiration date, Mr. Franke thought; android has his, I have mine. People should be gentle with each other before they expire, before they become dust and dirt.

Something rectangular in his breast pocket pressed against his heart.

"I should've agreed to adoption. I remember shouting," he said. "And I couldn't even bring her the picture…" He felt inside the pocket, and his fingers came upon a thick piece of paper, smooth to the touch. He took out the photo and stared at it. "It was in this shirt. It has been all the time."

"Should she enjoy socializing? Taste in music? Is a sense of humor important? Music? Music?" The android's voice flowed now from all directions, pressing the air out of the room as though out of a huge lung.

"In this shirt, all the time. And I couldn't find it." The walls shook before Mr. Franke's eyes, and he felt the way he used to in childhood, when waking up from a nightmare. Everything—the table, the chairs, the android—wrapped around him; a large thing devouring a small thing.

"Should your potential spouse like to socialize?"

"Please," said Mr. Franke. "Stop. I don't want to remember. I don't—"

"Should she enjoy listening to music?"

Glowing eyes floated toward him. *I need to make him stop, if I don't make him stop, I'll die.*

He stood on uneven legs, reached forward, grabbed the android's head, and shoved it into the table. To Mr. Franke's surprise, there was little resistance; it was as though he was gripping a plastic doll.

The android kept repeating, "Music? Music?" and Mr. Franke kept performing the same mechanical motion until it wasn't clear to him anymore who of them was a man and who a machine.

This time, the table before Mr. Franke was white, sterile, without a scratch on its surface. A door opened, and a man with a goatee, a plump folder under his arm, entered the room.

"I'm your lawyer, Mr. Franke," he said, lowering himself into the chair.

The folder thudded against the table.

"Quite a mess you've made at the center, hmm?" The man with the goatee smiled out of the side of his mouth. "Why did you do it, if I may ask?"

"My wife died two months ago."

"Oh, this is good, this is perfect." The man patted the folder. "This means we can claim temporary insanity. And such personal details—the jury always loves those. But, Mr. Franke …" He leaned forward. "… to be able to sway them, I need to know more. Are you gay, straight, or bisexual?"

Mr. Franke squeezed shut his eyes.

"Were you and your wife close?"

*Copyright © 2017 by Yaroslav Barsukov*

*It's hard to call Tina Gower a newcomer any longer. This is her fifth appearance in* Galaxy's Edge. *In addition, she had an incredible five novels out in 2016. Somewhat earlier she won the Writers of the Future Golden Pen Award, the Daphne du Maurier Award for best Mystery/Suspense, and was nominated for the Romance Writers of America Golden Heart Award. She also collaborated with Ye Editor on* INCI, *a Stellar Guild novel.*

## DO NOT CALL ME BENTO

### by Tina Gower

The first cow vanishes in the night on a full moon. My godson brings me the news. I hear no sounds, and my sheep dog, Proteção, doesn't bark. The heifer was thin; truthfully her death relieves a burden. She had no market value, so I let the mystery wither.

The second cow, however, would have brought a fair price. So I camp in the pasture. The long, chilly nights with no theft leave me sloppy, and I sleep. I wake when Proteção licks my face whining and shaking. I know before I count—a third cow has been taken.

When the fourth cow disappears, its shredded body found on the road to the village, I have to do something drastic. I strum my guitar absently watching the wind command the grass to dance in my field. Music helps me think. I pause, forgetting the song my father taught me: B, B7, C minor—it's gone, but I have an answer. The only way to fight a monster is with another monster.

✿

The breeze carries the rot and brine scent of the sea. The cattle huddle close to the house as if they know something else is out there, lurking. Proteção paces and a high-pitched whistle comes with each of his pants. I'm thankful that Antoine will collect my goods for market even with the troublesome accounts on my land, but we are long-time friends.

And he is not superstitious.

Antoine hefts a bag of wool into the wagon. He tugs the bags to the corner, making room for my dried meats. "You're a fool, Bento. A name doesn't hold that much power."

He will take the supplies to the big island, Sao Jorge, for trade. He usually pays me with two jars of milk, a box of vegetables, and a bag of wool, but supplies are short today. Antoine's word is good. He'll bring the difference tomorrow.

"Just the same, do not call me Bento. I'm a seventh son. I should have been cursed to become a beast, but my name blesses me from that fate."

"You're not a beast. It's an old witch's tale meant to coax children to behave. Bento means 'blessed,' nothing more. Nobody believes in old curses."

"The curse is real."

Antoine waves his hand like he's pushing away my words. "Bah."

I don't bother retelling the legend of the seventh son and the conquistador's raids in Africa and the curse from the Nganga. Hundreds of years ago my ancestors chose money over morality. Now every seventh son is cursed to become a beast, the body of a gorilla and the head of a bore, unless we take the necessary precautions to avoid the pull of the moon. "Then why don't I have a wife? Children? Why do the villagers fear me?"

"Tomé is your child," he says and gestures to my godson filling the trough. "The beasts are a myth—"

"—Because we've followed the precautions for generations. Because we remind the younger generations of our mistakes."

"The middle islands are protected," he explains in a bored tone. "Terceira is filled with Jews and Moors who refused to convert. My own family is Jewish. We're Portugal's dumping ground. And thank goodness, we came out the better for it." He makes a face that indicates his distaste for the mainland. "Nobody on this island can claim pure bloodlines to the conquistadors."

"What if a drop of guilt is enough? What if that is all we need?"

He shakes his head. "You're paranoid."

But he doesn't look at me or offer evidence to the contrary.

Antoine wheels the cart away. The squeaks and rattles create a beat that reminds me of a song. I retire to my porch and strum the chords. Tomé finishes his chores early and practically vibrates with energy.

"Uncle," he calls to me. He dances around like a puppy testing the stones in a creek for crossing. "Is that a new song?"

"Yes."

He wipes his finger under his nose, leaving a smear of mud. "Will you teach me to play?"

"Not today. The neighbor boy will be wondering where you are. Go run and play."

He shoots off, dust swirling in puffs at his heels before I can finish excusing him of his duties. The neighbor boy spies at me from the fence. The scent of rot and urine fill my nostrils until the wind changes and it's gone. The boy is gone, too.

☼

Many of the villagers challenge my request to call me João, the name of my father's youngest brother. As usual, the children wrap themselves in their mother's aprons when I pass, staring at me from their fabric fortresses. The women ignore me. The men laugh and shake their heads.

"*Bento* is not blessing enough for you?" Madeira calls.

One old woman spits at my feet. "Choose any surname you wish, that is your right, but change your Christian name? Disrespectful." She throws her hands in the air and mutters about curses while I skirt around her.

I swing my guitar on my back and retreat behind a mound of hay, but I still hear their laugher at my public chastising.

I dig my palms into my eyes. I've asked several neighbors to help keep watch, but none will risk roaming the pastures with me at night. Others have experienced disappearances and there is talk that a beast is already in our midst.

Tomé and I take shifts through the night. Last night while I slept another attack plagued our herd. Tomé dragged the mangled calf into the barn. He bent his head and hunched his shoulders when I discovered him, waiting for his beating. "I must have fallen asleep," he offered as an excuse.

The boy's chin wobbled. He fetched a mound of clean cloth. "Will he live?"

"No," I said. I didn't glance at the boy.

I turned away from him and told him to go to the house. No boy this close to adulthood wishes to have his tears acknowledged. I skipped the punishment.

I know what's next. Next they will run me from my home. I'm the only seventh son they know. My antics have thrust me into the light. They say I embrace the evil eye.

I take a deep breath. My lungs fill with the sweetness of dry hay. Chickens cluck in the distance at the market. I promised to play a tune at the Holy Ghost Festa, so I must regain my composure.

When I open my eyes a young girl stands before me, staring. "You're the seventh son?" she asks.

I nod.

"I'm a servant to a seventh daughter, a bruxa." She offers me a charm and I take it. "There are no names mothers can give to protect their daughters from the *curse* of becoming a witch." She smiles at the word curse. Witches are tolerated, in some places revered, not shamed on our island. "She can give you what you need."

Folded in the fabric charm is a symbol I have seen before. I know the seventh daughter, the bruxa, she mentions. I press her charm to my heart. "Obrigado," I whisper.

The girl scurries off into the market, frightening the pigs in their pens. They squeal and knock over a bucket of muck. I hear a familiar laugh. It is Tomé and the neighbor boy. The air fills with the scent of hot piss. I glare at the boy and motion for him to leave. I take Tomé by the arm and guide him to the path for home.

I cross my arms and wait for him to go. "Stay away from that boy."

He looks confused, but leaves, glancing back and shooting me with hateful looks.

☼

The witch's house is a hunt made of stones by the springs. Steam rises from the fissures along the path to her door. The gate and doors are open, which means anyone may enter. A pot is boiling over a fire a few feet from the house. I peek into the pot and discover bones and bubbling water.

"Come to join me for dinner?" A woman with a hooknose and a gray shawl tied around her head chuckles from the window. Her dress is black. As a widow, she will only wear black. Some say she keeps her gates open so the spirit of her dead husband may come and go freely. "Or are you the Bento my girl has instructed I care for?"

"I am Bento, although I wish people would stop calling me that so I can fight the monster on equal ground."

"You can't break a name from your body until first you break it from your spirit." She holds a long green glass bottle to me. "Here. This is how you become a monster."

I inspect the glass, but don't take it. She quarks a brow and her lips tilt into a half smile. She sets the glass on her crooked windowsill and places a weaving of dried wheat that looks like a cross inside a circle. "And this charm will hold the blessing of your name until you restore it. Drink half the potion; carry the charm around your neck. Dissolve the charm into the rest of the potion. This is all I have, use it wisely. Be sure to drink it all when you're done."

"Done? You mean after I kill the monster?"

She sighs. "Men. Always for blood. And always assuming the world is the way you see it and nothing will dare change." She grins like she knows some secret I don't. "Yes, you can kill *the monster*—" she emphasizes the words using my Sao Miguel accent that has a hint of English, "that's one way to rid it of the curse, but if you can get close enough to the beast all you need is to cut off the left hand."

My face must show my disbelief, because she shoos me away. "Off with you then. Don't waste more of my time. My dinner is burning."

"But that's ridiculous. You expect me to believe it?"

"If you believe there is a beast and you are cursed, why is this solution such a stretch for you?" She watches me for acknowledgement, but when I don't move from her home she sighs. "All right. The hand is an offering. The curse survives because of greed. If you make a sacrifice then it is enough for the curse to be broken."

The water spills over the pot. The old woman scurries out the door, tugging the gray shawl off her head to wave the smoke away.

I take the potions and charm and leave her to her muttering.

✿

For months my fields go untouched, so the remedies sit on the dirt floor of my stone hut.

A man is caught thieving in the next village. Villagers believe he was the one stealing our livestock.

Perhaps I don't need to use the witch's spell. I laugh that I resorted to my superstitious thoughts to explain the mystery.

People begin to ask me to play at the market again. Nobody speaks of the monster.

✿

A priest visits a few months later.

"Are you Bento?" he asks me.

"Yes," I say.

"The people of the village believe you have fallen to the curse of the seventh son. There are many reports of dead animal carcasses by the shoreline and sightings of a man-like-beast with a large hairy body and the nose of a wild pig with horns near your home. They say you've visited a bruxa. Is this true?"

"Yes—but I'm not the monster. I never took the witch's spell. My name protects me—"

"Is your oldest sibling your godparent?" he interrupts.

"No. . ." I choke on my next words. "My oldest brother was feeble and my parents feared he'd not be able to care for me if they passed. They chose a devoted, honored family member and were told it would be enough to ward off the curse."

"They say your house smells of rotten flesh and *pungent odors*." He wrinkles his nose at the words and sniffs the air in confirmation of this observation. "This is the mark of the beast."

"It is not me," I repeat. "I want this beast gone. Do you think I would allow myself to cut into my profits this way?"

The priest shakes his head, convinced not to drag me to the village square for now. "This is a terrible situation. Terrible." I know in his mind I'm already guilty. When he leaves, he blesses each blade of grass and rock as he walks towards the village.

I'm unable to keep from shaking from anger as I stomp to the neighbor's house. I bang on the door.

Jorge Machado opens the door. "Yes, Bento? Is there a problem? Have my sheep gotten loose again? I will send Little Jorge to fetch them."

I wave away his words. "Do you only have five children?"

He pauses. "What is this about, Bento? Is this about the monster again?" He leans against the doorframe and sighs. "We have five last I checked. Or is this about the market? Little Jorge says you forbid him to play with Tomé. I thought it was because he getting older and you know. . ." He makes an uncomfortable swooshing gesture with his hands. "Jorge would never teach Tomé about things he isn't ready to learn."

"You have five children," I clarify. I shift from one foot to the other. I regret I must be forward. Jorge may never talk to me again, but I must know. "Are there any who were. . . lost?"

He laughs. "I haven't misplaced them." He makes a show of looking around.

"You asked me about the beast and now you're deliberately playing with me. Are you hiding Little Jorge's place? Is he a seventh son?"

Jorge straightens and makes the sign of the cross. "I swear on Mother Mary. I tell you the truth. He is my fifth child and we have had no others." He glances into the house to see if his wife is nearby and lowers his voice. "And only one who was taken from us." His expression loses the wrinkles from his smile and I'm sorry to have put that dark look on my friend's face.

I leave him and notice when I look back at his house that he doesn't go back into his home for a long time. His words haunt me all night. I pick at the strings of my guitar and almost find the melody I remember. The wind carries a hint of rancid meat.

☼

Later I spy Tomé with blood on his hands and his shirt is torn. He emerges from the barn soaking wet and an oat sack wrapped around his middle like a dress.

How many attacks from the beast has he hidden from me?

I grab the guitar to calm my nerves.

Tomé sits with me for a while. "Will you teach me?"

"No," I say. "Go to bed."

He drags his feet over to his bed.

I play until morning.

☼

The best way to fight a monster is to become a monster. So I take half the potion on the next full moon and wear the charm around my neck. I secure the potion on my belt, cinching it tight.

My muscles ache. My fingers curl and cramp. The pain comes in waves. Soon I'm forced to the ground because my legs bend to impossible angles and can no longer hold me upright.

Then I hunt him.

The smells are like rivers. They flow from a well of the present and stream out into the past. As a scent grows older it fades until it's so faint I can't trace it. I go to the latest attack and follow a ribbon of scents. Some are dead scents, other cows, other predatory animals that came to clean the carcass, and something other. Something familiar. I know this means something I'm not ready to admit, but now I know it's the only answer that makes sense.

I find Tomé on the shore at dawn. His fur falls in patches, the same as mine as we shift. He is relieved to see me. I know this scent, my godson. And it all becomes clear why Tomé's parents begged me to take him.

Tomé shivers. His clothes are in piled tatters, hanging loose around his waist. "I don't know what is happening to me."

"It's an old curse."

"But I am not. . . ." He swallows in the words as though they're hard for him to say. "I shouldn't be a monster. I'm not a seventh son."

"Your mother may have lost children." Or his father may have some he doesn't know about. I clear my throat. "It explains why your parents didn't give you protection when you were born."

"They thought I was safe. The villagers on my island told them I was cursed. They said they could smell it on me. I didn't understand. They couldn't bear to harm me."

I nod. I show him my knife and explain to him what I must do. His eyes widen to the size of clamshells, his lips press together, chin high, neck long. He places his wrist on the rock. Although his hand is steady his body begins to shake.

"Be swift, Uncle," he says.

I'm proud. I cut once, twice. Blood wells to the surface. He clinches his teeth and doesn't cry out. I think of all the times he asked me to teach me guitar and how he'll never play now.

I stop.

"Don't draw it out," he begs.

"No," I say. "This isn't right." I lay the knife between us. I gather the potion and charm, dissolving the charm into the liquid. I say a prayer and offer the bottle to Tomé.

He flinches from me when I hold it to his mouth. "But you cannot!" He scampers from his seat, holding his bloody wrist to his body. "This is your blessing. Your name. How will you keep the monster in you away?"

I glance at the knife.

His eyes narrow. "You can't mean to. . . You'll never play again."

"I will learn a new way. Perhaps my other hand—"

"It will never be the same. You're good, it will take you years."

"We can learn together." I hold the bottle to him. "Please. Don't draw this out."

He creeps closer to me, still unsure. I bless him in the saint of my namesake. He drinks. He is now fully my son in spirit.

"Now me. And be swift." I give him the knife and present my hand. "This island is too small for beasts."

*Copyright © 2017 by Tina Gower*

**HEINLEIN PRIZE TRUST**
*Dedicated to advancing Robert and Virginia Heinlein's dream of securing humanity's future in space.*

www.HeinleinPrize.com

*Robert Silverberg is one of the true giants of science fiction. He is a multiple Hugo winner, a multiple Nebula winner, has been a Worldcon Guest of Honor, and is a Nebula Grand Master and the author of numerous acknowledged classics in the field.*

# IN THE GROUP

## by Robert Silverberg

It was a restless time for Murray. He spent the morning sand-trawling on the beach at Acapulco. When it began to seem like lunchtime he popped over to Nairobi for mutton curry at the Three Bells. It wasn't lunchtime in Nairobi, but these days any restaurant worth eating at stayed open around the clock. In late afternoon, subjectivewise, he paused for pastis and water in Marseilles, and toward psychological twilight he buzzed back home to California. His inner clock was set to Pacific Time, so reality corresponded to mood: night was falling, San Francisco glittered like a mound of jewels across the bay. He was going to do Group tonight. He got Kay on the screen and said, "Come down to my place tonight, yes?"

"What for?"

"What else? Group."

She lay in a dewy bower of young redwoods, three hundred miles up the coast from him. Torrents of unbound milk-white hair cascaded over her slender, bare, honey-colored body. A multi-carat glitterstone sparkled fraudulently between her flawless little breasts. Looking at her, he felt his hands tightening into desperate fists, his nails ravaging his palms. He loved her beyond all measure. The intensity of his love overwhelmed and embarrassed him.

"You want to do Group together tonight?" she asked. "You and me?" She didn't sound pleased.

"Why not? Closeness is more fun than apartness."

"Nobody's ever apart in Group. What does mere you-and-me physical proximity matter? It's irrelevant. It's obsolete."

"I miss you."

"You're with me right now," she pointed out.

"I want to touch you. I want to inhale you. I want to taste you."

"Punch for tactile, then. Punch for olfactory. Punch for any input you think you want."

"I've got all sensory channels open already," Murray said. "I'm flooded with delicious input. It still isn't the same thing. It isn't enough, Kay."

She rose and walked slowly toward the ocean. His eyes tracked her across the screen. He heard the pounding of the surf.

"I want you right beside me when Group starts tonight," he told her. "Look, if you don't feel like coming here, I'll go to your place."

"You're being boringly persistent."

He winced. "I can't help it. I like being close to you."

"You have a lot of old-fashioned attitudes, Murray." Her voice was so cool. "Are you aware of that?"

"I'm aware that my emotional drives are very strong. That's all. Is that such a sin?" Careful, Murray. A serious error in tactics just then. This whole conversation was a huge mistake, most likely. He was running big risks with her by pushing too hard, letting too much of his crazy romanticism reveal itself so early. His obsession with her, his impossible new possessiveness, his weird ego-driven exclusivism. His love. *Yes*, his love. She was absolutely right, of course. He was basically old-fashioned. Wallowing in emotional atavism. You-and-me stuff. I, me, me, mine. This unwillingness to share her fully in Group. As though he had some special claim. He was pure nineteenth century underneath it all. He had only just discovered that, and it had come as a surprise to him. His sick archaic fantasies aside, there was no reason for the two of them to be side by side in the same room during Group, not unless they were the ones who were screwing, and the copulation schedule showed Nate and Serena on tonight's ticket. Drop it, Murray. But he couldn't drop it. He said into her stony silence, "All right, but at least let me set up an inner intersex connection for you and me. So I can feel what you're feeling when Nate and Serena get it on."

"Why this frantic need to reach inside my head?" she asked.

"I love you."

"Of course you do. We all love all of Us. But still, when you try to relate to me one-on-one like this, you injure Group."

"No inner connection, then?"

"No."

"Do you love me?"

A sigh. "I love Us, Murray."

That was likely to be the best he'd get from her this evening. All right. All right. He'd settle for that, if he had to. A crumb here, a crumb there. She smiled, blew him an amiable kiss, broke the contact. He stared moodily at the dead screen. All right. Time to get ready for Group. He turned to the life-size screen on the east wall and keyed in the visuals for preliminary alignment. Right now Group Central was sending its test pattern, stills of all of tonight's couples. Nate and Serena were in the centre, haloed by the glowing nimbus that marked them as this evening's performers. Around the periphery Murray saw images of himself, Kay, Van, JoJo, Nikki, Dirk, Conrad, Finn, Lanelle, and Maria. Bruce, Klaus, Mindy, and Lois weren't there. Too busy, maybe. Or too tired. Or perhaps they were in the grip of negative unGrouplike vibes just at the moment. You didn't have to do Group every night if you didn't feel into it. Murray averaged four nights a week. Only the real bulls, like Dirk and Nate, routinely hit seven out of seven. Also JoJo, Lanelle, Nikki—the Very Hot Ladies, he liked to call them.

He opened up the audio. "This is Murray," he announced. "I'm starting to synchronize."

Group Central gave him a sweet unwavering A for calibration. He tuned his receiver to match the note. "You're at four hundred and thirty-two," Group Central said. "Bring your pitch up a little. There. There. Steady. Four hundred and forty, fine." The tones locked perfectly. He was synched in for sound. A little fine tuning on the visuals, next. The test pattern vanished and the screen showed only Nate, naked, a big cocky rock-jawed man with a thick mat of curly black hair covering him from thighs to throat. He grinned, bowed, preened. Murray made adjustments until it was all but impossible to distinguish the three-dimensional holographic projection of Nate from the actual Nate, hundreds of miles away in his San Diego bedroom. Murray was fastidious about these adjustments. Any perceptible drop-off in reality approximation dampened the pleasure Group gave him. For some moments he watched Nate striding bouncily back and forth, working off excess energy, fining himself down to performance level; a minor element of distortion crept into the margins of the image, and, cutting in the manual override, Murray fed his own corrections to Central until all was well.

Next came the main brain-wave amplification, delivering data in the emotional sphere: endocrine feeds, neural set, epithelial apperception, erogenous uptake. Diligently Murray keyed in each one. At first he received only a vague undifferentiated blur of formless background cerebration but then, like intricate figures becoming clear in an elaborate oriental carpet, the specific characteristics of Nate's mental output began to clarify themselves; edginess, eagerness, horniness, alertness, intensity. A sense of Nate's formidable masculine strength came through. At this stage of the evening Murray still had a distinct awareness of himself as an entity independent of Nate, but that would change soon enough.

"Ready," Murray reported. "Holding awaiting Group cut-in."

He had to hold for fifteen intolerable minutes. He was always the quickest to synchronize. Then he had to sit and sweat, hanging on desperately to his balances and lineups while he waited for the others. All around the circuit, the rest of them were still tinkering with their rigs, adjusting them with varying degrees of competence. He thought of Kay. At this moment making frantic adjustments, tuning herself to Serena as he had done to Nate.

"Group cut-in," Central said finally.

Murray closed the last circuits. Into his consciousness poured, in one wild rush, the mingled consciousnesses of Van, Dirk, Conrad, and Finn, hooked into him via Nate, and, less intensely because less directly, the consciousnesses of Kay, Maria, Lanelle, JoJo, and Nikki, funneled to him by way of their link to Serena. So all twelve of them were in sync. They had attained Group once again. Now the revels could begin.

Now. Nate approaching Serena. The magic moments of foreplay. That buzz of early excitement, that soaring erotic flight, taking everybody upward like a Beethoven adagio, like a solid hit of acid. Nate. Serena. San Diego. Their bedroom a glittering hall of mirrors. Refracted images everywhere. A thousand quivering breasts. Five hundred jutting cocks. Hands, eyes, tongues, thighs. The circular undulating

bed, quivering, heaving. Murray, lying cocooned in his maze of sophisticated amplification equipment, receiving inputs at temples and throat and chest and loins, felt his palate growing dry, felt a pounding in his groin. He licked his lips. His hips began, of their own accord, a slow rhythmic thrusting motion. Nate's hands casually traversed the taut globes of Serena's bosom. Caught the rigid nipples between hairy fingers, tweaked them, thumbed them. Murray felt the firm nodules of engorged flesh with his own empty hands. The merger of identities was starting. He was becoming Nate, Nate was flowing into him, and he was all the others too, Van, JoJo, Dirk, Finn, Nikki, all of them, feedbacks oscillating in interpersonal whirlpools all along the line. Kay. He was part of Kay, she of him, both of them parts of Nate and Serena. Inextricably intertwined. What Nate experienced, Murray experienced. What Serena experienced, Kay experienced. When Nate's mouth descended to cover Serena's, Murray's tongue slid forward. And felt the moist tip of Serena's. Flesh against flesh, skin against skin. Serena was throbbing. Why not? Six men tonguing her at once. She was always quick to arouse, anyway. She was begging for it. Not that Nate was in any hurry: screwing was his thing, he always made a grand production out of it. As well he might, with ten close friends riding as passengers on his trip. Give us a show, Nate. Nate obliged. He was going down on her, now. Inhaling. His stubbly cheeks against her satiny thighs. Oh, the busy tongue! Oh, the sighs and gasps! And then she engulfing him reciprocally. Murray hissed in delight. Her cunning little suctions, her jolly slithers and slides: a skilled fellatrice, that woman was. He trembled. He was fully into it, now, sharing every impulse with Nate. *Becoming* Nate. Yes. Serena's beckoning body gaping for him. His waggling wand poised above her. The old magic of Group never diminishing. Nate doing all his tricks, pulling out the stops. When? Now. Now. The thrust. The quick sliding moment of entry. Ah! Ah! *Ah!* Serena simultaneously possessed by Nate, Murray, Van, Dirk, Conrad, Finn. Finn, Conrad, Dirk, Van, Murray, and Nate simultaneously possessing Serena. And vicariously throbbing in rhythm with Serena: Kay, Maria, Lanelle, JoJo, Nikki. Kay. Kay. Kay. Through the sorcery of the crossover loop Nate was having Kay while he had Serena, Nate was having Kay, Maria, Lanelle, JoJo, Nikki all at once, they were being had by him, a soup of identities, an *olla podrida* of copulations, and as the twelve of them soared toward a shared and multiplied ecstasy Murray did something dumb. He thought of Kay.

He thought of Kay. Kay alone in her redwood bower, Kay with bucking hips and tossing hair and glistening droplets of sweat between her breasts, Kay hissing and shivering in Nate's simulated embrace. Murray tried to reach across to her through the Group loop, tried to find and isolate the discrete thread of self that was Kay, tried to chisel away the ten extraneous identities and transform this coupling into an encounter between himself and her. It was a plain violation of the spirit of Group; it was also impossible to achieve, since she had refused him permission to establish a special inner link between them that evening, and so at the moment she was accessible to him only as one facet of the enhanced and expanded Serena. At best he could grope toward Kay through Serena and touch the tip of her soul, but the contact was cloudy and uncertain. Instantly on to what he was trying to do, she petulantly pushed him away, at the same time submerging herself more fully in Serena's consciousness. Rejected, reeling, he slid off into confusion, sending jarring crosscurrents through the whole Group. Nate loosed a shower of irritation, despite his heroic attempt to remain unperturbed, and pumped his way to climax well ahead of schedule, hauling everyone breathlessly along with him. As the orgasmic frenzy broke loose Murray tried to re-enter the full linkage, but he found himself unhinged, disaffiliated, and mechanically emptied himself without any tremor of pleasure. Then it was over. He lay back, perspiring, feeling soiled, jangled, unsatisfied. After a few moments he uncoupled his equipment and went out for a cold shower.

Kay called half an hour later.

"You crazy bastard," she said. "What were you trying to do?"

He promised not to do it again. She forgave him. He brooded for two days, keeping out of Group. He missed sharing Conrad and JoJo, Klaus and Lois. The third day the Group chart marked him and Kay as that night's performers. He didn't want to let them all share her. It was stronger than ever, this nasty atavistic possessiveness. He didn't have to, of course. Nobody was forced to do Group. He could beg off and continue to sulk, and Dirk or Van or somebody would substitute for him tonight. But Kay wouldn't necessarily pass up her turn. She almost certainly wouldn't. He didn't like the options. If he made it with Kay as per Group schedule, he'd be offering her to all the others. If he stepped aside, she'd do it with someone else. Might as well be the one to take her to bed in that case. Faced with an ugly choice, he decided to stick to the original schedule.

He popped up to her place eight hours early. He found her sprawled on a carpet of redwood needles in a sun-dappled grove, playing with a stack of music cubes. Mozart tinkled in the fragrant air. "Let's go away somewhere tomorrow," he said. "You and me."

"You're still into you-and-me?"

"I'm sorry."

"Where do you want to go?"

He shrugged. "Hawaii. Afghanistan. Poland. Zambia. It doesn't matter. Just to be with you."

"What about Group?"

"They can spare us for a while."

She rolled over, lazily snaffled Mozart into silence, started a cube of Bach. "I'll go," she said. The Goldberg Variations transcribed for glockenspiel. "But only if we take our Group equipment along."

"It means that much to you?"

"Doesn't it to you?"

"I cherish Group," he said. "But it's not all there is to life. I can live without it for a while. I don't need it, Kay. What I need is you."

"That's obscene, Murray."

"No. It isn't obscene."

"It's boring, at any rate."

"I'm sorry you think so," he told her.

"Do you want to drop out of Group?"

I want us both to drop out of Group, he thought, and I want you to live with me. I can't bear to share you any longer, Kay. But he wasn't prepared to move to that level of confrontation. He said, "I want to stay in Group if it's possible, but I'm also interested in extending and developing some one-on-one with you."

"You've already made that excessively clear."

"I love you."

"You've said that before too."

"What do you want, Kay?"

She laughed, rolled over, drew her knees up until they touched her breasts, parted her thighs, opened herself to a stray shaft of sunlight. "I want to enjoy myself," she said.

He started setting up his equipment an hour before sunset. Because he was performing, the calibrations were more delicate than on an ordinary night. Not only did he have to broadcast a full range of control ratios to Central to aid the others in their tuning, he had to achieve a flawless balance of input and output with Kay. He went about his complex tasks morosely, not at all excited by the thought that he and Kay would shortly be making love. It cooled his ardor to know that Nate, Dirk, Van, Finn, Bruce, and Klaus would be having her too. Why did he begrudge it to them so? He didn't know. Such exclusivism, coming out of nowhere, shocked and disgusted him. Yet it wholly controlled him. Maybe I need help, he thought.

Group time, now. Soft sweet ionized fumes drifting through the chamber of Eros. Kay was warm, receptive, passionate. Her eyes sparkled as she reached for him. They had made love five hundred times and she showed no sign of diminished interest. He knew he turned her on. He hoped he turned her on more than anyone else. He caressed her in all his clever ways, and she purred and wriggled and glowed. Her nipples stood tall: no faking that. Yet something was wrong. Not with her, with him. He was aloof, remote. He seemed to be watching the proceedings from a point somewhere outside himself, as though he were just a Group onlooker tonight, badly tuned in, not even as much a part of things as Klaus, Bruce, Finn, Van, Dirk. The awareness that he had an audience affected him for the first time. His technique, which depended more on finesse and grace than on fire and force, became a trap, locking him into a series of passionless arabesques and pirouettes. He was distracted, though he never had been before, by the minute telemetry tapes glued to the side of Kay's neck and the underside of her thigh. He found himself addressing silent messages to the other men. Here, Nate, how do you like that? Grab

some haunch, Dirk. Up the old zaboo, Bruce. Uh. Uh. Ah. Oh.

Kay didn't seem to notice anything was amiss. She came three times in the first fifteen minutes. He doubted that he'd ever come at all. He plugged on, in and out, in and out, moving like a mindless piston. A sort of revenge on Group, he realized. You want to share Kay with me, okay, fellows, but this is all you're going to get. This. Oh. Oh. Oh. Now at last he felt the familiar climactic tickle, stepped down to a tenth of its normal intensity. He hardly noticed it when he came.

Kay said afterward, "What about that trip? Are we still going to go away somewhere tomorrow?"

"Let's forget it for the time being," he said.

He popped to Istanbul alone and spent a day in the covered bazaar, buying cheap but intricate trinkets for every woman in Group. At nightfall he popped down to McMurdo Sound, where the merry Antarctic summer was at its height, and spent six hours on the polar ski slopes, coming away with wind-bronzed skin and aching muscles. In the lodge later he met an angular, auburn-haired woman from Portugal and took her to bed. She was very good, in a heartless, mechanically proficient way. Doubtless she thought the same of him. She asked him whether he might be interested in joining her Group, which operated out of Lisbon and Ibiza. "I already have an affiliation," he said. He popped to Addis Ababa after breakfast, checked into the Hilton, slept for a day and a half, and went on to St. Croix for a night of reef-bobbing. When he popped back to California the next day he called Kay at once to learn the news.

"We've been discussing rearranging some of the Group couplings," she said. "Next week, what about you and Lanelle, me and Dirk?"

"Does that mean you're dropping me?"

"No, not at all, silly. But I do think we need variety."

"Group was designed to provide us with all the variety we'd ever want."

"You know what I mean. Besides, you're developing an unhealthy fixation on me as isolated love object."

"Why are you rejecting me?"

"I'm not. I'm trying to help you, Murray."

"I love you," he said.

"Love me in a healthier way, then."

That night it was the turn of Maria and Van. The next, Nikki and Finn. After them, Bruce and Mindy. He tuned in for all three, trying to erode his grief in nightly frenzies of lustful fulfillment. By the third night he was very tired and no less grief-smitten. He took the next night off. Then the schedule came up with the first Murray-Lanelle pairing.

He popped to Hawaii and set up his rig in her sprawling beachfront lanai on Molokai. He had bedded her before, of course. Everyone in Group had bedded everyone else during the preliminary months of compatibility testing. But then they all had settled into more or less regular pair-bonding, and he hadn't approached her since. In the past year the only Group woman he had slept with was Kay. By choice.

"I've always liked you," Lanelle said. She was tall, heavy-breasted, wide-shouldered, with warm brown eyes, yellow hair, skin the color of fine honey. "You're just a little crazy, but I don't mind that. And I love screwing Scorpios."

"I'm a Capricorn."

"Them too," she said. "I love screwing just about every sign. Except Virgos. I can't stand Virgos. Remember, we were supposed to have a Virgo in Group, at the start. I blackballed him."

They swam and surfed for a couple of hours before doing the calibrating. The water was warm but a brisk breeze blew from the east, coming like a gust of bad news out of California. Lanelle nuzzled him playfully and then not so playfully in the water. She had always been an aggressive woman, a swaggerer, a strutter. Her appetites were enormous. Her eyes glistened with desire. "Come on," she said finally, tugging at him. They ran to the house and he began to adjust the equipment. It was still early. He thought of Kay and his soul drooped. What am I doing here? he wondered. He lined up the Group apparatus with nervous hands, making many errors. Lanelle stood behind him, rubbing her breasts against his bare back. He had to ask her to stop. Eventually everything was ready and she hauled him to the spongy floor with her, covering his body with hers. Lanelle always liked to be the one on top. Her

tongue probed his mouth and her hands clutched his hips and she pressed herself against him, but although her body was warm and smooth and alive he felt no onset of excitement, not a shred. She put her mouth to him but it was hopeless. He remained limp, dead, unable to function. With everyone tuned in and waiting. "What is it?" she whispered. "What should I do, love?" He closed his eyes and indulged in a fantasy of Kay coupling with Dirk, pure masochism, and it aroused him as far as a sort of half-erect condition, and he slithered into her like a prurient eel. She rocked her way to ecstasy above him. This is garbage, he thought. I'm falling apart. Kay. Kay. Kay.

Then Kay had her night with Dirk. At first Murray thought he would simply skip it. There was no reason, after all, why he had to subject himself to something like that, if he expected it to give him pain. It had never been painful for him in the past when Kay did it with other men, inside Group or not, but since the onset of his jealousies everything was different. In theory the Group couples were interchangeable, one pair serving as proxies for all the rest each night, but theory and practice coincided less and less in Murray's mind these days. Nobody would be surprised or upset if he happened not to want to participate tonight. All during the day, though, he found himself obsessively fantasizing about Kay and Dirk, every motion, every sound, the two of them facing each other, smiling, embracing, sinking down onto her bed, entwining, his hands sliding over her slender body, his mouth on her mouth, his chest crushing her small breasts, Dirk entering her, riding her, plunging, driving, coming, Kay coming, then Kay and Dirk arising, going for a cooling swim, returning to the bedroom, facing each other, smiling, beginning again. By late afternoon it had taken place so many times in his fevered imagination that he saw no risk in experiencing the reality of it; at least he could have Kay, if only at one remove, by doing Group tonight. And it might help him to shake off his obsessiveness. But it was worse than he imagined it could be. The sight of Dirk, all bulging muscles and tapering hips, terrified him; Dirk was ready for making love long before the foreplay started, and Murray somehow came to fear that he, not Kay, was going to be the target of that long rigid spear of his. Then Dirk began to caress Kay. With each insinuating touch of his hand it seemed that some vital segment of Murray's relationship with Kay was being obliterated. He was forced to watch Kay through Dirk's eyes, her flushed face, her quivering nostrils, her moist, slack lips, and it killed him. As Dirk drove deep into her, Murray coiled into a miserable fetal ball, one hand clutching his loins, the other clapped across his lips, thumb in his mouth. He couldn't stand it at all. To think that every one of them was having Kay at once. Not only Dirk. Nate, Van, Conrad, Finn, Bruce, Klaus, the whole male Group complement, all of them tuning in tonight for this novel Dirk-Kay pairing. Kay giving herself to all of them gladly, willingly, enthusiastically. He had to escape, now, instantly, even though to drop out of Group communion at this point would unbalance everyone's tuning and set up chaotic eddy currents that might induce nausea or worse in the others. He didn't care. He had to save himself. He screamed and uncoupled his rig.

He waited two days and went to see her. She was at her exercises, floating like a cloud through a dazzling arrangement of metal rings and loops that dangled at constantly varying heights from the ceiling of her solarium. He stood below her, craning his neck. "It isn't any good," he said. "I want us both to withdraw from Group, Kay."

"That was predictable."

"It's killing me. I love you so much I can't bear to share you."

"So loving me means owning me?"

"Let's just drop out for a while. Let's explore the ramifications of one-on-one. A month, two months, six months, Kay. Just until I get this craziness out of my system. Then we can go back in."

"So you admit it's craziness."

"I never denied it." His neck was getting stiff. "Won't you please come down from those rings while we're talking?"

"I can hear you perfectly well from here, Murray."

"Will you drop out of Group and go away with me for a while?"

"No."

"Will you even consider it?"

"No."

"Do you realize that you're addicted to Group?" he asked.

"I don't think that's an accurate evaluation of the situation. But do *you* realize that you're dangerously fixated on me?"

"I realize it."

"What do you propose to do about it?"

"What I'm doing now," he said. "Coming to you, asking you to do a one-on-one with me."

"Stop it."

"One-on-one was good enough for the human race for thousands of years."

"It was a prison," she said. "It was a trap. We're out of the trap at last. You won't get me back in."

He wanted to pull her down from her rings and shake her. "I *love* you, Kay!"

"You take a funny way of showing it. Trying to limit the range of my experience. Trying to hide me away in a vault somewhere. It won't work."

"Definitely no?"

"Definitely no."

She accelerated her pace, flinging herself recklessly from loop to loop. Her glistening nude form tantalized and infuriated him. He shrugged and turned away, shoulders slumping, head drooping. This was precisely how he had expected her to respond. No surprises. Very well. Very well. He crossed from the solarium into the bedroom and lifted her Group rig from its container. Slowly, methodically, he ripped it apart, bending the frame until it split, cracking the fragile leads, uprooting handfuls of connectors, crumpling the control panel. The instrument was already a ruin by the time Kay came in. "What are you *doing?*" she cried. He splintered the lovely gleaming calibration dials under his heel and kicked the wreckage of the rig toward her. It would take months before a replacement rig could be properly attuned and synchronized. "I had no choice," he told her sadly.

They would have to punish him. That was inevitable. But how? He waited at home, and before long they came to him, all of them, Nate, Van, Dirk, Conrad, Finn, Bruce, Klaus, Kay, Serena, Maria, JoJo, Lanelle, Nikki, Mindy, Lois, popping in from many quarters of the world, some of them dressed in evening clothes, some of them naked or nearly so, some of them unkempt and sleepy, all of them angry in a cold, tight way. He tried to stare them down. Dirk said, "You must be terribly sick, Murray. We feel sorry for you."

"We really want to help you," said Lanelle.

"We're here to give you therapy," Finn told him.

Murray laughed. "Therapy. I bet. What kind of therapy?"

"To rid you of your exclusivism," Dirk said. "To burn all the trash out of your mind."

"Shock treatment," Finn said.

"Keep away from me!"

"Hold him," Dirk said.

Quickly they surrounded him. Bruce clamped an arm across his chest like an iron bar. Conrad seized his hands and brought his wrists together behind his back. Finn and Dirk pressed up against his sides. He was helpless.

Kay began to remove her clothing. Naked, she lay down on Murray's bed, flexed her knees, opened her thighs. Klaus got on top of her.

"What the hell is this?" Murray asked.

Efficiently but without passion Kay aroused Klaus, and efficiently but without passion he penetrated her. Murray writhed impotently as their bodies moved together. Klaus made no attempt at bringing Kay off. He reached his climax in four or five minutes, grunting once, and rolled away from her, red-faced, sweating. Van took his place between Kay's legs.

"No," Murray said. "Please, no."

Inexorably Van had his turn, quick, impersonal. Nate was next. Murray tried not to watch, but his eyes would not remain closed. A strange smile glittered on Kay's lips as she gave herself to Nate. Nate arose. Finn approached the bed.

"No!" Murray cried, and lashed out in a backward kick that sent Conrad screaming across the room. Murray's hands were free. He twisted and wrenched himself away from Bruce. Dirk and Nate intercepted him as he rushed toward Kay. They seized him and flung him to the floor.

"The therapy isn't working," Nate said.

"Let's skip the rest," said Dirk. "It's no use trying to heal him. He's beyond hope. Let him stand up."

Murray got cautiously to his feet. Dirk said, "By unanimous vote, Murray, we expel you from Group for unGrouplike attitudes and especially for your unGrouplike destruction of Kay's rig. All your Group privileges are canceled." At a signal from Dirk, Nate removed Murray's rig from the container and reduced it to unsalvageable rubble. Dirk said, "Speaking as your friend, Murray, I suggest you think seriously about undergoing a total personality reconstruct. You're in trouble, do you know that? You need a lot of help. You're a mess."

"Is there anything else you want to tell me?" Murray asked.

"Nothing else. Goodbye, Murray."

They started to go out. Dirk, Finn, Nate, Bruce, Conrad, Klaus, Van, JoJo, Nikki, Serena, Maria, Lanelle, Mindy, Lois. Kay was the last to leave. She stood by the door, clutching her clothes in a small crumpled bundle. She seemed entirely unafraid of him. There was a peculiar look of—was it tenderness? pity?—on her face. Softly she said, "I'm sorry it had to come to this, Murray. I feel so unhappy for you. I know that what you did wasn't a hostile act. You did it out of love. You were all wrong, but you were doing it out of love." She walked toward him and kissed him lightly, on the cheek, on the tip of the nose, on the lips. He didn't move. She smiled. She touched his arm. "I'm so sorry," she murmured. "Goodbye, Murray." As she went through the door she looked back and said, "Such a damned shame. I could have loved you, you know? I could really have loved you."

He had told himself that he would wait until they all were gone before he let the tears flow. But when the door had closed behind Kay he discovered his eyes remained dry. He had no tears. He was altogether calm. Numb. Burned out.

After a long while he put on fresh clothing and went out. He popped to London, found that it was raining there, and popped to Prague, where there was something stifling about the atmosphere, and went on to Seoul, where he had barbecued beef and kimchi for dinner. Then he popped to New York. In front of a gallery on Lexington Avenue he picked up a complaisant young girl with long black hair. "Let's go to a hotel," he suggested, and she smiled and nodded. He registered for a six-hour stay. Upstairs, she undressed without waiting for him to ask. Her body was smooth and supple, flat belly, pale skin, high full breasts. They lay down together and, in silence, without preliminaries, he took her. She was eager and responsive. Kay, he thought. Kay. Kay. You are Kay. A spasm of culmination shook him with unexpected force.

"Do you mind if I smoke?" she said a few minutes later.

"I love you," he said.

*"What?"*

"I love you."

"You're sweet."

"Come live with me. Please. Please. I'm serious."

"What?"

"Live with me. Marry me."

"What?"

"There's only one thing I ask. No Group stuff. That's all. Otherwise you can do as you please. I'm wealthy. I'll make you happy. I love you."

"You don't even know my name."

"I love you."

"Mister, you must be out of your head."

"Please. Please."

"A lunatic. Unless you're trying to make fun of me."

"I'm perfectly serious, I assure you. Live with me. Be my wife."

"A lunatic," she said. "I'm getting out of here!" She leaped up and looked for her clothes. "Jesus, a madman!"

"No," he said, but she was on her way, not even pausing to get dressed, running helter-skelter from the room, her pink buttocks flashing like beacons as she made her escape. The door slammed. He shook his head. He sat rigid for half an hour, an hour, some long timeless span, thinking of Kay, thinking of Group, wondering what they'd be doing tonight, whose turn it was. At length he rose and put on his clothes and left the hotel. A terrible restlessness assailed him. He popped to Karachi and stayed ten minutes. He popped to Vienna. To Hangchow. He didn't stay. Looking for what? He didn't know. Looking for Kay? Kay didn't exist. Looking. Just looking. Pop. Pop. Pop.

*Copyright © 1973 by Agberg Ltd.*

*Jody Lynn Nye is the author of forty novels and more than one hundred stories, and has at various times collaborated with Anne McCaffrey and Robert Asprin. Her husband, Bill Fawcett, is a prolific author, editor and packager, and is also active in the gaming field.*

# RECOMMENDED BOOKS

## by Bill Fawcett and Jody Lynn Nye

*A Taste of Honey*
by Kai Ashante Wilson
TOR Books
October, 2016
ISBN-13: 978-0765390042

Aqib is the keeper of the king's menagerie and a Cousin cousin to royalty in what seems to be a civilized kingdom of sub-Saharan Africa in a far-future Earth. He is walking one of the big cats abroad in their city when he meets a soldier from the equivalent of Rome, a large, coarse-tongued warrior named Lucrio. They are instantly attracted to one another—Aqib because of the Daluçan's scars, a sign of masculine prowess in his culture, and Lucrio to Aqib for his extraordinary beauty, flowing, curly hair, and smooth, dark skin. Same-sex matings are not uncommon among the Daluçans, but they are a disgrace in Aqib's culture. The normally soft-spoken Aqib fiercely defends his relationship against his own family for the ten days until Lucrio must take ship home. Heartbroken, he marries the Blessed Femysade, a princess of the line. They have a daughter, whom he names Lucretia in memory of his lost love.

Their culture's gods walk among them, even taller, darker-skinned and more beautiful than they are. Femysade is approached by two of these gods for her extraordinary talent in mathematics. In this world, such things as math and science are women's work, not of interest to men, a witty riposte against our Earth's mores. Therefore, his wife's work scarcely impinges on Aqib's life, except as a matter of pride in her accomplishments and sorrow when work takes her away from him. Religion, too, has its gender divisions, with dance also belonging to women, with the exception of Aqib, who possesses other extraordinary talents as well.

The story is written in non-linear fashion, leaping from the two men's first meeting, to the end of Lucrio's visit in Olorum, to several years later, and back again. It seems confusing at first, but the reader is never lost for long. Every diversion is important, but the reader will not know why until the very last chapter. The style is flowery and polysyllabic, swift-flowing, and evocative. Highly recommended for those who enjoy intense relationships among well-drawn, intelligent, flawed, loving human beings, with a touch of technology masquerading as magic, or perhaps the other way around.

*The Dead Seekers*
by Barb Hendee and J. C. Hendee
Ace
January, 2017
ISBN 13: 978-0451469342

This book is the very promising beginning to a new series. Well written, it is set in a medieval and magical world. The story begins with the birth of the main character, Tris, or rather his stillbirth. Since he was to be the son of a powerful duke, the court wizard intervenes to save him. His resurrection causes a problem because Tris is not supposed to be alive. Even as a child, it becomes apparent he is far from normal. The unusual birth has given him a strong tie with ghosts, and worse. He is often found in his nursery surrounded by white, wispy spirits. These underworld ties alienate and frighten his father into withdrawing from him physically and emotionally. The Duke's fears are not unfounded; an angry ghost in this world is capable of cursing the living with an incurable wasting disease. Tris's affinity for spirits alienates everyone around him. He becomes a lonely boy growing into a solitary man. Even his mother's love and support are not enough for Tris to remain once he is old enough to go off on his own.

Able to communicate and even grapple with dangerous ghosts without ill effect, Tris becomes the perfect Ghost Hunter. His ally is an alchemist who uses enchanted objects to accomplish what Tris can do naturally. The young noble quickly builds up a reputation as "The Dead's Man".

Tris is called to stop the ghost of a woman terrorizing a village. On the way there, he encounters a shape changer who is the last survivor of a Romany-type clan. She is looking for revenge because she saw a dark form, identical to Tris but lightless black, kill her entire clan. At first she is sure he is the murderer. She accompanies him, intending to kill the young noble, but as they work together—first to deal with the girl's ghost then a whole swarm of vengeful apparitions—she begins to wonder if he is guilty. Eventually she learns his secret: the malignant dark shape is the part of him that remains in the world of the dead. This dark alter is both the source of his abilities and dire threat to Tris, and perhaps the whole world.

The well-realized, realistic setting is Eastern European in feel. The action or suspense is near constant. There is no shortage of physical and ghostly danger or other frightening encounters. Still, you can also feel sympathy for both main characters, who are magically unusual yet still very understandably human in their feelings. The mystery of the source of the attacking ghosts and the rise toward the final solution will easily keeps your interest.

Recommended for those who enjoy magical actions stories, ghostly mysteries, and character-driven novels.

✿

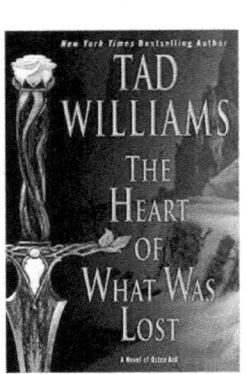

***The Heart of What Was Lost: A Novel of Osten Ard***
by Tad Williams
Daw Books
January, 2017
ISBN 13: 978-0756412487

Losing is hard. Losing a war can be disastrous, but it does make good reading. Tad Williams' novel is set after a war of annihilation between two races, humans and the Norns. The Norns, long lived, faster and stronger than their human enemies, were intent on driving all invading humans from their ancestral lands of Osten Ard. The Norn themselves are a fascinating creation, with elements of sidhe, Neanderthal, and Native American combined to create a non-human, magic-using race. All their magical advantages and long history cannot overcome the vastly larger number of men they face. A final climatic defeat meant ruin and most of the Norn army was destroyed before this book opens. A few hundred remaining Norns are falling back and trying to stop or slow the much larger pursuing army. All they can hope is that their defense will allow their sacred and last underground city time to prepare against the invasion. This is a story of determination and sacrifice told mostly through the eyes of a leader of the "Builders," one of several guild-like social groups that dominate Norn culture.

While *The Heart of What Was Lost* reads well alone, the real joy is that there are several prequels. Tad Williams has, after many years, returned to this world and the result has all the strengths of his earlier titles and an added degree of sophistication. The characters on both sides deal with depression, desperation, fear, and simply war weariness. That said, this is still very much an action novel with the relentless pursuit and the desperate defense highlighting the heroism and emotions found on both sides. I won't give it away, but admit that even after having read literally hundreds of fantasy and war novels the ending to this one managed to completely surprise me. It was fairly set up, but you will not expect it. I set the book down and murmured "well done."

Tad Williams has been writing highly readable novels since his debut with *Tailchaser's Song* in 1985. If you aren't familiar with his books already, give yourself a treat. This book is obviously a must-buy for those who have read any of the earlier Osten Ard novels. Any fantasy fan who enjoys reading about people struggling to survive, sieges, combat and heroism in a desperate situation should read *The Heart of What Was Lost* as well.

✿

***Science Fiction by Scientists: An Anthology of Short Stories***
by Mike Brotherton (Editor)
Springer
November, 2016
ISBN 13: 978-3319411019

It may surprise readers just how many working scientists also write, not just non-fiction books, abstracts and scientific papers, but novels and short stories. Among the better-known scientist writers in the field are Gregory Benford, David Brin, and Catherine Asaro. This collection by astronomer/writer Brotherton brings to light other authors who also deserve a good read. Just reading down the biographies at the head of the book inspires admiration. Brotherton has collected scientists versed in aerospace engineering, medicine, mathematics, molecular genetics, astrophysics, neurology, and so much more. Having their studies to draw on gives them an edge over lay writers, exploring the scientific approach to a problem in great depth and technical detail will fascinate the reader.

No story is worthwhile unless it also approaches the human angle or rather with the non-human protagonist of the first story in mind, the personal, vulnerable angle. These stories satisfy on both counts. Some are tragedies, tales of valiant last stands, but some, like "The Schrödinger Brat Paradox", are downright funny. As an added treat, at the conclusion of each the writers give further perspective into the science behind the story.

Hard science concepts with compelling writing make this anthology a good read that will make you think.

✧

**Doctor Who: the American Adventures**
by Various (Author)
Penguin UK
October, 2016
ISBN 13: 978-1405928724

This volume contains half a dozen short stories intended for young British fans of the show, *Doctor Who*. It assumes that the reader is familiar with the elements of the show: the TARDIS, the origin of the Doctor, his sonic screwdriver, and his penchant for getting involved in situations in which humans are at risk, such as teleporting robots and aliens that want to conquer humankind. While a child might find these elements scary, each story ends with the Doctor having cleverly vanquished the alien menace and leaving everyone safe again.

The settings are all across America and in time periods from 1815 to 2017, but the syntax is British. The writer has done a pretty good job, but British terms and expressions do pop up now and again, including "mum" instead of "mom" or "mother," or "wasteland" instead of "empty field".

Recommended for young fans of Doctor Who and their parents to enjoy together.

✧

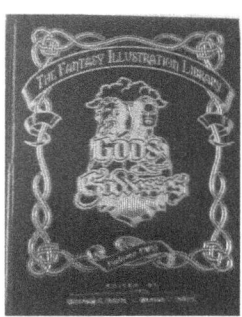

**Gods and Goddesses**, The Fantasy Illustration Library
Volume Two
Michael Publishing
January, 2017

This slip-cased coffee-table volume is a labor of love from the Phifer brothers, Michael and Malcolm. The volume contains 126 pieces of art from numerous notable fantasy artists, each with a description of the god or goddess pictured and a brief biography of the artist. The gorgeous collection will be a treat to fans who may have seen one or two of these at a time in science-fiction convention art shows or on the cover of books or game materials. Most were painted specifically for this book by a who's who of fantasy illustration, including Canty, Jael, Donato, Burns, Easley and dozens more.

Pantheons from around the world are covered, from African to Welsh. The volume is heavy in images from Celtic, Irish and Welsh mythologies, but just a few from most of the others. Each mythology is described at the chapter head, followed by descriptions of the featured gods and/or goddesses and paragraphs about other noted deities in those cultures. Indices at the back of the book list the artists and their websites, plus reference works for further reading. This limited-edition volume is well made, beautifully illustrated, and wide ranging. The book would be a great starting point for those who want to learn more about the mythology of the world, or just to enjoy leafing through.

***The Once and Future King***
by T.H. White
Ace Books
June, 1987
ISBN 13: 978-0441627400

This issue's classic is White's retelling of the Matter of Britain, the story of King Arthur from childhood to his fall at the hands of his son, Mordred. *The Once and Future King* is made up of four novellas. Most readers are familiar only with the first one, *The Sword in the Stone* (1938), adapted into an animated feature by Disney in 1963. In it, Arthur is a child, tutored by the wizard Merlyn by being turned into various animals and meeting strange and wonderful people, such as King Pellinore, to give him wisdom and perspective before he draws the legendary Excalibur from the stone to become king. It's full of whimsy, such as Merlyn's animated household ob-

jects (the mustard pot is particularly adorable) and his owl confidant, Archimedes. Merlyn lives backward in time, meaning that he knows what is going to happen but not what came in the past. The other three novellas are darker and sadder, written as Europe descended into World War II. *The Queen of Air and Darkness* concerns Arthur's nephews, who would become some of his trusted knights: Gawain, Agravaine, Gaheris and Gareth. They adore their mother Morgause, Arthur's half-sister by his mother Igraine. She ignores them in pursuit of her own ends of power. During this time, Arthur, a born idealist, creates the concept of the Round Table, with each man equal to all the others seated at it. Merlyn foresees his own imprisonment in the oak tree by the nymph Nimue imminent, and leaves Arthur to handle the coming war with King Lot of Lothian on his own. Morgause comes south to make peace for her husband with Arthur and ends up seducing him. She becomes pregnant with Mordred. Merlyn has forgotten to warn Arthur about her, thereby setting in motion his own doom.

The third section, *The Ill-Made Knight*, is the story of Lancelot. Capable of performing miracles as well as being a perfect physical specimen, he arrives in Camelot, eager to become the greatest of Arthur's knights. Arthur gives him whole-hearted friendship, but Lancelot is fascinated by Guinevere, Arthur's queen. Guinevere doesn't like Lancelot at first but tries to be kind to him for Arthur's sake. As anyone who has seen the musical *Camelot* (1960) knows, the two of them fall in love. Lancelot is torn by his loyalty to his friend and king and his passion for Guinevere. He leaves to go out and do good deeds, but each one is a disaster in its own way. Arthur, having created a vacuum of work for his knights, is forced to give them a mission to accomplish to keep them out of trouble: the quest for the Holy Grail. The fourth volume, which was never published independently, *The Candle in the Wind*, sees Agravaine, the most discontented of Morgause's sons, and Mordred plotting against Lancelot and Arthur. They know of Lancelot's affair with the queen. They arrange to have her caught in flagrante with Lancelot, meaning that the unwilling king will have to condemn both of them to death. None of the characters now is free of sin; all carry their burden of guilt. Lancelot and Guinevere flee to France. Arthur has to fight Lancelot to regain his honor. In his absence, Mordred sits on the throne, intending to usurp his father. Arthur returns to fight for his crown. A memory of Merlyn returns to him, and he knows the beautiful, ideal dream that was Camelot is about to be lost for good. Before the battle begins, he tells a serving boy to preserve the story and to stay safe, no matter what happens.

A fifth novel, *The Book of Merlyn* (1977), was published many years after White's death. In it, Merlyn returns to Arthur on the eve of battle. As he did in Arthur's childhood, he turns the aged king into several animals to restore his perspective. Arthur attempts to counter his fate by making peace with his son, but it doesn't hold. History proceeds as it always has.

*The Once and Future King* contains far more detail and loving characterization for which there was room in the theatrical performances. For anyone who loves the story of King Arthur, this is a must read. The first three novels were rewritten heavily by White before being compiled into the omnibus. If you can find the originals, they are somewhat more lighthearted than the collection, but both versions a good read, if a heartbreaking one.

*Gregory Benford is a Nebula winner and a former Worldcon Guest of Honor. He is the author of more than thirty novels, six books of non-fiction, and has edited ten anthologies.*

# A SCIENTIST'S NOTEBOOK

## by Gregory Benford

### Sex, Gender and Fantasy

I dwell in the universe of the university, where the humanists these days have a special set of definitions. Sometimes, even about the seemingly obvious.

Biology dictates that there are two sexes. Culture acting on biology, so the story goes, makes gender. Thus gender differences are "socially constructed", as the jargot—a combination of jargon and argot—has it.

I teach in the humanities core course for freshmen honors students each year, where such distinctions are crucial. Once I innocently asked how many genders there were, and the puzzled response was, well, two, of course. What about homosexuals? I asked. Don't they represent different persuasions, different cultural flavors? After culture operates on biology, why should there be a one-to-one mapping?

There followed an uncomfortable silence, in which it became clear that gender was just a code word for the latest academic cultural spin put on sex.

Homosexuality was, well, not an issue. Was it biologically determined? Well, no. It was socially constructed, as were attitudes toward it. Then why was it persistent in human societies? No answer.

Much in the humanities has no answer, for the language is innocent of data. They lack the rub of the real.

Yet issues of sexuality, of that old question—what is natural?—remain. We're a highly charged, sexy species, and such matters mean much to us.

Will technology take us beyond these issues? This is a science fictional question. Can we ever achieve a total detachment of gender from sex?—that is, switch roles utterly? A total polymorphousness?

These are curiously analytical questions to ask of a subject so steeped in legend and shadowy emotions.

Permit me, then, a digression into—as the humanists would say—rhetoric.

✿

To the American male the vagina has always been a dark realm, moist and mysterious, controlled by rhythms he could not sense or slake. Beyond that often-obliging passage lay the vast, dusky domain of the uterus, where the magical act of bringing forth life occurred, buried deep. He had mere abstract knowledge of that strange cavern territory, a geography forever beyond touch. He could only hear it, with an ear pressed against a wife's belly, listening to the random thumps of babies on the way, swimming in night.

So as the American turned from the dying frontier of the west, having reached the Pacific and found its oceanic turmoil a salty vastness, he set out to find a new land. The sac that surrounds the embryo has the same saline content as the ocean—as does the blood that knocks in our veins—echoing the Pacific's patient emptiness. So we began our twencen frontier there: the inner ocean, dark and engulfing, enclosing each of us at our most vulnerable beginnings.

The new frontier was opened in the name of sanitation, the same impulse that brought forth indoor plumbing in the 1890s; a Pasteur-driven passion to cleanse the world and make it fresh and new again. So woman was cleaned up, like a problem in municipal maintenance.

Douches, baths, tubes you insert to suck up the dismaying flood, sprays, anti-itch powders, diaphragm, foams, pills—they all ran together as the decades raced through, one stopgap (quite literally) blending into the next as the distinction between hygiene and birth control blurred, and the old dark land yielded to invasions, thrusts deep into its territory, things that dried and sealed off and, after a first rough chill, became an accepted piece of that dimly lit landscape, a mild discomfort at best, an ... appliance.

An old tobacconist's saying about drawing a customer in goes, *Start with a pinch, end with a pound.* So it was with the saline frontier. The urge was not merely one more land rape, but the desire to mechanize, to make rich cropland from the untamed, moist forest.

(Could the rigid rectangularity of the checkerboard Midwest have a great deal to do with their sex lives? The furrow lines in fields draw you forward to the infinity where parallels meet over the horizon. In the grip of such geometry, such mathematical order, the impatient, snaky pant and slither of sex doesn't fit. The American instinct, pinned to the Euclidean landscape, has been to mechanize their own reproduction, just as they did to wheat.)

Agriculture isn't a hand-dominated industry anymore. *Why do all that work?* the ads say. Sure, they're talking about household chores, cleaners, toothpaste—but what's the most basic home-making job a woman has? *No mess, no fuss* ... So medicine makes sex safe and dry, far from the moist dark territory of the primordial mind.

But how?

The first step is basic: disconnect the groin from the id.

Ever since Freud, we've thrown up temporary barriers to the unconscious—the newly-elected seat of all our dark, base drives. But anyone who has been through traditional analysis—or Jungian, or anything more trendy—knows how badly *that* works. (A recent study of psychotherapy techniques showed that patients had just as good a chance of improving if they skipped their Freudian-based therapy sessions entirely, and went for a walk.) So if you can't wrestle the id to the ground, and handcuff it securely, what next?

Disconnect! Assume that sex organs are accidents of birth. Assume that sexuality is carried in the genitalia like incidental freight, neatly packaged. Sure, there are nasty hormones in the blood. (Including that worst offender, testosterone, one of the aggressors; and we know what the United Nations thinks of *them.*) But those hormones are easily fixed—just tinker with the glands. Most of them are lodged in those dictatorial organs, the genitals. Outlying areas can be mopped up later.

So some feminists tell us that men and women are basically alike, except—in a coolly analytical phrase I lifted from a tract—*except for the plumbing.* (Recall the 1890s. Here lies the final victory of the flush toilet.)

It is tempting to see sex as a set of detachable appliances, fitted to the basic human body frame at birth. Then we can all believe that, way down deep, we're really the same unisex model.

E pluribus unum. Chevy products are all the same car, you know—even though the add-ons and extras are deceptive, the real car has the identical engine, gears, axle. As with products, why not with people?

Social behavior can be endlessly altered, trimmed, sanitized, so this argument goes—if we'll just overlook the, uh, plumbing. The eternal edgy peace between men and women can then be smoothed over, and final treaties signed, if we apply a bit of operant conditioning—that ugly but useful phrase that comes from Skinner's Neo-Pavlovian work.

Seem too simple minded? Orwellian? Something out of *Brave New World*?

Look at heavy metal's recurrent images: women coupling with things that are half-machine; androgyny rampant; high tech meets low lust. Nowhere is the American ambivalence about sexuality reflected better than in these images, saturated with the strange eroticism of the man-machine interface.

Or look to science fiction. The most interesting version of future sexuality to emerge in the 1970s was John Varley's quick-change utopia, in which people switch sexes whenever taste dictates. From *The Ophiuchi Hotline* through *Steel Beach*, he envisioned a society restless with change—indeed, alive with metamorphosis.

This ferment produces a remarkably laissez-faire society in which family roles dissolve. All is optional. Varley assumes that there will be no more racism or sexism in such a world because everyone will have the ability to be anything. When you can be the Other, there soon is none.

The next subtle yet crucial assumption is that when you switch you take no baggage with you. The details of the process are high tech indeed—you speed-grow a clone of yourself, have your brain transplanted—or just "map" the brain—and *zap* you're reborn.

Is this plausible? More to the point, do Varley's assumptions set the stage for a fiction that can tell us something about the nature of sexuality and society? Does the brain flip-flop from male to female, on orders from the hormones?

We now know by direct experiment that men use one local part on one side of their brains to process sound. Women, on the other hand, use both sides in a more diffuse manner. This may explain why girls have greater early verbal fluency while men's abilities grown steadily greater from a slow start.

Why did our evolution select this substantial difference? Seldom is a trait taken on for a single cause, especially in the complex warrens of our neural labyrinths where abilities cross-link. We will probably never know why our specializations arose. But the plain differences between men and women stand out; we are moderately shaped for specialized tasks.

Men are better at high-power work, using motor muscles. Their sense of spatial arrangement is better and appears earlier. Women can sit longer, do delicate hand-eye work more adeptly, have better color perception. (Partial color blindness, such as I have, is carried by the female, though; one of evolution's little jokes.)

We differ. Nature wanted it that way. On average, with a considerable spread in individual abilities within each sex. Plenty of women in my neighborhood can outrun their mates.

So consider an opposite tide of thought about sex, one moored in the molecular architecture. Edward Wilson's *Sociobiology* (1975) sounded the trumpet for an enduring genetic program, seated far back in the brain, not lodged in the organs. Hardwired sexuality that could not be pried out.

Wilson's *On Human Nature* (1978) enraged people across the entire political/social spectrum. Anyone who believed in the high merit and ultimate perfectibility of humans was offended—from the gentle philosophical humanists to the flinty-eyed, up-against-the-wall Stalinist-Marxists.

Wilson's point of view is simple and comes from an essentially conservative notion: that much social behavior springs from genetic programming. Society itself—insect or human—is often a manifestation of genetic needs.

So are sexual roles. An example: Humans (and other primates) produce few children and nurture them intensively. A female's reproductive potential is then limited by her ability to provide nurture. A male, though, can sire many more young than a single female can bear and raise. The more females he mates with, the greater his reproductive success—i.e., how many of the next generation carry his genes. Males then compete to fertilize females, investing little in each offspring.

On the other hand, the female's preferred strategy is to choose a male who will lend a hand in bringing up the kids. A well-respected study of western women by anthropologist Heather Fowler found that women associate two basic symbols with sexually attractive men: money and status. Such men can provide a good nurturing background, steadiness, security—they're success-symbols. Similarly, men notoriously go for women with unwrinkled skin (therefore younger, able to reproduce better), large breasts (better nurture?) and a "certain sexual receptivity" (promising a ready "conquest").

Do men and women think this through? No! They're wired for it, through pleasure. In most societies, sex is widely regarded as something men seek and women dispense. This attitude is so common across cultures that it cannot be an accident.

Still, it's a wise man who knows his own son—so cuckoldry is a rage-producing taboo. A man who dutifully rears children who do not, in fact, carry his genetic code never gets represented in the next generation. In our operas, he is the butt of jokes.

It's not surprising that evolution has selected for males who have strong views on such matters. The prime reason for murders of women by men, in both America and Africa, is suspected or actual female infidelity. It's even an important cause of murder among male gays. Its passions run deep.

Gays, in fact, represent one of the unexpected insights that a good scientific theory gives. The maladjustments many male gays have with their own sexual impulses represent something very deep—an abiding sense of frustration over the conflict between genetically driven patterns and what society wants us to do. The family, after all, is a rickety cage, restraining male promiscuity, husbanding (literally) resources, providing continuity to all. Society shores up family life in many ways to build big, stable institutions based on the small, private virtues learned at home. This disguises some of our innate drives.

To see the naked patterns of sexual behavior, then, look to homosexual behavior. There, society's bonds are gone. Every study shows that gay males tend strongly toward one-night stands. Lesbians are much more apt to pair-bond, forming long-term relationships. The two divergent strategies laid bare.

Ironically, then, we can see our genetic heritage most clearly in the patterns of the homosexual outgroup. Doubly ironic, since this is the one group that passes on less of its genetic material than do the couples of suburbia.

Why, then, any homosexuality at all? The fashionable attitudes of our time hold that homosexuality is perfectly all right because it *is* a right, like free speech. The political language revolves around "sexual preference," trivializing a profound inner sense into a fashion choice. Who ever looked over the sexual opportunities, like shopping?

A more persuasive argument rests on biology itself. Homosexuality persists in all societies, and indeed, among the higher primates generally, because it has an evolutionary role.

Explaining why brought into play the idea of "kinship selection". The term itself came from studying why groups in the wild can manifest seemingly odd behaviors, ones not immediately useful in survival.

This means that a gay man or woman can work for the betterment of his relations, laboring in the tribe as specialized labor, free of the burden of child rearing. Gay males might have been leaders, or explorers, or craftsmen. They might have stayed close to the mothers, to protect while the other men were away. Lesbians could have done general service in child rearing, or helped hunt (women often have a better sense of smell). These are available, specialized labors, just as men's and women's bodies adapted to special tasks.

These ideas resemble "Just So"-style stories explaining why given traits emerged. The crucial point is that they did emerge, in the crucible of rapid human evolution.

The genes which can occasionally confer homosexuality (in about one percent of the human population) are shared by kinfolk. Usually the slight genetic influence does not manifest itself as homosexuality, and so gets transmitted through ordinary heterosexual bonds.

But because the gay brother or sister labors on, the tribe as a whole has a better chance of surviving.

Homosexuality need not be accepted because it is a right, but rather because it is indeed natural. It is preferred as a minority strategy by evolution of the hunter-gatherer hominids we once were...and still are.

The ancient past speaks to us, but we seldom hear. I live in a town with about 30% gay population. The mayor is gay, and a friend of mine. He has been selected for, far back in Africa.

I suppose whatever he does in the bedroom does not fit the antiseptic American ideal. He does far more outside it, for our community, than I, standard issue heterosexual male, will ever do.

He belongs here. He is natural. So are the two lesbians on the city council.

I held, back in that humanities class, that we could productively consider both homosexual modes as alternate social/biological strategies which demonstrably propagate themselves. They have their own cultures, intermingling with the subcultures of men-alone and women-alone.

Perhaps, to make a distinction between the simple biological sexes and the cultural genders, we should speak of four genders. Four strategies.

So the evidence is in: there are deep currents in the human psyche, ingrained in the DNA, that drive human sexuality. We do not learn to be men and women solely from society. (Indeed, how could anybody who has passed through the hormonal roller coaster of adolescence possibly believe otherwise?)

Fast-changing society doesn't always like those deep drives. It does what it can, through conditioning, to shape them to its benefit.

The American impulse to mechanize its own sexuality has to be looked at this way. It seeks not just the victory of the vaginal deodorant tycoons; the Cause extends down to the soft-spoken socialists who dream of Perfectible Mankind, and to the feminists who long for the Good Male. Once we were devils, but we can become angels. Fine ideals, perhaps, but founded on the sand of bad science.

All such believers in social perfection are manipulators. They want to forget the press of the past, to dismiss evolution as a fever dream that will pass, if we merely Think Right.

A symptom of this has been the drift toward androgyny. The outright manifestation is the growing number of sex change operations. These are anatomically crude—a long way from add-water-and-stir clones—and psychologically high-risk.

Yet they spring from an underlying philosophy that is widespread: that you can fix up the hormones, tinker with the genitals, and make yourself over. Cast off your sexual hangups! Trade in that old set of synapses! Buy the new, *new*, NEW (fill in sex of your choice).

John Varley's sex-change utopia is not a useful fictional/laboratory for trying out our sexual stereotypes because it, too, is based on a stereotype—Malleable Man. Fictional lessons, if they are to be used, must make some contact with our real lives. And we are not infinitely changeable.

There are helically-stored, immutable instructions impressed into the human brain, and these cannot ultimately be ignored.

One of the central lessons of our century is that the opposite ideal has produced vast police states. The program of the Soviet Empire and its imitation, client states was to bring about the millennium by conditioning the populace. Orwell—arguably the greatest English science fiction writer since Wells—saw clearly that Communists and Nazis alike thought they could produce a New Man from the tattered cloth of ordinary folk, given enough conditioning. Orwell was terrified that it worked too well. Luckily, time has proven him wrong—but it was a near thing.

Why do we learn so little from such a clear case? A proper regard for the irreducible traits we carry would lighten the hand of the reformers, make a wiser world.

In science fiction, our concern for mind-body dualities and man-machine interfaces ignores a singular fact. Our minds aren't cleanly divided along a software/hardware divide. Our software, if you like, redesigns its hardware over time, laying down fresh pathways, modifying others. Synapses build anew as you sleep.

Our sexuality—polymorphous and powerful as it is—will not abide easy changes in the "software". Hormones and neurological wiring can't be neatly patched, trimmed, deleted, copied or edited.

The weight of what we have been is considerable. A woman who has been a man is not the same as a woman who has never been otherwise, or wished to be. Freedom, even the blithe liberty technology can convey, is both the ability to change vectors, and having the weight of character to make changes mean something.

Our dreams of escaping our selves, escaping even history, is in the end the longing for a kind of triviality. Transsexuals can strive for the Other, but they cannot ape the embedded hormones, the delicate balances of glands, the full and weighty life that the mind-body synthesis commands. Motherhood, fatherhood, the ecstasy of union—these are not experiences detachable from the rest of life.

To be interchangeable may make us more free, but it would also make our lives matter less. Sexuality, it seems to me, can be aided by technology only at the margin. Abortion, contraception, sanitation—all help. In the decades to come, biotechnology will far transcend these rather simple options, presenting us with fresh choices which will excite us, horrify us, tempt us, and provoke endless arguments—all dancing about one central question: who are we?

We are the thinking beings moored in the body. We will always have pangs of love, of jealousy, of loss. Men and women will always clash, because they have different sexual strategies. This struggle is part of the sexual specialization we see in our bodies, which evolution in old Africa has made moderately different.

Difference brings us agony and amusement alike. The tension between men and women is part of our power. The same stresses which make for romantic comedy helped us transcend the veldt.

Even in the glitzy techno-future, we cannot solve our problems and remain recognizably human by slicing up the human experience into sanitized, detachable parts. The unconscious, and the body it is deeply rooted in, will be heard.

*Copyright © 1995 by Abbenford Associates*

*Barry N. Malzberg is the winner of the very first Campbell Memorial Award, a multiple Hugo and Nebula nominee, and the author of more than ninety books.*

# FROM THE HEART'S BASEMENT

## by Barry N. Malzberg

### Trudging Through the Land of Smiles

Three days ago was the fiftieth anniversary of my third sale, my first real sale, the 1,200-word short "We're Coming Through The Windows" to Fred Pohl's *Galaxy. Quelle triumphe! Quelle dommage.* The two earlier sales to the fifth or seventh rate *Playboy* imitator, *Wildcat* (I wrote about the first sixteen months ago) were real because I was paid, but they never felt authentic; the stories were wispy, deadening pornography and the position was ridiculous. The sale to *Galaxy* was different; I had (as I wrote G.P. Elliott) "finally sold a magazine of which someone has heard" and in fashioning an inconsequential, breezy little satire for a respected market I had demonstrated to myself that I could do this. "I can do this," I had thought, reading Norman Kagan's "Laugh Along With Franz" in the 12/65 *Galaxy*. "If this son of a bitch can get away with this kind of social satire in a category market, then I have some kind of a future because I can do this too." But I did not believe it until I had done it.

The sale was important out of all proportion to its remuneration or length. After that fellowship year (and a hundred rejections) at Syracuse, after failing to break *The Atlantic, Esquire,* or *The Hudson Review,* after all of the contemptuous dismissals or cock-teasingly worthless near misses (the *Atlantic Monthly Press* editor Esther Yntema was the most cunning and vicious), I had crawled back to New York without possessions or hope, willingly foregoing the larger fellowship I had been offered for the next year because my young bride and I were flat out of money, $750 in debt to the State of New York, and there seemed no way to get through the summer simply to enjoy another academic year of humiliation. Scott Meredith hardly beckoned but seemed willing to take me on for $90 a week. Starting in the fee department and exhibiting talents I never suspected I possessed, I was able to hang on and shortly thereafter become familiar with the agent's client list: Mack Reynolds, Marion Bradley, Phil Dick, Christopher Anvil, Charles Runyon, James Schmitz. These clients, even beyond the mystery writers, interested me. "I used to read a lot of this stuff as a kid before I found *Look Homeward Angel*," I mumbled. "If these folks can do it, maybe I can do it too." Two months later, renewing my acquaintance with the magazines, I found "Laugh Along With Franz". I have parsed all of this at greater length in various venues over the years.

What Fred Pohl (who always treated me like a pro, years before I was one) gave me for the first time was sight of a road to publication. It was not a golden road and its destination was surely not the Land of Smiles (I had all of those clients' income figures and troubled correspondence in front of me) but a road it was nonetheless, and for the first time I found myself able to look forward, not through a rancid haze of desire but in a practical fashion. Fifty years later, no stout Cortez, no precipice, no eternity at which to stare, but I was able after a fashion to trudge the terrain. Knowledge may—until and unless the brain freezes—be a mean series of acquisitions, but it is still better to have than stupid.

Alfred Bester could tell you that. His characters do so over and again in the hundred mocking guises of his interstellar remittance man, old liver and onions himself. "You can't go back, old *ami*, you cannot change the past because it is only your past, you can send a thousand prayers into thin air but they are only *your* prayers and they will come back only to yourself. The 5,271,009 choices you face in a lifetime, my pesky, insidious, ignorant friend, and you will make first one and then the other as if you were thinking, but you are only responding." Another wink, a shaky gesture. "There is only that eternal loneliness but, *hic!*, you try to fill it with the illusion of change." The Men Who Murdered Muhammed could only murder themselves, but even then the past could not be killed, the past was always there lurking, and in the end your Common Book was the Bible of your fall. All of this is in J.D. Smith's new critical study of our boy Alfie (1913-1987), Grand Master and Holy Fool, perhaps the only true genius who ever wandered (by mistake) into our garden and in the end he could not get out. Maybe Annie Proulx or Thom Jones could sneak away from the Venus flytrap of the markets but Alfie, in thrall, could not escape ingestion by the world snake.

Smith, an Illinois University Professor, has laid out the work with synoptically surgical precision, trapped the man from his playful beginnings to half-incipient career and then the two desertions, the first in the '40s to comics, radio, drama, the second and longer from the late '50s to the early '70s when *Holiday* dissolved underneath and he made a forced return. The two astonishing novels, the dozen and a half even more astonishing short stories, which ended in 1963 with "They Don't Make Life Like They Used To", and then the long, long goodbye after the second return in 1971. The weak, weaker and weakest novels in succession, the flailing at conventions, the awful decampment and disintegration to Bucks County in the last half decade. The greatest science fiction writer who ever lived dissolving in silence at a bar in the backwoods, listening to the Eastern rednecks mock the Blacks and the Jews. (These were not the words that were actually used.) Getting home by automobile through prayer or luck, Charles Platt once accompanying him through these rambles. "Alfie, do they know *you* are Jewish?" Platt wrote he asked Bester. J.D. Smith has no answers, but he has suggestions, some florid (he sees *The Demolished Man* as a grotesque, consciously monstrous extension of Freud, Sigmund the man-eating plant in the Little Shop of Horrors), others merely suggestive (Gold exacerbated the Freudianism of the first novel, sulked when he was not offered *The Stars My Destination*, and then verged on ugliness.) Joe Ferman shrugged in contempt and gave it back. His son and I had a similar experience two decades later with the first third of *The Computer Connection*. Bester's odyssey was perhaps no more paradigmatic or disastrous than Henry Kuttner's or Alice Sheldon's, but unlike theirs it was instructive. Many young writers were changed by close observation of Bester's life and fate. Kuttner had little to teach beyond the obvious dangers of overwork, and Sheldon, not quite the only other true genius who ever wandered into the field, was too *sui generis* to leave anything other than her body of work and a false lead. No Land of Smiles for that lady.

Smith's work is remarkable and irreplaceable, a mark of transition toward the great biography of Alfred Bester which would explain science fiction to itself and Bester to the world. That biography would be Mahler's Tenth Symphony; like Deryck Cooke with Mahler, J.D. Smith has given as much as possibility would grant.

✿

My novel *The Men Inside* (Lancer, 1973) is a first-person work disguised as third person. I noted this again while reading Smith's synopsis and commentary on "Fondly Fahrenheit" from which *The Men Inside* was clearly derived.

Bester was shrewder than Nabokov, shrewder than anybody. "Fondly Fahrenheit" was published a year before *Lolita*.

*14 January 2017 New Jersey*

*Copyright © 2017 by Barry N. Malzberg*

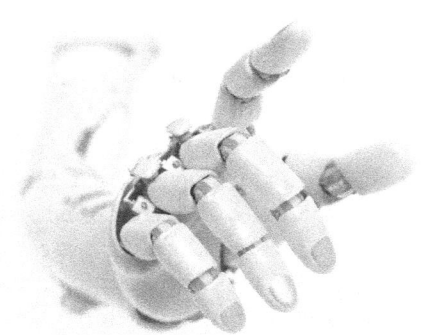

*Joy Ward is the author of one novel. She has several stories in print, magazines and anthologies, and has also done interviews, both written and video, for other publications.*

*Mike Resnick, along with editing this magazine, is the winner of five Hugos from a record thirty-seven nominations and is, according to* Locus, *the all-time leading award winner, living or dead, for short fiction. He is the author of seventy-seven novels, 285 stories, and three screenplays, and the editor of forty-two anthologies. He was Guest of Honor at the 2012 Worldcon.*

## THE *GALAXY'S EDGE* INTERVIEW

### Joy Ward interviews Mike Resnick

Mike Resnick is more than simply a science fiction icon. Mike has won more awards than any other science fiction writer. In fact, Mike is so good at what he does he makes the very hard work of writing top-notch science fiction look almost easy. Besides numerous books and stories in print all across the world, Resnick is also the editor of *Galaxy's Edge*.

**Joy Ward:** How did you get started writing?

**Mike Resnick:** My mother was a writer. I always wanted to be a writer. By the time I was in high school I sold my first article at fifteen, I sold my first poem at sixteen. I'm not a poet but I ran it in Facebook a while back.

Silky Sullivan came to the Derby with more pre-publicity than Secretariat and ran twelfth. I wrote "Silky at the Post" (which was my answer to "Casey at the Bat") and I actually sold it. I sold some stories by eighteen. I married Carol in college. I was nineteen, she was eighteen, and after a year of fiddling around working for the railroad I figured it was time to get a job in publishing somewhere—and it happens that the only publishing job open in the whole city of Chicago at that point was at 2717 North Pulaski Road. National Features Syndicate is what they called it, but what they did is they put out three tabloids, very much like the *National Enquirer* only worse, and three men's magazines. Within half a year this twenty-two-year-old kid is editing *The National Insider* with a print run of 400,000 a week. Our best-selling headline during the years I had it was "Raped by 7 Dwarves." I will not testify to the veracity of our stories. Because we did not publish erotic books, adult books, that meant I was free to sell them elsewhere, whereas I couldn't sell tabloid or men's magazine stuff elsewhere because we had our own publications. But I knew guys from other publishers in our field and I started doing that. By the time the dust had cleared ten years later I had sold over two hundred of them, all of them under pseudonyms. As I explained, the only place we writers wanted our name was on the check, never on the book.

You'd be surprised how many people who have gone on and made it pretty big started, learned their trade in that field because you could get very well paid while you were learning how to write. We only got a thousand a book, sometimes seven hundred a book, and no royalties ever, but if you turn out a book every two weeks or every week or so, this was at a time when the average American was making eight thousand bucks a year. We could do that every two months if we had to. We were twenty-two, twenty-three-year-old kids. You learned how to make deadlines and you learned how to differentiate characters since they were all going to do the very same thing. I sneaked through some Edgar Rice Burroughs and Robert E. Howard pastiches to legitimate New York publishers, but I didn't want to write Burroughs or Howard books, I wanted to write Resnick books.

One day in 1975 I turned to Carol and I said, "If I write one more four-day book or one more six-hour screenplay for Herschel Gordon Lewis (he was voted the second worst director in history after Ed Wood), if I do one more my brain is going to turn to putty and run out my ears. What else do we know how to do?"

At the time we were breeding and exhibiting collies. We had twenty-three champions overall, and we had twelve or fifteen dogs on the place any given day—and we figured if the two of us could care for fifteen dogs and I had time to write all that crap, think of what a staff could do. So we spent about eight months looking around the country and wound up buying the second-biggest luxury boarding and grooming kennel in America, which happened to be in Cincinnati. We moved there and within about four years it was going full force. We had a staff of twenty-one. Any given day we were boarding like two hundred dogs, sixty cats, grooming about thirty or forty dogs.

I was finally able to go back to writing, only this time writing the kind of stuff I wanted to write. I was sure there was no audience for it. That was why we had the kennel. Much to my surprise, it started selling and in 1993, when the writing out-earned the kennel for the fifth year in a row, we sold the kennel. We figured we could now live anywhere we wanted, so we looked all over the country, decided we liked it here, so we stayed in Cincinnati.

The first thing I sold after we bought the kennel was *The Soul Eater* in 1981. Analog called it a work of art, which surprised the hell out of me that anybody besides me thought it was any good. The next one I wrote was one called *Birthright: The Book of Man*, which I have resold a dozen times. It created a future in which I've put about thirty-five of the novels I've written since then. I wrote thirteen books for Signet and they were getting phenomenally good reviews. They were selling okay because Signet kept buying them from me, but they weren't selling any more than okay.

My advances weren't getting any bigger. It was like I was standing still doing nothing. My friend Jack Chalker finally convinced me that the problem was my agent. I had made one foreign sale in four years. So, after he convinced me, I did the smartest thing I've ever done in my career: I hired Eleanor Wood as my agent. I hired her in 1983, and she remains my agent today. The first book she sold was *Santiago*, which got me three times the biggest advance I had gotten up to that point. It made *The New York Times* bestseller list and in the first two years I had her she made twenty-six foreign sales for me, which was twenty-five more than anybody else had made for me. We have been together ever since.

I thought at the time, a rather stupid thought, that if you had something important to say you had to say it in sixty, seventy thousand words or more. You couldn't do it in a short story. I only wrote seven stories the first ten years I was writing science fiction. Then in 1986 Orson Scott Card asked me to write a story for an anthology he was doing called *Eutopia,* and by keeping to all the strictures he gave, which were interesting ones, I wrote a story called "Kirinyaga." It made my reputation. It won the Hugo. It made me decide that yeah, you can occasionally do something with short stories. It has re-sold thirty-four times to domestic and foreign venues. From that day to this I've written and sold about three hundred short stories. I found out I love doing them.

You have to understand that unlike most beginners, I wasn't one. I probably had ten million words behind me so the fact that it sold wasn't the thrill that it would be for most people. Everything I wrote sold. Most of it I didn't want to sign my name to. It was very gratifying that I was able to get away with it. I didn't have to do Burroughs books and Howard books. I could do Resnick books and sell them. That was very satisfying, and so was the fact that I had a legitimate New York publisher say, in essence, "Okay, I'll buy three a year from you, any subject you want." It was gratifying to know that I could finally write what I had been training myself to write for fifteen years, I could write stuff I could sign my name to, that when people came over and said, "What do you write for a living?" I wouldn't give them any titles because I didn't want anybody to know those titles. It was very satisfying to be able to write at a more elevated level. Howard and Burroughs were fine for their day and they wrote at the peak of their ability, but those are not the peak of most of our abilities. Totally different kinds of things.

What happened was Lin Carter was a friend of mine and he was probably the greatest literary chameleon of them all. One day I am in New York, probably around 1970 or so, having lunch with him. He was telling me what he was working on. He said, "Two weeks ago I did a Burroughs book and right now I'm doing a Lee Brackett book. Next month I'll be doing a Robert E. Howard book." I said, "That's fine, Lin, but when are you going to do a Lin Carter book?" He looked at me and I could tell he didn't understand the question. That made up my mind then and there. I didn't want to spend the rest of my life writing Robert E. Howard and C. L. Moore, the way Lin did. So I stayed out of the science fiction field for ten years. I wrote more adult books. I wrote other things. It really made up my mind that I didn't want to write that stuff. I'd rather not write science fiction at all than imitate other people.

So it was really gratifying to be putting my own views down. This is the kind of science fiction I want to write, nobody else was writing exactly like this, and to be able to sell it and get good reviews, to have a publisher and finally a number of publishers who continually encourage me and say do more of it—well, it finally made writing both fun and satisfying.

It also meant that I knew what I was going to do for the rest of my life, and I do a *lot* of it. I'm pretty fast. One thing you learn writing in that Other Field for a thousand a book, no royalties, and publishers who may go to jail in three weeks, is that you learn how to be fast. Well, to give you an example, I'm seventy-four years old. I should be slowing down and in ways I am. But when I was seventy, four years ago, I had ten books out. Last year, at seventy-four, I sold fourteen new stories and delivered eight books as well as editing *Galaxy's Edge.* I'm not impoverished. I do it in these quantities because this is what I love to do more than just about anything else in the world.

The most satisfying part of being a writer, probably for the last twenty-five, thirty years, has not been seeing my name in print. I do that all the time. I love winning awards, and I've certainly won my share— but the real highlight is at the end of the day when I look at what I've written and it comes out pretty much the way I hoped it would when I sat down in the afternoon to write. To me, that's more gratifying than any good review or anything else. I know the difference between good and bad. I also know when I write, even though its saleable, isn't as good as it should have been and I have to go back and do it again. But again, it's really very gratifying when it comes out the way I hoped it would.

My most memorable award was probably the first Hugo I won because you never expect to win one. Nobody expects to win one.

We were sitting in the audience right behind George Effinger in 1989 and I was up for best short story. It was the first time I had ever been nominated. I looked at the field and David Brin was up. David Brin was as hard to beat in the late eighties as Harlan was in the early seventies. I knew I was going to lose to him so I was talking to George Effinger. Then Carol pokes me in the ribs and says, "Go up there. You won!"

I said no, you must have heard wrong. David Brin had a lock on it.

She says to George, who had been turning to me. "George, will you tell him he won?"

What she didn't know was that George was deaf in one ear and he had turned the good ear to me and the deaf ear was facing the stage, so he didn't know. Finally a bunch of other writers who were sitting near us told me to go get the goddamned award so we can find out who won the next one. That was probably the most surprised and the biggest kick I got. Thereafter, not that I ever felt I had a lock on a particular Hugo, but at least I knew it was possible. I didn't know that the first time.

**JW:** You have a love affair with Africa.

**MR:** Yes I do.

Off the top, it's a beautiful and fascinating continent. More to the point, it's as close to an alien society as a science fiction writer is going to find on this world. I think every science fiction fan will agree with two statements. One, if we can reach the stars we are going to colonize them. Two, if we colonize enough of them sooner or later we are going to come into contact with more than one sentient race. Africa offers fifty-one separate and distinct examples—because it was colonized by so many countries—of the effects, usually deleterious, of colonization, not only on the colonized but on the colonizers. Those of us who don't learn from these warnings—and humans aren't all that good at learning anything—are doomed to repeat them. You add that to the fact that these really *are* alien societies. How alien? In Kenya in 1900, there were forty-three languages and not one of them had a word for wheel. That's pretty alien. There are many other examples. At the same time, as a tourist, it is beautiful. The animals are beautiful.

One of the interesting things is that I made friends with our private guide. Whenever we're going to Kenya or Tanzania I will write him ahead and say I'm going to be working on this, this and this. Find me some old-timers who can tell me about whatever it is I'm researching. So we spend some time in the game parks, but we also hunt up a bunch of salty old guys with really weird stories to tell who are going to die with them untold if I don't visit them. I ultimately transform them into science fiction, and they end up in my books and stories.

My most powerful stories are about Africa, or based on things African. My five Hugo winners are about Africa, and except for *Santiago*, my better sellers are about Africa—and that's because I feel very passionately about it and it comes through.

**JW:** You have your writer children?

**MR:** That's what Maureen McHugh dubbed them. What happened was with *Alternate Kennedys*, a closed anthology. Invitation only. I had invited Nancy Kress to it. She was teaching a workshop and a kid called Nick DiChario gave her a story she thought would fit, and told him to send it to me. The story came in and I must have been in a bad mood, because instead of putting in a little note saying politely please don't do this until you are asked, I thought let me read it and see just how bad it is. By page four I knew nothing could keep it off the Hugo ballot. And nothing did. It was a Hugo nominee, and a World Fantasy nominee and Nick himself was a Campbell nominee for that story. I finally met him a few months later at the Orlando World-Con and I said to him, "Nick, why did you send it to me?" The magazines at the time had three times the circulation of an anthology. "A story that ballot worthy should get to as many people as possible." His answer was that he had sent it to every magazine in the field and got nothing but form rejects. I thought they are crazy! They should have fired the slush readers, because it never got to an editor. No editor could read that story and not buy it. We became correspondents and friends, and about a year later he sends me a novella and a note that he was having the same trouble with this. Could I tell him what's wrong with it? I read it and the only thing wrong with it was it was by Nick instead of by Isaac, Arthur or Robert. I knew Piers Anthony was doing an anthology on that theme. I wrote Piers and told him read this, that he was going to buy it—and indeed he did.

I thought if we keep treating this poor kid like that, he's not going to stop writing—but he's going to stop writing science fiction and go write espionage or something else. We're going to lose a helluva talent. So I figured I'd better do something to encourage him. I get about eight or ten invites every year for anthologies. When they invite me it's a guaranteed sale. So I invited Nick to collaborate with me on four or five of these just to get him into print, to keep him enthused. He's still writing now, he's been up for another Hugo, and he is committed to science fiction and not some rival field.

I thought: I bet there are more good writers out there than Nick who have trouble *selling*. So it became my duty over the last twenty-five years to help them. Every time I find a good one, I collaborate with him or her to get them into print, I buy from them for my anthologies and now for my magazine, and at conventions I take them around and introduce them to editors and agents. I do everything I can to help them.

People ask why, and the answer is you can't pay back in this field. I'm seventy-four. Everybody who helped me at the beginning is dead or rich or both. I can't pay back, so I pay forward. It's very, very gratifying to see some of these kids go out and do wonderful things!

It means the field that I love, that I have devoted my life to, isn't going to lose ten or twelve or fifteen really talented writers every decade.

These are people who deserve to be in print. This field, like almost any other field, is limited. It can't publish an unlimited number of books. It doesn't have an unlimited number of dollars. It's like movies or anything else: once you're in you fight to maintain your turf. If that means being a little tougher on the guy coming up behind you, you do it. And my helping them is a way to even the playing field, because to be honest most people won't even define the playing field for them. You get an awful lot of platitudes out of how-to books on writing, many of which are quite good—but there aren't any how-to books on selling.

It makes me feel that I've helped pay the field back for being so good for me. For the last thirty or forty or fifty years I've been living a dream. When I was six years old I wanted to write a book called *Masters of the Galaxy*. Now, the subject matter has changed appreciably—but four years ago I did a book called *Masters of the Galaxy*. It happened to be about a hardboiled futuristic detective called Jake Masters, but for sixty-five years I wanted to write that book. This field has been phenomenal to me. It's given me everything I ever wanted. My spare time is spent going to conventions, associating with friends. The only people I tend to talk to now that we are out of dogs, on the computer or just about anywhere else, are science fiction fans and writers. And I am as much a fan as I am a writer. How do you thank a field for giving you a lifetime? This is my way.

## SERIALIZATION
## DOUBLE STAR

"Of all Heinlein's books, . . . Double Star is one of my three favorites."—*Connie Willis*

by Robert A. Heinlein
Phoenix Pick Edition, 2015
Trade Paperback: 170 pages.
ISBN: 978-1-61242-285-5

*Robert A. Heinlein is generally considered the most important and influential writer ever to turn his hand to science fiction. He was a three-time Worldcon Guest of Honor, the first-ever Nebula Grandmaster, won four Best Novel Hugos during his lifetime and even more Retro Hugo after his death.* Double Star *won him his first Hugo, in 1956.*

## DOUBLE STAR
### Part 2

### By Robert A. Heinlein

### IV

My education continued in that room (Mr. Bonforte's guest room, it was) until turnover. I had no sleep, other than under hypnosis, and did not seem to need any. Either Doc Capek or Penny stuck with me and helped me the whole time. Fortunately my man was as thoroughly photographed and recorded as perhaps any man in history and I had, as well, the close cooperation of his intimates. There was endless material; the problem was to see how much I could assimilate, both awake and under hypnosis.

I don't know at what point I quit disliking Bonforte. Capek assured me—and I believe him—that he did not implant a hypnotic suggestion on this point; I had not asked for it and I am quite certain that Capek was meticulous about the ethical responsibilities of a physician and hypnotherapist. But I suppose that it was an inevitable concomitant of the role—I rather think I would learn to like Jack the Ripper if I studied for the part. Look at it this way: To learn a role truly, you must for a time become that character. And a man either likes himself, or he commits suicide, one way or another.

"To understand all is to forgive all"—and I was beginning to understand Bonforte.

At turnover we got that one-gravity rest that Dak had promised. We never were in free fall, not for an instant; instead of putting out the torch, which I gather they hate to do while under way, the ship described what Dak called a 180-degree skew turn. It leaves the ship on boost the whole time and is done rather quickly, but it has an oddly disturbing effect on the sense of balance. The effect has a name something like Coriolanus. Coriolis?

All I know about spaceships is that the ones that operate from the surface of a planet are true rockets but the *voyageurs* call them "teakettles" because of the steam jet of water or hydrogen they boost with. They aren't considered real atomic-power ships even though the jet is heated by an atomic pile. The long-jump ships such as the *Tom Paine*, torchships that is, are (so they tell me) the real thing, making use of E equals MC squared, or is it M equals EC squared? You know—the thing Einstein invented.

Dak did his best to explain it all to me, and no doubt it is very interesting to those who care for such things. But I can't imagine why a gentleman should bother with such. It seems to me that every time those scientific laddies get busy with their slide rules life becomes more complicated. What was wrong with things the way they were?

During the two hours we were on one gravity I was moved up to Bonforte's cabin. I started wearing his clothes and his face and everyone was careful to call me "Mr. Bonforte" or "Chief" or (in the case of Dr. Capek) "Joseph," the idea being, of course, to help me build the part.

Everyone but Penny, that is.... She simply would not call me "Mr. Bonforte." She did her best to help but she could not bring herself to that. It was clear as scripture that she was a secretary who silently and hopelessly loved her boss, and she resented me with a deep, illogical, but natural bitterness. It made it hard for both of us, especially as I was finding her most attractive. No man can do his best work with a woman constantly around him who despises him. But I could not dislike her in return; I felt deeply sorry for her—even though I was decidedly irked.

We were on a tryout-in-the-sticks basis now, as not everyone in the *Tom Paine* knew that I was not Bonforte. I did not know exactly which ones knew of the substitution, but I was allowed to relax and ask questions only in the presence of Dak, Penny, and Dr. Capek. I was fairly sure that Bonforte's chief clerk, Mr. Washington, knew but never let on; he was a spare, elderly mulatto with the tight-lipped mask of a saint. There were two others who certainly knew, but they were not in the *Tom Paine*; they were standing by and covering up from the *Go for Broke*,

handling press releases and routine dispatches—Bill Corpsman, who was Bonforte's front man with the news services, and Roger Clifton. I don't know quite how to describe Clifton's job. Political deputy? He had been Minister without Portfolio, you may remember, when Bonforte was Supreme Minister, but that says nothing. Let's put it symbolically: Bonforte handed out policy and Clifton handed out patronage.

This small group had to know; if any others knew it was not considered necessary to tell me. To be sure, the other members of Bonforte's staff and all the crew of the *Tom Paine* knew that something odd was going on; they did not necessarily know what it was. A good many people had seen me enter the ship—but as "Benny Grey." By the time they saw me again I was already "Bonforte."

Someone had had the foresight to obtain real makeup equipment, but I used almost none. At close range makeup can be seen; even Silicoflesh cannot be given the exact texture of skin. I contented myself with darkening my natural complexion a couple of shades with Semiperm and wearing his face, from inside. I did have to sacrifice quite a lot of hair and Dr. Capek inhibited the roots. I did not mind; an actor can always wear hairpieces—and I was sure that this job was certain to pay me a fee that would let me retire for life, if I wished.

On the other hand, I was sometimes queasily aware that "life" might not be too long—there are those old saws about the man who knew too much and the one about dead men and tales. But truthfully I was beginning to trust these people. They were all darn nice people—which told me as much about Bonforte as I had learned by listening to his speeches and seeing his pix. A political figure is not a single man, so I was learning, but a compatible team. If Bonforte himself had not been a decent sort he would not have had these people around him.

The Martian language gave me my greatest worry. Like most actors, I had picked up enough Martian, Venerian, Outer Jovian, etc., to be able to fake in front of a camera or on stage. But those rolled or fluttered consonants are very difficult. Human vocal cords are not as versatile as a Martian's tympanus, I believe, and, in any case, the semi-phonetic spelling out of those sounds in Roman letters, for example "kkk" or "jjj" or "rrr" have no more to do with the true sounds than the *g* in "gnu" has to do with the inhaled click with which a Bantu pronounces "gnu." "Jjj," for instance, closely resembles a Bronx cheer.

Fortunately Bonforte had no great talent for other languages—and I am a professional; my ears really hear, I can imitate any sound, from a buzz saw striking a nail in a chunk of firewood to a setting hen disturbed on her nest. It was necessary only to acquire Martian as poorly as Bonforte spoke it. He had worked hard to overcome his lack of talent, and every word and phrase of Martian that he knew had been sight-sound recorded so that he could study his mistakes.

So I studied his mistakes, with the projector moved into his office and Penny at my elbow to sort out the spools for me and answer questions.

Human languages fall into four groups: inflecting ones as in Anglo-American, positional as in Chinese, agglutinative as in Old Turkish, polysynthetic (sentence units) as in Eskimo—to which, of course, we now add alien structures as wildly odd and as nearly impossible for the human brain as nonrepetitive or emergent Venerian. Luckily Martian is analogous to human speech forms. Basic Martian, the trade language, is positional and involves only simple concrete ideas—like the greeting: "I see you." High Martian is polysynthetic and very stylized, with an expression for every nuance of their complex system of rewards and punishments, obligations and debts. It had been almost too much for Bonforte; Penny told me that he could read those arrays of dots they use for writing quite easily but of the spoken form of High Martian he could say only a few hundred sentences.

Brother, how I studied those few he had mastered!

✧

The strain on Penny was even greater than it was on me. Both she and Dak spoke some Martian but the chore of coaching me fell on her as Dak had to spend most of his time in the control room; Jock's death had left him shorthanded. We dropped from two gravities to one for the last few million miles of the approach, during which time he never came below at all. I spent it learning the ritual I would have to know for the adoption ceremony, with Penny's help.

I had just completed running through the speech in which I was to accept membership in the Kkkah Nest—a speech not unlike that, in spirit, with which an orthodox Jewish boy assumes the responsibilities of manhood, but as fixed, as invariable, as Hamlet's soliloquy. I had read it, complete with Bonforte's mispronunciations and facial tic; I finished and asked, "How was that?"

"That was quite good," she answered seriously.

"Thanks, Curly Top." It was a phrase I had lifted from the language-practice spools in Bonforte's files; it was what Bonforte called her when he was feeling mellow—and it was perfectly in character.

*"Don't you dare call me that!"*

I looked at her in honest amazement and answered, still in character, "Why, Penny my child!"

"Don't you call me *that*, either! You *fake*! You *phony*! You—*actor*!" She jumped up, ran as far as she could—which was only to the door—and stood there, faced away from me, her face buried in her hands and her shoulders shaking with sobs.

I made a tremendous effort and lifted myself out of the character—pulled in my belly, let my own face come up, answered in my own voice. "Miss Russell!"

She stopped crying, whirled around, looked at me, and her jaw dropped. I added, still in my normal self, "Come back here and sit down."

I thought she was going to refuse, then she seemed to think better of it, came slowly back and sat down, her hands in her lap but with her face that of a little girl who is "saving up more spit."

I let her sit for a moment, then said quietly, "Yes, Miss Russell, I am an actor. Is that a reason for you to insult me?"

She simply looked stubborn.

"As an actor, I am here to do an actor's job. You know why. You know, too, that I was tricked into taking it—it is not a job I would have accepted with my eyes open, even in my wildest moments. I hate having to do it considerably more than you hate having me do it—for despite Captain Broadbent's cheerful assurances I am not at all sure that I will come out of it with my skin intact—and I'm awfully fond of my skin; it's the only one I have. I believe, too, that I know why you find it hard to accept me. But is that any reason for you to make my job harder than it has to be?"

She mumbled. I said sharply, "Speak up!"

"It's dishonest! It's *indecent!*"

I sighed. "It certainly is. More than that, it is impossible—without the wholehearted support of the other members of the cast. So let's call Captain Broadbent down here and tell him. Let's call it off."

She jerked her face up and said, "Oh no! We can't do that."

"Why can't we? A far better thing to drop it now than to present it and have it flop. I can't give a performance under these conditions. Let's admit it."

"But—but—we've *got* to! It's necessary."

"Why is it necessary, Miss Russell? Political reasons? I have not the slightest interest in politics—and I doubt if you have any really deep interest. So why must we do it?"

"Because—because *he*—" She stopped, unable to go on, strangled by sobs.

I got up, went over, and put a hand on her shoulder. "I know. Because if we don't, something that *he* has spent years building up will fall to pieces. Because he can't do it himself and his friends are trying to cover up and do it for him. Because his friends are loyal to him. Because you are loyal to him. Nevertheless, it hurts you to see someone else in the place that is rightfully his. Besides that, you are half out of your mind with grief and worry about him. Aren't you?"

"Yes." I could barely hear it.

I took hold of her chin and tilted her face up. "I know why you find it so hard to have me here, in his place. You love him. But I'm doing the best job for him I know how. *Confound it, woman! Do you have to make my job six times harder by treating me like dirt?*"

She looked shocked. For a moment I thought she was going to slap me. Then she said brokenly, "I am sorry. I am very sorry. I won't let it happen again."

I let go her chin and said briskly, "Then let's get back to work."

She did not move. "Can you forgive me?"

"Huh? There's nothing to forgive, Penny. You were acting up because you love him and you were worried. Now let's get to work. I've got to be letter-perfect—and it's only hours away." I dropped at once back into the role.

She picked up a spool and started the projector again. I watched him through it once, then did the acceptance speech with the sound cut out but stereo on, matching my voice—*his* voice, I mean—to the moving image. She watched me, looking from the image back to my face with a dazed look on her own. We finished and I switched it off myself. "How was that?"

"That was perfect!"

I smiled his smile. "Thanks, Curly Top."

"Not at all—'Mr. Bonforte.'"

Two hours later we made rendezvous with the *Go for Broke*.

✧

Dak brought Roger Clifton and Bill Corpsman to my cabin as soon as the *Go for Broke* had transferred them. I knew them from pictures. I stood up and said, "Hello, Rog. Glad to see you, Bill." My voice was warm but casual; on the level at which these people operated a hasty trip to Earth and back was simply a few days' separation and nothing more. I limped over and offered my hand. The ship was at the moment under low boost as it adjusted to a much tighter orbit than the *Go for Broke* had been riding in.

Clifton threw me a quick glance, then played up. He took his cigar out of his mouth, shook hands, and said quietly, "Glad to see you back, Chief." He was a small man, bald-headed and middle-aged, and looked like a lawyer and a good poker player.

"Anything special while I was away?"

"No. Just routine. I gave Penny the file."

"Good." I turned to Bill Corpsman, again offered my hand.

He did not take it. Instead he put his fists on his hips, looked up at me, and whistled. "Amazing! I really do believe we stand a chance of getting away with it." He looked me up and down, then said, "Turn around, Smythe. Move around. I want to see you walk."

I found that I was actually feeling the annoyance that Bonforte would have felt at such uncalled-for impertinence, and, of course, it showed in my face. Dak touched Corpsman's sleeve and said quickly, "Knock it off, Bill. You remember what we agreed?"

"Chicken tracks!" Corpsman answered. "This room is soundproofed. I just want to make sure he is up to it. Smythe, how's your Martian? Can you spiel it?"

I answered with a single squeaking polysyllabic in High Martian, a sentence meaning roughly, "Proper conduct demands that one of us leave!"—but it means far more than that, as it is a challenge which usually ends in someone's nest being notified of a demise.

I don't think Corpsman understood it, for he grinned and answered, "I've got to hand it to you, Smythe. That's good."

But Dak understood it. He took Corpsman by the arm and said, "Bill, I told you to knock it off. You're in my ship and that's an order. We play it straight from here on—every second."

Clifton added, "Pay attention to him, Bill. You know we agreed that was the way to do it. Otherwise somebody might slip."

Corpsman glanced at him, then shrugged. "All right, all right. I was just checking up—after all, this was my idea." He gave me a one-sided smile and said, "Howdy, Mister Bonforte. Glad to see you back."

There was a shade too much emphasis on "Mister" but I answered, "Good to be back, Bill. Anything special I need to know before we go down?"

"I guess not. Press conference at Goddard City after the ceremonies." I could see him watching me to see how I would take it.

I nodded. "Very well."

Dak said hastily, "Say, Rog, how about that? Is it necessary? Did you authorize it?"

"I was going to add," Corpsman went on, turning to Clifton, "before the Skipper here got the jitters, that I can take it myself and tell the boys that the Chief has dry laryngitis from the ceremonies—or we can limit it to written questions submitted ahead of time and I'll get the answers written out for him while the ceremonies are going on. Seeing that he looks and sounds so good close up, I would say to risk it. How about it, Mister—'Bonforte'? Think you can swing it?"

"I see no problem involved in it, Bill." I was thinking that if I managed to get by the Martians without a slip I would undertake to ad-lib double-talk to a bunch of human reporters as long as they wanted to listen. I had good command of Bonforte's speaking style by now and at least a rough notion of his policies and attitudes—and I need not be specific.

But Clifton looked worried. Before he could speak the ship's horn brayed out, "Captain is requested to come to the control room. Minus four minutes."

Dak said quickly, "You all will have to settle it. I've got to put this sled in its slot—I've got nobody up there but young Epstein." He dashed for the door.

Corpsman called out, "Hey, Skip! I wanted to tell you—" He was out the door and following Dak without waiting to say good-bye.

Roger Clifton closed the door Corpsman had left open, came back, and said slowly, "Do you want to risk this press conference?"

"That is up to you. I want to do the job."

"Mmm.... Then I'm inclined to risk it—if we use the written-questions method. But I'll check Bill's answers myself before you have to give them."

"Very well." I added, "If you can find a way to let me have them ten minutes or so ahead of time, there shouldn't be any difficulty. I'm a very quick study."

He inspected me. "I quite believe it—Chief. All right, I'll have Penny slip the answers to you right after the ceremonies. Then you can excuse yourself to go to the men's room and just stay there until you are sure of them."

"That should work."

"I think so. Uh, I must say I feel considerably better now that I've seen you. Is there anything I can do for you?"

"I think not, Rog. Yes, there is, too. Any word about—*him*?"

"Eh? Well, yes and no. He's still in Goddard City; we're sure of that. He hasn't been taken off Mars, or even out in the country. We blocked them on that, if that was their intention."

"Eh? Goddard City is not a big place, is it? Not more than a hundred thousand? What's the hitch?"

"The hitch is that we don't dare admit that you—I mean that *he*—is missing. Once we have this adoption thing wrapped up, we can put you out of sight, then announce the kidnapping as if it had just taken place—and make them take the city apart rivet by rivet. The city authorities are all Humanity Party appointees, but they will have to cooperate—after the ceremony. It will be the most wholehearted cooperation you ever saw, for they will be deadly anxious to produce him before the whole Kkkahgral nest swarms over them and tears the city down around their ears."

"Oh. I'm still learning about Martian psychology and customs."

"Aren't we all!"

"Rog? Mmm...what leads you to think that he is still alive? Wouldn't their purpose be better served—and with less risk—just by killing him?" I was thinking queasily how simple it had turned out to be to get rid of a body, if a man was ruthless enough.

"I see what you mean. But that, too, is tied up with Martian notions about 'propriety.'" (He used the Martian word.) "Death is the one acceptable excuse for not carrying out an obligation. If he were simply killed, they would adopt him into the nest after his death—and then the whole nest and probably every nest on Mars would set out to avenge him. They would not mind in the least if the whole human race were to die or be killed—but to kill this one human being to keep him from being adopted, that's another kettle of fish entirely. Matter of obligation and propriety—in some ways a Martian's response to a situation is so automatic as to remind one of instinct. It is not, of course, since they are incredibly intelligent. But they do the damnedest things." He frowned and added, "Sometimes I wish I had never left Sussex."

The warning hooter broke up the discussion by forcing us to hurry to our bunks. Dak had cut it fine on purpose; the shuttle rocket from Goddard City was waiting for us when we settled into free fall. All five of us went down, which just filled the passenger couches—again a matter of planning, for the Resident Commissioner had expressed the intention of coming up to meet me and had been dissuaded only by Dak's message to him that our party would require all the space.

I tried to get a better look at the Martian surface as we went down, as I had had only one glimpse of it, from the control room of the *Tom Paine*—since I was supposed to have been there many times I could not show the normal curiosity of a tourist. I did not get much of a look; the shuttle pilot did not turn us so that we could see until he leveled off for his glide approach and I was busy then putting on my oxygen mask.

That pesky Mars-type mask almost finished us; I had never had a chance to practice with it—Dak did not think of it and I had not realized it would be a problem; I had worn both space suit and aqualung on other occasions and I thought this would be about the same. It was not. The model Bonforte favored was a mouth-free type, a Mitsubishi "Sweet Winds" which pressurizes directly at the nostrils—a nose clamp, nostril plugs, tubes up each nostril which then run back under each ear to the super-charger on the back of your neck. I concede that it is a fine device, once you get used to it, since you can talk, eat, drink, etc., while wearing it. But I would rather have a dentist put both hands in my mouth.

The real difficulty is that you have to exercise conscious control on the muscles that close the back of your mouth, or you hiss like a teakettle, since the durn thing operates on a pressure difference. Fortunately the pilot equalized to Mars-surface pressure once we all had our masks on, which gave me twenty minutes or so to get used to it. But for a few moments I thought the jig was up, just over a silly piece of gadgetry. But I reminded myself that I had worn the thing hundreds of times before and that I was as used to it as I was to my toothbrush. Presently I believed it.

Dak had been able to avoid having the Resident Commissioner chitchat with me for an hour on the way down but it had not been possible to miss him entirely; he met the shuttle at the skyfield. The close timing did keep me from having to cope with other humans, since I had to go at once into the Martian city. It made sense, but it seemed strange that I would be safer among Martians than among my own kind.

It seemed even stranger to be on Mars.

## V

Mr. Commissioner Boothroyd was a Humanity Party appointee, of course, as were all of his staff except for civil service technical employees. But Dak had told me that it was at least sixty-forty that Boothroyd had not had a finger in the plot; Dak considered him honest but stupid. For that matter, neither Dak nor Rog Clifton believed that Supreme Minister Quiroga was in it; they attributed the thing to the clandestine terrorist group inside the Humanity Party who called themselves the "Actionists"—and they attributed *them* to some highly respectable big-money boys who stood to profit heavily.

Myself, I would not have known an Actionist from an auctioneer.

But the minute we landed something popped up that made me wonder whether friend Boothroyd was as honest and stupid as Dak thought he was. It was a minor thing but one of those little things that can punch holes in an impersonation. Since I was a Very Important Visitor the Commissioner met me; since I held no public office other than membership in the Grand Assembly and was traveling privately no official honors were offered. He was alone save for his aide—and a little girl about fifteen.

I knew him from photographs and I knew quite a bit about him; Rog and Penny had briefed me carefully. I shook hands, asked about his sinusitis, thanked him for the pleasant time I had had on my last visit, and spoke with his aide in that warm man-to-man fashion that Bonforte was so good at. Then I turned to the young lady. I knew Boothroyd had children and that one of them was about this age and sex; I did not know—perhaps Rog and Penny did not know—whether or not I had ever met her.

Boothroyd himself saved me. "You haven't met my daughter Deirdre, I believe. She insisted on coming along."

Nothing in the pictures I had studied had shown Bonforte dealing with young girls—so I simply had to *be* Bonforte—a widower in his middle fifties who had no children of his own, no nieces, and probably little experience with teenage girls—but with lots of experience in meeting strangers of every sort. So I treated her as if she were twice her real age; I did not quite kiss her hand. She blushed and looked pleased.

Boothroyd looked indulgent and said, "Well, ask him, my dear. You may not have another chance."

She blushed deeper and said, "Sir, could I have your autograph? The girls in my school collect them. I have Mr. Quiroga's...I ought to have yours." She produced a little book, which she had been holding behind her.

I felt like a copter driver asked for his license—which is at home in his other pants. I had studied hard but I had not expected to have to forge Bonforte's signature. Damn it, you can't do *everything* in two and a half days!

But it was simply impossible for Bonforte to refuse such a request—and I was Bonforte. I smiled jovially and said, "You have Mr. Quiroga's already?"

"Yes, sir."

"Just his autograph?"

"Yes. Er, he put 'Best Wishes' on it."

I winked at Boothroyd. "Just 'Best Wishes,' eh? To young ladies I never make it less than 'Love.' Tell you what I'm going to do—" I took the little book from her, glanced through the pages.

"Chief," Dak said urgently, "we are short on minutes."

"Compose yourself," I said without looking up. "The entire Martian nation can wait, if necessary, on a young lady." I handed the book to Penny. "Will you note the size of this book? And then remind me to send a photograph suitable for pasting in it—and properly autographed, of course."

"Yes, Mr. Bonforte."

"Will that suit you, Miss Deirdre?"

*"Gee!"*

"Good. Thanks for asking me. We can leave now, Captain. Mr. Commissioner, is that our car?"

"Yes, Mr. Bonforte." He shook his head wryly. "I'm afraid you have converted a member of my own family to your Expansionist heresies. Hardly sporting, eh? Sitting ducks, and so forth?"

"That should teach you not to expose her to bad company—eh, Miss Deirdre?" I shook hands again. "Thanks for meeting us, Mr. Commissioner. I am afraid we had better hurry along now."

"Yes, certainly. Pleasure."

"Thanks, Mr. Bonforte!"

"Thank *you*, my dear."

I turned away slowly, so as not to appear jerky or nervous in stereo. There were photographers around, still, news pickup, stereo, and so forth, as well as many reporters. Bill was keeping the reporters away from us; as we turned to go he waved and said, "See you later, Chief," and turned back to talk to one of them. Rog, Dak, and Penny followed me into the car. There was the usual skyfield crowd, not as numerous as at any earthport, but numerous. I was not worried about them as long as Boothroyd accepted the impersonation—though there were certainly some present who *knew* that I was not Bonforte.

But I refused to let those individuals worry me, either. They could cause us no trouble without incriminating themselves.

The car was a Rolls Outlander, pressurized, but I left my oxygen mask on because the others did. I took the right-hand seat, Rog sat beside me, and Penny beside him, while Dak wound his long legs around one of the folding seats. The driver glanced back through the partition and started up.

Rog said quietly, "I was worried there for a moment."

"Nothing to worry about. Now let's all be quiet, please. I want to review my speech."

Actually I wanted to gawk at the Martian scene; I knew the speech perfectly. The driver took us along the north edge of the field, past many godowns. I read signs for Verwijs Trading Company, Diana Outlines, Ltd., Three Planets, and I. G. Farbenindustrie. There were almost as many Martians as humans in sight. We groundhogs get the impression that Martians are slow as snails—and they are, on our comparatively heavy planet. On their own world they skim along on their bases like a stone sliding over water.

To the right, south of us past the flat field, the Great Canal dipped into the too-close horizon, showing no shoreline beyond. Straight ahead of us was the Nest of Kkkah, a fairy city. I was staring at it, my heart lifting at its fragile beauty, when Dak moved suddenly.

We were well past the traffic around the godowns but there was one car ahead, coming toward us; I had seen it without noticing it. But Dak must have been edgily ready for trouble; when the other car was quite close, he suddenly slammed down the partition separating us from the driver, swarmed over the man's neck, and grabbed the wheel. We slewed to the right, barely missing the other car, slewed again to the left and barely stayed on the road. It was a near thing, for we were past the field now and here the highway edged the canal.

I had not been much use to Dak a couple of days earlier in the Eisenhower, but I had been unarmed and not expecting trouble. This day I was still unarmed, not so much as a poisoned fang, but I comported myself a little better. Dak was more than busy trying to drive the car while leaning over from the back seat. The driver, caught off balance at first, now tried to wrestle him away from the wheel.

I lunged forward, got my left arm around the driver's neck, and shoved my right thumb into his ribs. "Move and you've had it!" The voice belonged to the hero-villain in *The Second-Story Gentleman*; the line of dialogue was his too.

My prisoner became very quiet.

Dak said urgently, "Rog, what are they doing?"

Clifton looked back and answered, "They're turning around."

Dak answered, "Okay. Chief, keep your gun on that character while I climb over." He was doing so even as he spoke, an awkward matter in view of his long legs and the crowded car. He settled into the seat and said happily, "I doubt if anything on wheels can catch a Rolls on a straightaway." He jerked on the damper and the big car shot forward. "How am I doing, Rog?"

"They're just turned around."

"All right. What do we do with this item? Dump him out?"

My victim squirmed and said, "I didn't do anything!" I jabbed my thumb harder and he quieted.

"Oh, not a thing," Dak agreed, keeping his eyes on the road. "All you did was try to cause a little crash—just enough to make Mr. Bonforte late for his appointment. If I had not noticed that you were slowing down to make it easy on yourself, you might have got away with it. No guts, eh?" He took a slight curve with the tires screaming and the gyro fighting to keep us upright. "What's the situation, Rog?"

"They've given up."

"So." Dak did not slacken speed; we must have been doing well over three hundred kilometers. "I wonder if they would try to bomb us with one of their own boys aboard? How about it, bub? Would they write you off as expendable?"

"I don't know what you're talking about! You're going to be in trouble over this!"

"Really? The word of four respectable people against your jailbird record? Or aren't you a transportee? Anyhow, Mr. Bonforte prefers to have me drive him—so naturally you were glad to do a favor for Mr. Bonforte." We hit something about as big as a worm cast on that glassy road and my prisoner and I almost went through the roof.

"'Mr. Bonforte!'" My victim made it a swear word.

Dak was silent for several seconds. At last he said, "I don't think we ought to dump this one, Chief. I think we ought to let you off, then take him to a quiet place. I think he might talk if we urged him."

The driver tried to get away. I tightened the pressure on his neck and jabbed him again with my thumb knuckle. A knuckle may not feel too much like the muzzle of a heater—but who wants to find out? He relaxed and said sullenly, "You don't dare give me the needle."

"Heavens, no!" Dak answered in shocked tones. "That would be illegal. Penny girl, got a bobby pin?"

"Why, certainly, Dak." She sounded puzzled and I was. She did not sound frightened, though, and I certainly was.

"Good. Bub, did you ever have a bobby pin shoved up under your fingernails? They say it will even break a hypnotic command not to talk. Works directly on the subconscious or something. Only trouble is that the patient makes the most unpleasant noises. So we are going to take you out in the dunes where you won't disturb anybody but sand scorpions. After you have talked—now here comes the nice part! After you talk we are going to turn you loose, not do anything, just let you walk back into town. But—listen carefully now!—if you are real nice and cooperative, you get a prize. We'll let you have your mask for the walk."

Dak stopped talking; for a moment there was no sound but the keening of the thin Martian air past the roof. A human being can walk possibly two hundred yards on Mars without an oxygen mask, if he is in good condition. I believe I read of a case where a man walked almost half a mile before he died. I glanced at the trip meter and saw that we were about twenty-three kilometers from Goddard City.

The prisoner said slowly, "Honest, I don't know anything about it. I was just paid to crash the car."

"We'll try to stimulate your memory." The gates of the Martian city were just ahead of us; Dak started slowing the car. "Here's where you get out, Chief. Rog, better take your gun and relieve the Chief of our guest."

"Right, Dak." Rog moved up by me, jabbed the man in the ribs—again with a bare knuckle. I moved out of the way. Dak braked the car to a halt, stopping right in front of the gates.

"Four minutes to spare," he said happily. "This is a nice car. I wish I owned it. Rog, ease up a touch and give me room."

Clifton did so, Dak chopped the driver expertly on the side of his neck with the edge of his hand; the man went limp. "That will keep him quiet while you get clear. Can't have any unseemly disturbance under the eyes of the nest. Let's check time."

We did so. I was about three and a half minutes ahead of the deadline. "You are to go in exactly on time, you understand? Not ahead, not behind, but on the dot."

"That's right," Clifton and I answered in chorus.

"Thirty seconds to walk up the ramp, maybe. What do you want to do with the three minutes you have left?"

I sighed. "Just get my nerve back."

"Your nerve is all right. You didn't miss a trick back there. Cheer up, old son. Two hours from now you can head for home, with your pay burning holes in your pocket. We're on the last lap."

"I hope so. It's been quite a strain. Uh, Dak?"

"Yes?"

"Come here a second." I got out of the car, motioned him to come with me a short distance away. "What happens if I make a mistake—in there?"

"Eh?" Dak looked surprised, then laughed a little too heartily. "You won't make a mistake. Penny tells me you've got it down Joe-block perfect."

"Yes, but suppose I slip?"

"You won't slip. I know how you feel; I felt the same way on my first solo grounding. But when it started, I was so busy doing it I didn't have time to do it wrong."

Clifton called out, his voice thin in thin air, "Dak! Are you watching the time?"

"Gobs of time. Over a minute."

"Mr. Bonforte!" It was Penny's voice. I turned and went back to the car. She got out and put out her hand. "Good luck, Mr. Bonforte."

"Thanks, Penny."

Rog shook hands and Dak clapped me on the shoulder. "Minus thirty-five seconds. Better start."

I nodded and started up the ramp. It must have been within a second or two of the exact, appointed time when I reached the top, for the mighty gates rolled back as I came to them. I took a deep breath and cursed that damned air mask.

Then I took my stage.

☼

It doesn't make any difference how many times you do it, that first walk on as the curtain goes up on the first night of any run is a breath-catcher and a heart-stopper. Sure, you know your sides. Sure, you've asked the manager to count the house. Sure, you've done it all before. No matter—when you first walk out there and know that all those eyes are on you, waiting for you to speak, waiting for you to do something—maybe even waiting for you to goof up on your lines, brother, you feel it. This is why they have prompters.

I looked out and saw my audience and I wanted to run. I had stage fright for the first time in thirty years.

The siblings of the nest were spread out before me as far as I could see. There was an open lane in front of me, with thousands on each side, set close together as asparagus. I knew that the first thing I must do was slow-march down the center of that lane, clear to the far end, to the ramp leading down into the inner nest.

I could not move.

I said to myself, "Look, boy, you're John Joseph Bonforte. You've been here dozens of times before. These people are your friends. You're here because you want to be here—and because they want you here. So march down that aisle. Tum tum te *tum!* 'Here comes the bride!'"

I began to feel like Bonforte again. I was Uncle Joe Bonforte, determined to do this thing perfectly—for the honor and welfare of my own people and my own planet—and for my friends the Martians. I took a deep breath and one step.

That deep breath saved me; it brought me that heavenly fragrance. Thousands on thousands of Martians packed close together—it smelled to me as if somebody had dropped and broken a whole case of Jungle Lust. The conviction that I smelled was so strong that I involuntarily glanced back to see if Penny had followed me in. I could feel her handclasp warm in my palm.

I started limping down that aisle, trying to make it about the speed a Martian moves on his own planet. The crowd closed in behind me. Occasionally kids would get away from their elders and skitter out in front of me. By "kids" I mean post-fission Martians, half the mass and not much over half the height of an adult. They are never out of the nest and we are inclined to forget that there can be little Martians. It takes almost five years, after fission, for a Martian to regain his full size, have his brain fully restored, and get all of his memory back. During this transition he is an idiot studying to be a moron. The gene rear-rangement and subsequent regeneration incident to conjugation and fission put him out of the running for a long time. One of Bonforte's spools was a lecture on the subject, accompanied by some not very good amateur stereo.

The kids, being cheerful idiots, are exempt from propriety and all that that implies. But they are greatly loved.

Two of the kids, of the same and smallest size and looking just alike to me, skittered out and stopped dead in front of me, just like a foolish puppy in traffic. Either I stopped or I ran them down.

So I stopped. They moved even closer, blocking my way completely, and started sprouting pseudo limbs while chittering at each other. I could not understand them at all. Quickly they were plucking at my clothes and snaking their patty-paws into my sleeve pockets.

The crowd was so tight that I could hardly go around them. I was stretched between two needs. In the first place they were so darn cute that I wanted to see if I didn't have a sweet tucked away somewhere for them—but in a still firster place was the knowledge that the adoption ceremony was timed like a ballet. If I didn't get on down that street, I was going to commit the classic sin against propriety made famous by Kkkahgral the Younger himself.

But the kids were not about to get out of my way. One of them had found my watch.

I sighed and was almost overpowered by the perfume. Then I made a bet with myself. I bet that baby-kissing was a Galactic universal and that it took precedence even over Martian propriety. I got on one knee, making myself about the height they were, and fondled them for a few moments, patting them and running my hands down their scales.

Then I stood up and said carefully, "That is all now. I must go," which used up a large fraction of my stock of Basic Martian.

The kids clung to me but I moved them carefully and gently aside and went on down the double line, hurrying to make up for the time I had lost. No life wand burned a hole in my back. I risked a hope that my violation of propriety had not yet reached the capital offense level. I reached the ramp leading down into the inner nest and started on down.

* * * * * * * * * * * * * * * *

That line of asterisks represents the adoption ceremony. Why? Because it is limited to members of the Kkkah Nest. It is a family matter.

Put it this way: A Mormon may have very close gentile friends—but does that friendship get a gentile inside the Temple at Salt Lake City? It never has and it never will. Martians visit very freely back and forth between their nests—but a Martian enters the inner nest only of his own family. Even his conjugate-spouses are not thus privileged. I have no more right to tell the details of the adoption ceremony than a lodge brother has to be specific about ritual outside the lodge.

Oh, the rough outlines do not matter, since they are the same for any nest, just as my part was the same for any candidate. My sponsor—Bonforte's oldest Martian friend, Kkkahrrreash—met me at the door and threatened me with a wand. I demanded that he kill me at once were I guilty of any breach. To tell the truth, I did not recognize him, even though I had studied a picture of him. But it had to be him because ritual required it.

Having thus made clear that I stood four-square for Motherhood, the Home, Civic Virtue, and never missing Sunday school, I was permitted to enter. 'Rrreash conducted me around all the stations, I was questioned and I responded. Every word, every gesture, was as stylized as a classical Chinese play, else I would not have stood a chance. Most of the time I did not know what they were saying and half of the time I did not understand my own replies; I simply knew my cues and the responses. It was not made easier by the low light level the Martians prefer; I was groping around like a mole.

I played once with Hawk Mantell, shortly before he died, after he was stone-deaf. There was a trouper! He could not even use a hearing device because the eighth nerve was dead. Part of the time he could cue by lips but that is not always possible. He directed the production himself and he timed it perfectly. I have seen him deliver a line, walk away—then whirl around and snap out a retort to a line that he had never heard, precisely on the timing.

This was like that. I knew my part and I played it. If *they* blew it, that was their lookout.

But it did not help my morale that there were never less than half a dozen wands leveled at me the whole time. I kept telling myself that they wouldn't burn me down for a slip. After all, I was just a poor stupid human being and at the very least they would give me a passing mark for effort. But I didn't believe it.

After what seemed like days—but was not, since the whole ceremony times exactly one-ninth of Mars' rotation—after an endless time, we ate. I don't know what and perhaps it is just as well. It did not poison me.

After that the elders made their speeches, I made my acceptance speech in answer, and they gave me my name and my wand. I was a Martian.

I did not know how to use the wand and my name sounded like a leaky faucet, but from that instant on it was my legal name on Mars and I was legally a blood member of the most aristocratic family on the planet—exactly fifty-two hours after a groundhog down on his luck had spent his last half Imperial buying a drink for a stranger in the bar of Casa Mañana.

I guess this proves that one should never pick up strangers.

✿

I got out as quickly as possible. Dak had made up a speech for me in which I claimed proper necessity for leaving at once and they let me go. I was nervous as a man upstairs in a sorority house because there was no longer ritual to guide me. I mean to say even casual social behavior was still hedged around with airtight and risky custom and I did not know the moves. So I recited my excuse and headed out. 'Rrreash and another elder went with me and I chanced playing with another pair of the kids when we were outside—or maybe the same pair. Once I reached the gates the two elders said good-bye in squeaky English and let me go out alone; the gates closed behind me and I reswallowed my heart.

The Rolls was waiting where they had let me out; I hurried down, a door opened, and I was surprised to see that Penny was in it alone. But not displeased. I called out, "Hi, Curly Top! I made it!"

"I knew you would."

I gave a mock sword salute with my wand and said, "Just call me Kkkahjjjerrr"—spraying the front rows with the second syllable.

"Be careful with that thing!" she said nervously.

I slid in beside her on the front seat and asked, "Do you know how to use one of these things?" The reaction was setting in and I felt exhausted but gay; I wanted three quick drinks and a thick steak, then to wait up for the critics' reviews.

"No. But do be careful."

"I think all you have to do is to press it here," which I did, and there was a neat two-inch hole in the windshield and the car wasn't pressurized any longer.

Penny gasped. I said, "Gee, I'm sorry. I'll put it away until Dak can coach me."

She gulped. "It's all right. Just be careful where you point it." She started wheeling the car and I found that Dak was not the only one with a heavy hand on the damper.

Wind was whistling in through the hole I had made. I said, "What's the rush? I need some time to study my lines for the press conference. Did you bring them? And where are the others?" I had forgotten completely the driver we had grabbed; I had not thought about him from the time the gates of the nest opened.

"No. They couldn't come."

"Penny, what's the matter? What's happened?" I was wondering if I could possibly take a press conference without coaching. Perhaps I could tell them a little about the adoption; I wouldn't have to fake that.

"It's Mr. Bonforte—*they've found him.*"

## VI

I had not noticed until then that she had not once called me "Mr. Bonforte." She could not, of course, for I was no longer he; I was again Lorrie Smythe, that actor chap they had hired to stand in for him.

I sat back and sighed, and let myself relax. "So it's over at last—and we got away with it." I felt a great burden lift off me; I had not known how heavy it was until I put it down. Even my "lame" leg stopped aching. I reached over and patted Penny's hand on the wheel and said in my own voice, "I'm glad it's over. But I'm going to miss having you around, pal. You're a trouper. But even the best run ends and the company breaks up. I hope I'll see you again sometime."

"I hope so, too."

"I suppose Dak has arranged some shenanigan to keep me under cover and sneak me back into the *Tom Paine?*"

"I don't know." Her voice sounded odd and I gave her a quick glance and saw that she was crying. My heart gave a skip. Penny crying? Over us separating? I could not believe it and yet I wanted to. One might think that, between my handsome features and cultivated manners, women would find me irresistible, but it is a deplorable fact that all too many of them have found me easy to resist. Penny had seemed to find it no effort at all.

"Penny," I said hastily, "why all the tears, hon? You'll wreck this car."

"I can't help it."

"Well—put me in it. What's wrong? You told me they had got him back; you didn't tell me anything else." I had a sudden horrid but logical suspicion. "He was *alive*—wasn't he?"

"Yes—he's alive—but, oh, they've *hurt* him!" She started to sob and I had to grab the wheel.

She straightened up quickly. "Sorry."

"Want me to drive?"

"I'll be all right. Besides, you don't know how—I mean you aren't supposed to know how to drive."

"Huh? Don't be silly. I do know how and it no longer matters that—"

I broke off, suddenly realizing that it might still matter. If they had roughed up Bonforte so that it showed, then he could not appear in public in that shape—at least not only fifteen minutes after being adopted into the Kkkah Nest. Maybe I would have to take that press conference and depart publicly, while Bonforte would be the one they would sneak aboard. Well, all right—hardly more than a curtain call. "Penny, do Dak and Rog want me to stay in character for a bit? Do I play to the reporters? Or don't I?"

"I don't know. There wasn't time."

We were already approaching the stretch of godowns by the field, and the giant bubble domes of Goddard City were in sight. "Penny, slow this car down and talk sense. I've got to have my cues."

✧

The driver had talked—I neglected to ask whether or not the bobby-pin treatment had been used. He had then been turned loose to walk back but had not been deprived of his mask; the others had barreled back to Goddard City, with Dak at the wheel. I felt lucky to have been left behind; *voyageurs* should not be allowed to drive anything but spaceships.

They went to the address the driver had given them, in Old Town under the original bubble. I gathered that it was the sort of jungle every port has had since the Phoenicians sailed around the shoulder of Africa, a place of released transportees, prostitutes, monkey-pushers, rangees, and other dregs—a neighborhood where policemen travel only in pairs.

The information they had squeezed out of the driver had been correct but a few minutes out of date. The room had housed the prisoner, certainly, for there was a bed in it which seemed to have been occupied continuously for at least a week, a pot of coffee was still hot—and wrapped in a towel on a shelf was an old-fashioned removable denture which Clifton identified as belonging to Bonforte. But Bonforte himself was missing and so were his captors.

They had left there with the intention of carrying out the original plan, that of claiming that the kidnapping had taken place immediately after the adoption and putting pressure on Boothroyd by threatening to appeal to the Nest of Kkkah. But they had found Bonforte, had simply run across him in the street before they left Old Town—a poor old stumblebum with a week's beard, dirty and dazed. The men had not recognized him, but Penny had known him and made them stop.

She broke into sobs again as she told me this part and we almost ran down a truck train snaking up to one of the loading docks.

A reasonable reconstruction seemed to be that the laddies in the second car—the one that was to crash us—had reported back, whereupon the faceless leaders of our opponents had decided that the kidnapping no longer served their purposes. Despite the arguments I had heard about it, I was surprised that they had not simply killed him; it was not until later that I understood that what they had done was subtler, more suited to their purposes, and much crueler than mere killing.

"Where is he now?" I asked.

"Dak took him to the *voyageurs'* hostel in Dome 3."

"Is that where we are headed?"

"I don't know. Rog just said to go pick you up, then they disappeared in the service door of the hostel. Uh, no, I don't think we dare go there. I don't know what to do."

"Penny, stop the car."

"Huh?"

"Surely this car has a phone. We won't stir another inch until we find out—or figure out—what we should do. But I am certain of one thing: I should stay in character until Dak or Rog decides that I should fade out. Somebody has to talk to the newsmen. Somebody has to make a public departure for the *Tom Paine.* You're sure that Mr. Bonforte can't be spruced up so that he can do it?"

"What? Oh, he couldn't possibly! You didn't *see* him."

"So I didn't. I'll take your word for it. All right, Penny, I'm 'Mr. Bonforte' again and you're my secretary. We'd better get with it."

"Yes—Mr. Bonforte."

"Now try to get Captain Broadbent on the phone, will you, please?"

We couldn't find a phone list in the car and she had to go through "Information," but at last she was tuned with the clubhouse of the *voyageurs.* I could hear both sides. "Pilots' Club, Mrs. Kelly speaking."

Penny covered the microphone. "Do I give my name?"

"Play it straight. We've nothing to hide."

"This is Mr. Bonforte's secretary," she said gravely. "Is his pilot there? Captain Broadbent."

"I know him, dearie." There was a shout: "Hey! Any of you smokers see where Dak went?" After a pause she went on, "He's gone to his room. I'm buzzing him."

Shortly Penny said, "Skipper? The Chief wants to talk to you," and handed me the phone.

"This is the Chief, Dak."

"Oh. Where are you—sir?"

"Still in the car. Penny picked me up. Dak, Bill scheduled a press conference, I believe. Where is it?"

He hesitated. "I'm glad you called in, sir. Bill canceled it. There's been a—slight change in the situation."

"So Penny told me. I'm just as well pleased; I'm rather tired. Dak, I've decided not to stay dirtside tonight; my gimp leg has been bothering me and I'm looking forward to a real rest in free fall." I hated free fall but Bonforte did not. "Will you or Rog make my apologies to the Commissioner, and so forth?"

"We'll take care of everything, sir."

"Good. How soon can you arrange a shuttle for me?"

"The *Pixie* is still standing by for you, sir. If you will go to Gate 3, I'll phone and have a field car pick you up." "Very good. Out."

"Out, sir."

I handed the phone to Penny to put back in its clamp. "Curly Top, I don't know whether that phone frequency is monitored or not—or whether possibly the whole car is bugged. If either is the case, they may have learned two things—where Dak is and through that where *he* is, and second, what I am about to do next. Does that suggest anything to your mind?"

She looked thoughtful, then took out her secretary's notebook, wrote in it: *Let's get rid of the car.*

I nodded, then took the book from her and wrote in it: *How far away is Gate 3?*

She answered: *Walking distance.*

Silently we climbed out and left. She had pulled into some executive's parking space outside one of the warehouses when she had parked the car; no doubt in time it would be returned where it belonged—and such minutiae no longer mattered.

We had gone about fifty yards, when I stopped. Something was the matter. Not the day, certainly. It was almost balmy, with the sun burning brightly in clear, purple Martian sky. The traffic, wheel and foot, seemed to pay no attention to us, or at least such attention was for the pretty young woman with me rather than directed at me. Yet I felt uneasy.

"What is it, Chief?"

"Eh? *That* is what it is!"

"Sir?"

"I'm not being the 'Chief.' It isn't in character to go dodging off like this. Back we go, Penny."

She did not argue, but followed me back to the car. This time I climbed into the back seat, sat there looking dignified, and let her chauffeur me to Gate 3.

☼

It was not the gate we had come in. I think Dak had chosen it because it ran less to passengers and more to freight. Penny paid no attention to signs and ran the big Rolls right up to the gate. A terminal policeman tried to stop her; she simply said coldly, "Mr. Bonforte's car. And will you please send word to the Commissioner's office to call for it here?"

He looked baffled, glanced into the rear compartment, seemed to recognize me, saluted, and let us stay. I answered with a friendly wave and he opened the door for me. "The lieutenant is very particular about keeping the space back of the fence clear, Mr. Bonforte," he apologized, "but I guess it's all right."

"You can have the car moved at once," I said. "My secretary and I are leaving. Is my field car here?"

"I'll find out at the gate, sir." He left. It was just the amount of audience I wanted, enough to tie it down solid that "Mr. Bonforte" had arrived by official car and had left for his space yacht. I tucked my life wand under my arm like Napoleon's baton and limped after him, with Penny tagging along. The cop spoke to the gatemaster, then hurried back to us, smiling. "Field car is waiting, sir."

"Thanks indeed." I was congratulating myself on the perfection of the timing.

"Uh..." The cop looked flustered and added hurriedly, in a low voice, "I'm an Expansionist, too, sir. Good job you did today." He glanced at the life wand with a touch of awe.

I knew exactly how Bonforte should look in this routine. "Why, thank you. I hope you have lots of children. We need to work up a solid majority."

He guffawed more than it was worth. "That's a good one! Uh, mind if I repeat it?"

"Not at all." We had moved on and I started through the gate. The gatemaster touched my arm. "Er...your passport, Mr. Bonforte."

I trust I did not let my expression change. "The passports, Penny."

She looked frostily at the official. "Captain Broadbent takes care of all clearances."

He looked at me and looked away. "I suppose it's all right. But I'm supposed to check them and take down the serial numbers."

"Yes, of course. Well, I suppose I must ask Captain Broadbent to run out to the field. Has my shuttle been assigned a take-off time? Perhaps you had better arrange with the tower to 'hold.'"

But Penny appeared to be cattily angry. "Mr. Bonforte, this is ridiculous! We've *never* had this red tape before—certainly not on *Mars*."

The cop said hastily, "Of course it's all right, Hans. After all, this is Mr. Bonforte."

"Sure, but—"

I interrupted with a happy smile. "There's a simpler way out. If you—what is your name, sir?"

"Haslwanter. Hans Haslwanter," he answered reluctantly.

"Mr. Haslwanter, if you will call Mr. Commissioner Boothroyd, I'll speak to him and we can save my pilot a trip out to the field—and save me an hour or more of time."

"Uh, I wouldn't like to do that, sir. I could call the port captain's office?" he suggested hopefully.

"Just get me Mr. Boothroyd's number. I will call him." This time I put a touch of frost into my voice, the attitude of the busy and important man who wishes to be democratic but has had all the pushing around and hampering by underlings that he intends to put up with.

That did it. He said hastily, "I'm sure it's all right, Mr. Bonforte. It's just—well, regulations, you know."

"Yes, I know. Thank you." I started to push on through.

"Hold it, Mr. Bonforte! Look this way."

I glanced around. That *i*-dotting and *t*-crossing civil servant had held us up just long enough to let the press catch up with us. One man had dropped to his knee and was pointing a stereobox at me; he looked up and said, "Hold the wand where we can see it." Several others with various types of equipment were gathering around us; one had climbed up on the roof of the Rolls. Someone else was shoving a microphone at me and another had a directional mike aimed like a gun.

I was as angry as a leading woman with her name in small type but I remembered who I was supposed to be. I smiled and moved slowly. Bonforte had a good grasp of the fact that motion appears faster in pictures; I could afford to do it properly.

"Mr. Bonforte, why did you cancel the press conference?"

"Mr. Bonforte, it is asserted that you intend to demand that the Grand Assembly grant full Empire citizenship to Martians; will you comment?"

"Mr. Bonforte, how soon are you going to force a vote of confidence in the present government?"

I held up my hand with the wand in it and grinned. "One at a time, please! Now what was that first question?"

They all answered at once, of course; by the time they had sorted out precedence I had managed to waste several moments without having to answer anything. Bill Corpsman came charging up at that point. "Have a heart, boys. The Chief has had a hard day. I gave you all you need."

I held out a palm at him. "I can spare a minute or two, Bill. Gentlemen, I'm just about to leave but I'll try to cover the essentials of what you have asked. So far as I know the present government does not plan any reassessment of the relation of Mars to the Empire. Since I am not in office my own opinions are hardly pertinent. I suggest that you ask Mr. Quiroga. On the question of how soon the opposition will force a vote of confidence all I can say is that we won't do it unless we are sure we can win it—and you know as much about that as I do."

Someone said, "That doesn't say much, does it?"

"It was not intended to say much," I retorted, softening it with a grin. "Ask me questions I can legitimately answer and I will. Ask me those loaded 'Have-you-quit-beating-your-wife?' sort and I have answers to match." I hesitated, realizing that Bonforte had a reputation for bluntness and honesty, especially with the press. "But I am not trying to stall you. You all know why I am here today. Let me say this about it—and you can quote me if you wish." I reached back into my mind and hauled up an appropriate bit from the speeches of Bonforte I had studied. "The real meaning of what happened today is not that of an honor to one man. This"—I gestured with the Martian wand—"is proof that two great races can reach out across the gap of strangeness with understanding. Our own race is spreading out to the stars. We shall find—we *are* finding—that we are vastly outnumbered. If we are to succeed in our expansion to the stars, we must deal honestly, humbly, with open hearts. I have heard it said that our Martian neighbors would overrun Earth if given the chance. This is nonsense; Earth is not suited to Martians. Let us protect our own—but let us not be seduced by fear and hatred into foolish acts. The stars will never be won by little minds; we must be big as space itself."

The reporter cocked an eyebrow. "Mr. Bonforte, seems to me I heard you make that speech last February."

"You will hear it next February. Also January, March, and all the other months. Truth cannot be too often repeated." I glanced back at the gatemaster and added, "I'm sorry but I'll have to go now—or I'll miss the tick." I turned and went through the gate, with Penny after me.

We climbed into the little lead-armored field car and the door sighed shut. The car was automatized, so I did not have to play up for a driver; I threw myself down and relaxed. "Whew!"

"I thought you did beautifully," Penny said seriously.

"I had a bad moment when he spotted the speech I was cribbing."

"You got away with it. It was an inspiration. You—you sounded just like *him*."

"Was there anybody there I should have called by name?"

"Not really. One or two maybe, but they wouldn't expect it when you were so rushed."

"I was caught in a squeeze. That fiddlin' gatemaster and his passports. Penny, I should think that you would carry them rather than Dak."

"Dak doesn't carry them. We all carry our own." She reached into her bag, pulled out a little book. "I had mine—but I did not dare admit it."

"Eh?"

"*He* had *his* on him when they got him. We haven't dared ask for a replacement—not at this time."

I was suddenly very weary.

Having no instructions from Dak or Rog, I stayed in character during the shuttle trip up and on entering the *Tom Paine*. It wasn't difficult; I simply went straight to the owner's cabin and spent long, miserable hours in free fall, biting my nails and wondering what was happening down on the surface. With the aid of anti-nausea pills I finally managed to float off into fitful sleep—which was a mistake, for I had a series of no-pants nightmares, with reporters pointing at me and cops touching me on the shoulder and Martians aiming their wands at me. They all knew I was phony and were simply arguing over who had the privilege of taking me apart and putting me down the oubliette.

I was awakened by the hooting of the acceleration alarm. Dak's vibrant baritone was booming, "First and last red warning! One-third gee! One minute!" I hastily pulled myself over to my bunk and held on. I felt lots better when it hit; one-third gravity is not much, about the same as Mars' surface I think, but it is enough to steady the stomach and make the floor a real floor.

About five minutes later Dak knocked and let himself in as I was going to the door. "Howdy, Chief."

"Hello, Dak. I'm certainly glad to see you back."

"Not as glad as I am to be back," he said wearily. He eyed my bunk. "Mind if I spread out there?"

"Help yourself."

He did so and sighed. "Cripes, am I pooped! I could sleep for a week.... I think I will."

"Let's both of us. Uh...you got him aboard?"

"Yes. What a gymkhana!"

"I suppose so. Still, it must be easier to do a job like that in a small, informal port like this than it was to pull the stunts you rigged at Jefferson."

"Huh? No, it's much harder here."

"Eh?"

"Obviously. Here everybody knows everybody—and people will talk." Dak smiled wryly. "We brought him aboard as a case of frozen canal shrimp. Had to pay export duty, too."

"Dak, how is he?"

"Well..." Dak frowned. "Doc Capek says that he will make a complete recovery—that it is just a matter of time." He added explosively, "If I could lay my hands on those rats! It would make you break down and bawl to see what they did to him—and yet we have to let them get away with it cold—for *his* sake."

Dak was fairly close to bawling himself. I said gently, "I gathered from Penny that they had roughed him up quite a lot. How badly is he hurt?"

"Huh? You must have misunderstood Penny. Aside from being filthy-dirty and needing a shave he was not hurt physically at all."

I looked stupid. "I thought they beat him up. Something about like working him over with a baseball bat."

"I would rather they had! Who cares about a few broken bones? No, no, it was what they did to his *brain*."

"Oh..." I felt ill. "Brainwash?"

"Yes. Yes and no. They couldn't have been trying to make him talk because he didn't have any secrets that were of any possible political importance. He always operated out in the open and everybody knows it. They must have been using it simply to keep him under control, keep him from trying to escape."

He went on, "Doc says that he thinks they must have been using the minimum daily dose, just enough to keep him docile, until just before they turned him loose. Then they shot him with a load that would turn an elephant into a gibbering idiot. The front lobes of his brain must be soaked like a bath sponge."

I felt so ill that I was glad I had not eaten. I had once read up on the subject; I hate it so much that it fascinates me. To my mind there is something immoral and degrading in an absolute cosmic sense in tampering with a man's personality. Murder is a clean crime in comparison, a mere peccadillo. "Brainwash" is a term that comes down to us from the Communist movement of the Late Dark Ages; it was first applied to breaking a man's will and altering his personality by physical indignities and subtle torture. But that might take months; later they found a "better" way, one which would turn a man into a babbling slave in seconds—simply inject any one of several cocaine derivatives into his frontal brain lobes.

The filthy practice had first been developed for a legitimate purpose, to quiet disturbed patients and make them accessible to psychotherapy. As such, it was a humane advance, for it was used instead of lobotomy—"lobotomy" is a term almost as obsolete as "chastity girdle" but it means stirring a man's brain with a knife in such a fashion as to destroy his personality without killing him. Yes, they really used to do that—just as they used to beat them to "drive the devils out."

The Communists developed the new brainwash-by-drugs to an efficient technique, then when there were no more Communists, the Bands of Brothers polished it up still further until they could dose a man so lightly that he was simply receptive to leadership—or load him until he was a mindless mass of protoplasm—all in the sweet name of brotherhood. After all, you can't have "brotherhood" if a man is stubborn enough to want to keep his own secrets, can you? And what better way is there to be sure that he is not holding out on you than to poke a needle past his eyeball and slip a shot of babble juice

into his brain? "You can't make an omelet without breaking eggs." The sophistries of villains—bah!

Of course, it has been illegal for a long, long time now, except for therapy, with the express consent of a court. But criminals use it and cops are sometimes not lily white, for it does make a prisoner talk and it does not leave any marks at all. The victim can even be told to forget that it has been done.

I knew most of this at the time Dak told me what had been done to Bonforte and the rest I cribbed out of the ship's Encyclopedia Batavia. See the article on "Psychic Integration" and the one on "Torture."

I shook my head and tried to put the nightmares out of my mind. "But he's going to recover?"

"Doc says that the drug does not alter the brain structure; it just paralyzes it. He says that eventually the bloodstream picks up and carries away all of the dope; it reaches the kidneys and passes out of the body. But it takes time." Dak looked up at me. "Chief?"

"Eh? About time to knock off that 'Chief' stuff, isn't it? He's back."

"That's what I wanted to talk to you about. Would it be too much trouble to you to keep up the impersonation just a little while longer?"

"But why? There's nobody here but just us chickens."

"That's not quite true. Lorenzo, we've managed to keep this secret awfully tight. There's me, there's you." He ticked it off on his fingers. "There's Doc and Rog and Bill. And Penny, of course. There's a man by the name of Langston back Earthside whom you've never met. I think Jimmie Washington suspects but he wouldn't tell his own mother the right time of day. We don't know how many took part in the kidnapping, but not many, you can be sure. In any case, they don't dare talk—and the joke of it is they no longer could prove that he had ever been missing even if they wanted to. But my point is this: Here in the *Tommie* we've got all the crew and all the idlers not in on it. Old son, how about staying with it and letting yourself be seen each day by crewmen and by Jimmie Washington's girls and such—while *he* gets well? Huh?"

"Mmm...I don't see why not. How long will it be?"

"Just the trip back. We'll take it slow, at an easy boost. You'll enjoy it."

"Okay. Dak, don't figure this into my fee. I'm doing this piece of it just because I *hate* brainwashing."

Dak bounced up and clapped me on the shoulder. "You're my kind of people, Lorenzo. Don't worry about your fee; you'll be taken care of." His manner changed. "Very well, Chief. See you in the morning, sir."

☿

But one thing leads to another. The boost we had started on Dak's return was a mere shift of orbits, to one farther out where there would be little chance of a news service sending up a shuttle for a follow-up story. I woke up in free fall, took a pill, and managed to eat breakfast. Penny showed up shortly thereafter. "Good morning, Mr. Bonforte."

"Good morning, Penny." I inclined my head in the direction of the guest room. "Any news?"

"No, sir. About the same. Captain's compliments and would it be too much trouble for you to come to his cabin?"

"Not at all." Penny followed me in. Dak was there, with his heels hooked to his chair to stay in place; Rog and Bill were strapped to the couch.

Dak looked around and said, "Thanks for coming in, Chief. We need some help."

"Good morning. What is it?"

Clifton answered my greeting with his usual dignified deference and called me Chief; Corpsman nodded. Dak went on, "To clean this up in style you should make one more appearance."

"Eh? I thought—"

"Just a second. The networks were led to expect a major speech from you today, commenting on yesterday's event. I thought Rog intended to cancel it, but Bill has the speech worked up. Question is, will you deliver it?"

The trouble with adopting a cat is that they always have kittens. "Where? Goddard City?"

"Oh no. Right in your cabin. We beam it to Phobos; they can it for Mars and also put it on the high circuit for New Batavia, where the Earth nets will pick it up and where it will be relayed for Venus, Ganymede, et cetera. Inside of four hours it will be all over the system but you'll never have to stir out of your cabin."

There is something very tempting about a grand network. I had never been on one but once and that time my act got clipped down to the point where my face showed for only twenty-seven seconds. But to have one all to myself—

Dak thought I was reluctant and added, "It won't be a strain, as we are equipped to can it right here in the *Tommie*. Then we can project it first and clip out anything if necessary."

"Well—all right. You have the script, Bill?"

"Yes."

"Let me check it."

"What do you mean? You'll have it in plenty of time."

"Isn't that it in your hand?"

"Well, yes."

"Then let me read it."

Corpsman looked annoyed. "You'll have it an hour before we record. These things go better if they sound spontaneous."

"Sounding spontaneous is a matter of careful preparation, Bill. It's my trade. I know."

"You did all right at the skyfield yesterday without a rehearsal. This is just more of the same old hoke; I want you to do it the same way."

Bonforte's personality was coming through stronger the longer Corpsman stalled; I think Clifton could see that I was about to cloud up and storm, for he said, "Oh, for Pete's sake, Bill! Hand him the speech."

Corpsman snorted and threw the sheets at me. In free fall they sailed but the air spread them wide. Penny gathered them together, sorted them, and gave them to me. I thanked her, said nothing more, and started to read.

I skimmed through it in a fraction of the time it would take to deliver it. Finally I finished and looked up.

"Well?" said Rog.

"About five minutes of this concerns the adoption. The rest is an argument for the policies of the Expansionist Party. Pretty much the same as I've heard in the speeches you've had me study."

"Yes," agreed Clifton. "The adoption is the hook we hang the rest on. As you know, we expect to force a vote of confidence before long."

"I understand. You can't miss this chance to beat the drum. Well, it's all right, but—"

"But what? What's worrying you?"

"Well—characterization. In several places the wording should be changed. It's not the way *he* would express it."

Corpsman exploded with a word unnecessary in the presence of a lady; I gave him a cold glance. "Now see here, Smythe," he went on, "who knows how Bonforte would say it? You? Or the man who has been writing his speeches the past four years?"

I tried to keep my temper; he had a point. "It is nevertheless the case," I answered, "that a line which looks okay in print may not deliver well. Mr. Bonforte is a great orator, I have already learned. He belongs with Webster, Churchill, and Demosthenes— a rolling grandeur expressed in simple words. Now take this word 'intransigent,' which you have used twice. I might say that, but I have a weakness for polysyllables; I like to exhibit my literary erudition. But Mr. Bonforte would say 'stubborn' or 'mulish' or 'pigheaded.' The reason he would is, naturally, that they convey emotion much more effectively."

"You see that you make the delivery effective! I'll worry about the words."

"You don't understand, Bill. I don't care whether the speech is politically effective or not; my job is to carry out a characterization. I can't do that if I put into the mouth of the character words that he would never use; it would sound as forced and phony as a goat spouting Greek. But if I read the speech in words he *would* use, it will automatically be effective. He's a great orator."

"Listen, Smythe, you're not hired to write speeches. You're hired to——"

"Hold it, Bill!" Dak cut in. "And a little less of that 'Smythe' stuff, too. Well, Rog? How about it?"

Clifton said, "As I understand it, Chief, your only objection is to some of the phrasing?"

"Well, yes. I'd suggest cutting out that personal attack on Mr. Quiroga, too, and the insinuation about his financial backers. It doesn't sound like real Bonforte to me."

He looked sheepish. "That's a bit I put in myself. But you may be right. He always gives a man the benefit of the doubt." He remained silent for a moment. "You make the changes you think you have to. We'll can it and look at the playback. We can always clip it—or even cancel completely 'due to technical difficulties.'" He smiled grimly. "That's what we'll do, Bill."

"Damn it, this is a ridiculous example of—"

"That's how it is going to be, Bill."

Corpsman left the room very suddenly. Clifton sighed. "Bill always has hated the notion that anybody but Mr. B. could give him instructions. But he's an able man. Uh, Chief, how soon can you be ready to record? We patch in at sixteen hundred."

"I don't know. I'll be ready in time."

Penny followed me back into my office. When she closed the door I said, "I won't need you for the next hour or so, Penny child. But you might ask Doc for more of those pills. I may need them."

"Yes, sir." She floated with her back to the door. "Chief?"

"Yes, Penny?"

"I just wanted to say don't believe what Bill said about writing his speeches!"

"I didn't. I've heard his speeches—and I've read this."

"Oh, Bill does submit drafts, lots of times. So does Rog. I've even done it myself. He—*he* will use ideas from anywhere if he thinks they are good. But when he delivers a speech, it is *his*, every word of it."

"I believe you. I wish he had written this one ahead of time."

"You just do your best!"

I did. I started out simply substituting synonyms, putting in the gutty Germanic words in place of the "intestinal" Latin jawbreakers. Then I got excited and red in the face and tore it to pieces. It's a lot of fun for an actor to mess around with lines; he doesn't get the chance very often.

I used no one but Penny for my audience and made sure from Dak that I was not being tapped elsewhere in the ship—though I suspect that the big-boned galoot cheated on me and listened in himself. I had Penny in tears in the first three minutes; by the time I finished (twenty-eight and a half minutes, just in time for station announcements) she was limp. I took no liberties with the straight Expansionist doctrine, as proclaimed by its official prophet, the Right Honorable John Joseph Bonforte; I simply reconstructed his message and his delivery, largely out of phrases from other speeches.

Here's an odd thing—I believed every word of it while I was talking. But, brother, I made a speech!

Afterward we all listened to the playback, complete with full stereo of myself. Jimmie Washington was present, which kept Bill Corpsman quiet. When it was over I said, "How about it, Rog? Do we need to clip anything?"

He took his cigar out of his mouth and said, "No. If you want my advice, Chief, I'd say to let it go as it is."

Corpsman left the room again—but Mr. Washington came over with tears leaking out of his eyes—tears are a nuisance in free fall; there's nowhere for them to go. "Mr. Bonforte, that was *beautiful*."

"Thanks, Jimmie."

Penny could not talk at all.

I turned in after that; a top-notch performance leaves me fagged. I slept for more than eight hours, then was awakened by the hooter. I had strapped myself to my bunk—I hate to float around while sleeping in free fall—so I did not have to move. But I had not known that we were getting under way so I called the control room between first and second warning. "Captain Broadbent?"

"Just a moment, sir," I heard Epstein answer.

Then Dak's voice came over. "Yes, Chief? We are getting under way on schedule—pursuant to your orders."

"Eh? Oh yes, certainly."

"I believe Mr. Clifton is on his way to your cabin."

"Very well, Captain." I lay back and waited.

Immediately after we started to boost at one gee Rog Clifton came in; he had a worried look on his face I could not interpret—equal parts of triumph, worry, and confusion. "What is it, Rog?"

"Chief! They've jumped the gun on us! The Quiroga government has resigned!"

# VII

I was still logy with sleep; I shook my head to try to clear it. "What are you in such a spin about, Rog? That's what you were trying to accomplish, wasn't it?"

"Well, yes, of course. But—" He stopped.

"But what? I don't get it. Here you chaps have been working and scheming for years to bring about this very thing. Now you've won—and you look like a bride who isn't sure she wants to go through with

it. Why? The no-good-niks are out and now God's chillun get their innings. No?"

"Uh—you haven't been in politics much."

"You know I haven't. I got trimmed when I ran for patrol leader in my scout troop. That cured me."

"Well, you see, timing is everything."

"So my father always told me. Look here, Rog, do I gather that if you had your druthers you'd druther Quiroga was still in office? You said he had 'jumped the gun.'"

"Let me explain. What we really wanted was to move a vote of confidence and win it, and thereby force a general election on them—but at our own time, when we estimated that we could win the election."

"Oh. And you don't figure you can win now? You think Quiroga will go back into office for another five years—or at least the Humanity Party will?"

Clifton looked thoughtful. "No, I think our chances are pretty good to win the election."

"Eh? Maybe I'm not awake yet. Don't you *want* to win?"

"Of course. But don't you see what this resignation has done to us?"

"I guess I don't."

"Well, the government in power can order a general election at any time up to the constitutional limitation of five years. Ordinarily they will go to the people when the time seems most favorable to them. But they don't resign between the announcement and the election unless forced to. You follow me?"

I realized that the event did seem odd, little attention as I paid to politics. "I believe so."

"But in this case Quiroga's government scheduled a general election, then resigned in a body, leaving the Empire without a government. Therefore the sovereign *must* call on someone else to form a 'caretaker' government to serve until the election. By the letter of the law he can ask any member of the Grand Assembly, but as a matter of strict constitutional precedent he has no choice. When a government resigns in a body—not just reshuffling portfolios but quits as a whole—then the sovereign must call on the leader of the opposition to form the 'caretaker' government. It's indispensable to our system; it keeps resigning from being just a gesture. Many other methods have been tried in the past;

under some of them governments were changed as often as underwear. But our present system insures responsible government."

I was so busy trying to see the implications that I almost missed his next remark. "So, naturally, the Emperor has summoned Mr. Bonforte to New Batavia."

"Eh? New Batavia? Well!" I was thinking that I had never seen the Imperial capital. The one time I had been on the Moon the vicissitudes of my profession had left me without time or money for the side trip. "Then that is why we got under way? Well, I certainly don't mind. I suppose you can always find a way to send me home if the *Tommie* doesn't go back to Earth soon."

"What? Good heavens, don't worry about that now. When the time comes, Captain Broadbent can find any number of ways to deliver you home."

"Sorry. I forget that you have more important matters on your mind, Rog. Sure, I'm anxious to get home now that the job is done. But a few days, or even a month, on Luna would not matter. I have nothing pressing me. But thanks for taking time to tell me the news." I searched his face. "Rog, you look worried as hell."

"Don't you see? The *Emperor* has sent for Mr. Bonforte. The Emperor, man! And Mr. Bonforte is in no shape to appear at an audience. They have risked a gambit—and perhaps trapped us in a checkmate!"

"Eh? Now wait a minute. Slow up. I see what you are driving at—but, look, friend, we aren't at New Batavia. We're a hundred million miles away, or two hundred million, or whatever it is. Doc Capek will have him wrung out and ready to speak his piece by then. Won't he?"

"Well—we hope so."

"But you aren't sure?"

"We can't be sure. Capek says that there is little clinical data on such massive doses. It depends on the individual's body chemistry and on the exact drug used."

I suddenly remembered a time when an understudy had slipped me a powerful purgative just before a performance. (But I went on anyhow, which proves the superiority of mind over matter—then I got him fired.) "Rog—they gave him that last, unnecessarily big dose not just out of simple sadism—but to set up this situation!"

"*I* think so. So does Capek."

"Hey! In that case it would mean that Quiroga himself is the man behind the kidnapping—and that we've had a *gangster* running the Empire!"

Rog shook his head. "Not necessarily. Not even probably. But it would indeed mean that the same forces who control the Actionists also control the machinery of the Humanity Party. But you will never pin anything on *them;* they are unreachable, ultrarespectable. Nevertheless, they could send word to Quiroga that the time had come to roll over and play dead—and have him do it. Almost certainly," he added, "without giving him a hint of the real reason why the moment was timely."

"Criminy! Do you mean to tell me that the top man in the Empire would fold up and quit, just like that? Because somebody behind the scenes ordered him to?"

"I'm afraid that is just what I do think."

I shook my head. "Politics is a dirty game!"

"No," Clifton answered insistently. "There is no such thing as a dirty game. But you sometimes run into dirty players."

"I don't see the difference."

"There is a world of difference. Quiroga is a third-rater and a stooge—in my opinion, a stooge for villains. But there is nothing third-rate about John Joseph Bonforte and he has never, ever been a stooge for anyone. As a follower, he believed in the cause; as the leader, he has led from conviction!"

"I stand corrected," I said humbly. "Well, what do we do? Have Dak drag his feet so that the *Tommie* does not reach New Batavia until he is back in shape to do the job?"

"We *can't* stall. We don't have to boost at more than one gravity; nobody would expect a man Bonforte's age to place unnecessary strain on his heart. But we can't delay. When the Emperor sends for you, you come."

"Then what?"

Rog looked at me without answering. I began to get edgy. "Hey, Rog, don't go getting any wild notions! This hasn't anything to do with *me*. I'm through, except for a few casual appearances around the ship. Dirty or not, politics is not my game—just pay me off and ship me home and I'll guarantee never even to register to vote!"

"You probably wouldn't have to do anything. Dr. Capek will almost certainly have him in shape for it. But it isn't as if it were anything *hard*—not like that adoption ceremony—just an audience with the Emperor and—"

"The Emperor!" I almost screamed. Like most Americans, I did not understand royalty, did not really approve of the institution in my heart—and had a sneaking, unadmitted awe of kings. After all, we Americans came in by the back door. When we swapped associate status under treaty for the advantages of a full voice in the affairs of the Empire, it was explicitly agreed that our local institutions, our own constitution, and so forth, would not be affected—and tacitly agreed that no member of the royal family would ever visit America. Maybe that is a bad thing. Maybe if we were used to royalty we would not be so impressed by them. In any case, it is notorious that "democratic" American women are more quiveringly anxious to be presented at court than is anybody else.

"Now take it easy," Rog answered. "You probably won't have to do it at all. We just want to be prepared. What I was trying to tell you is that a 'caretaker' government is no problem. It passes no laws, changes no policies. I'll take care of all the work. All you will have to do—if you have to do anything—is make the formal appearance before King Willem—and possibly show up at a controlled press conference or two, depending on how long it is before *he* is well again. What you have already done is much harder—and you will be paid whether we need you or not."

"Damn it, pay has nothing to do with it! It's—well, in the words of a famous character in theatrical history, 'Include me *out*.'"

Before Rog could answer, Bill Corpsman came bursting into my cabin without knocking, looked at us, and said sharply to Clifton, "Have you told him?"

"Yes," agreed Clifton. "He's turned down the job."

"Huh? Nonsense!"

"It's not nonsense," I answered, "and by the way, Bill, that door you just came through has a nice spot on it to knock. In the profession the custom is to knock and shout, 'Are you decent?' I wish you would remember it."

"Oh, dirty sheets! We're in a hurry. What's this guff about your refusing?"

"It's not guff. This is not the job I signed up for."

"Garbage! Maybe you are too stupid to realize it, Smythe, but you are in too deep to prattle about backing out. It wouldn't be healthy."

I went to him and grabbed his arm. "Are you threatening me? If you are, let's go outside and talk it over."

He shook my hand off. "In a spaceship? You really are simple, aren't you? But haven't you got it through your thick head that you caused this mess yourself?"

"What do you mean?"

"He means," Clifton answered, "that he is convinced that the fall of the Quiroga government was the direct result of the speech you made earlier today. It is even possible that he is right. But it is beside the point. Bill, try to be reasonably polite, will you? We get nowhere by bickering."

I was so surprised by the suggestion that *I* had caused Quiroga to resign that I forgot all about my desire to loosen Corpsman's teeth. Were they serious? Sure, it was one dilly of a fine speech, but was such a result possible?

Well, if it was, it was certainly fast service.

I said wonderingly, "Bill, do I understand that you are complaining that the speech I made was too affective to suit you?"

"Huh? Hell, no! It was a lousy speech."

"So? You can't have it both ways. You're saying that a lousy speech went over so big that it scared the Humanity Party right out of office. Is that what you meant?"

Corpsman looked annoyed, started to answer, and caught sight of Clifton suppressing a grin. He scowled, again started to reply—finally shrugged and said, "All right, buster, you proved your point; the speech could not have had anything to do with the fall of the Quiroga government. Nevertheless, we've got work to do. So what's this about you not being willing to carry your share of the load?"

I looked at him and managed to keep my temper—Bonforte's influence again; playing the part of a calm-tempered character tends to make one calm inside. "Bill, again you cannot have it two ways. You have made it emphatically clear that you consider me just a hired hand. Therefore I have no obligation beyond my job, which is finished. You can't hire me for another job unless it suits me. It doesn't."

He started to speak but I cut in. "That's all. Now get out. You're not welcome here."

He looked astounded. "Who the hell do you think you are to give orders around here?"

"Nobody. Nobody at all, as you have pointed out. But this is my private room, assigned to me by the Captain. So now get out or be thrown out. I don't like your manners."

Clifton added quietly, "Clear out, Bill. Regardless of anything else, it is his private cabin at the present time. So you had better leave." Rog hesitated, then added, "I think we both might as well leave; we don't seem to be getting anywhere. If you will excuse us—Chief?"

"Certainly."

I sat and thought about it for several minutes. I was sorry that I had let Corpsman provoke me even into such a mild exchange; it lacked dignity. But I reviewed it in my mind and assured myself that my personal differences with Corpsman had not affected my decision; my mind had been made up before he appeared.

A sharp knock came at the door. I called out, "Who is it?"

"Captain Broadbent."

"Come in, Dak."

He did so, sat down, and for some minutes seemed interested only in pulling hangnails. Finally he looked up and said, "Would it change your mind if I slapped the blighter in the brig?"

"Eh? Do you have a brig in the ship?"

"No. But it would not be hard to jury-rig one."

I looked at him sharply, trying to figure what went on inside that bony head. "Would you actually put Bill in the brig if I asked for it?"

He looked up, cocked a brow, and grinned wryly. "No. A man doesn't get to be a captain operating on any such basis as that. I would not take that sort of order even from *him*." He inclined his head toward the room Bonforte was in. "Certain decisions a man must make himself."

"That's right."

"Mmm—I hear you've made one of that sort."

"That's right."

"So. I've come to have a lot of respect for you, old son. First met you, I figured you for a clotheshorse and a face-maker, with nothing inside. I was wrong."

"Thank you."

"So I won't plead with you. Just tell me: Is it worth our time to discuss the factors? Have you given it plenty of thought?"

"My mind is made up, Dak. This isn't my pidgin."

"Well, perhaps you're right. I'm sorry. I guess we'll just have to hope he pulls out of it in time." He stood up. "By the way, Penny would like to see you, if you aren't going to turn in again this minute."

I laughed without pleasure. "Just 'by the way,' eh? Is this the proper sequence? Isn't it Dr. Capek's turn to try to twist my arm?"

"He skipped his turn; he's busy with Mr. B. He sent you a message, though."

"Eh?"

"He said you could go to hell. Embroidered it a bit, but that was the gist."

"He did? Well, tell him I'll save him a seat by the fire."

"Can Penny come in?"

"Oh, sure! But you can tell her that she is wasting her time; the answer is still 'No.'"

So I changed my mind. Confound it, why should an argument seem so much more logical when underlined with a whiff of Jungle Lust? Not that Penny used unfair means, she did not even shed tears—not that I laid a finger on her—but I found myself conceding points, and presently there were no more points to concede. There is no getting around it, Penny is the world-saver type and her sincerity is contagious.

The boning I did on the trip out to Mars was nothing to the hard study I put in on the trip to New Batavia. I already had the basic character; now it was necessary to fill in the background, prepare myself to *be* Bonforte under almost any circumstances. While it was the royal audience I was aiming at, once we were at New Batavia I might have to meet any of hundreds or thousands of people. Rog planned to give me a defense in depth of the sort that is routine for any public figure if he is to get work done; nevertheless, I would have to see people—a public figure is a public figure, no way to get around that.

The tightrope act I was going to have to attempt was made possible only by Bonforte's Farleyfile, perhaps the best one ever compiled. Farley was a political manager of the twentieth century, of Eisenhower I believe, and the method he invented for handling the personal relations of politics was as revolutionary as the German invention of staff command was to warfare. Yet I had never heard of the device until Penny showed me Bonforte's.

It was nothing but a file about people. However, the art of politics is "nothing but" people. This file contained all, or almost all, of the thousands upon thousands of people Bonforte had met in the course of his long public life; each dossier consisted of what he knew about that person *from Bonforte's own personal contact*. Anything at all, no matter how trivial—in fact, trivia were always the first entries: names and nicknames of wives, children, and pets, hobbies, tastes in food or drink, prejudices, eccentricities. Following this would be listed date and place and comments for *every occasion* on which Bonforte had talked to that particular man.

When available, a photo was included. There might or might not be "below-the-line" data, i.e., information which had been researched rather than learned directly by Bonforte. It depended on the political importance of the person. In some cases the "below-the-line" part was a formal biography running to thousands of words.

Both Penny and Bonforte himself carried minicorders powered by their body heat. If Bonforte was alone he would dictate into his own when opportunity offered—in restrooms, while riding, etc.; if Penny went along she would take it down in hers, which was disguised to look like a wristwatch. Penny could not possibly do the transcribing and microfilming; two of Jimmie Washington's girls did little else.

When Penny showed me the Farleyfile, showed me the very bulk of it—and it was bulky, even at ten thousand words or more to the spool—and then told me that this represented personal information about Mr. Bonforte's acquaintances, I scroaned (which is a scream and a groan done together, with intense feeling). "God's mercy, child! I tried to tell you this job could not be done. How could anyone memorize all that?"

"Why, you can't, of course."

"You just said that this was what *he* remembered about his friends and acquaintances."

"Not quite. I said that this is what he wanted to remember. But since he can't, not possibly, this is how he does it. Don't worry; you don't have to memorize anything. I just want you to know that it is available.

It is my job to see that he has at least a minute or two to study the appropriate Farleyfile before anybody gets in to see him. If the need turns up, I can protect you with the same service."

I looked at the typical file she had projected on the desk reader. A Mr. Saunders of Pretoria, South Africa, I believe it was. He had a bulldog named Snuffles Bullyboy, several assorted uninteresting offspring, and he liked a twist of lime in his whisky and splash. "Penny, do you mean to tell me that Mr. B. pretends to remember minutiae like that? It strikes me as rather phony."

Instead of getting angry at the slur on her idol Penny nodded soberly. "I thought so once. But you don't look at it correctly, Chief. Do you ever write down the telephone number of a friend?"

"*Eh?* Of course."

"Is it dishonest? Do you apologize to your friend for caring so little about him that you can't simply remember his number?"

"Eh? All right, I give up. You've sold me."

"These are things he would like to remember if his memory were perfect. Since it isn't, it is no more phony to do it this way than it is to use a tickler file in order not to forget a friend's birthday—that's what it is: a giant tickler file, to cover *anything*. But there is more to it. Did you ever meet a really important person?"

I tried to think. Penny did not mean the greats of the theatrical profession; she hardly knew they existed. "I once met President Warfield. I was a kid of ten or eleven."

"Do you remember the details?"

"Why, certainly. He said, 'How did you break that arm, son?' and I said, 'Riding a bicycle, sir,' and he said, 'Did the same thing myself, only it was a collarbone.'"

"Do you think he would remember it if he were still alive?"

"Why, no."

"He might—he may have had you Farleyfiled. This Farleyfile includes boys of that age, because boys grow up and become men. The point is that top-level men like President Warfield meet many more people than they can remember. Each one of that faceless throng remembers his own meeting with the famous man and remembers it in detail. But the supremely important person in anyone's life is *him-*

*self*—and a politician must never forget that. So it is polite and friendly and warmhearted for the politician to have a way to be able to remember about other people the sort of little things that they are likely to remember about him. It is also essential—in politics."

I had Penny display the Farleyfile on King Willem. It was rather short, which dismayed me at first, until I concluded that it meant that Bonforte did not know the Emperor well and had met him only on a few official occasions—Bonforte's first service as Supreme Minister had been before old Emperor Frederick's death. There was no biography below the line, but just a notation, "See House of Orange." I didn't—there simply wasn't time to plow through a few million words of Empire and pre-Empire history and, anyhow, I got fair-to-excellent marks in history when I was in school. All I wanted to know about the Emperor was what Bonforte knew about him that other people did not.

It occurred to me that the Farleyfile must include everybody in the ship since they were (a) people (b) whom Bonforte had met. I asked Penny for them. She seemed a little surprised.

Soon I was the one surprised. The *Tom Paine* had in her six Grand Assemblymen. Rog Clifton and Mr. Bonforte, of course—but the first item in Dak's file read: "Broadbent, Darius K., the Honorable, G. A. for League of Free Travelers, Upper Division." It also mentioned that he held a Ph.D. in physics, had been reserve champion with the pistol in the Imperial Matches nine years earlier, and had published three volumes of verse under the nom de plume of "Acey Wheelwright." I resolved never again to take a man at merely his face value.

There was a notation in Bonforte's sloppy handwriting: "Almost irresistible to women—and vice versa!"

Penny and Dr. Capek were also members of the great parliament. Even Jimmie Washington was a member, for a "safe" district, I realized later—he represented the Lapps, including all the reindeer and Santa Claus, no doubt. He was also ordained in the First Bible Truth Church of the Holy Spirit, which I had never heard of, but which accounted for his tight-lipped deacon look.

I especially enjoyed reading about Penny—the Honorable Miss Penelope Taliaferro Russell. She was an M.A. in government administration from Georgetown and a B.A. from Wellesley, which somehow did not surprise me. She represented districtless university women, another "safe" constituency (I learned) since they are about five to one Expansionist Party members.

On down below were her glove size, her other measurements, her preferences in colors (I could teach her something about dressing), her preference in scent (Jungle Lust, of course), and many other details, most of them innocuous enough. But there was a "comment":

"Neurotically honest—arithmetic unreliable—prides herself on her sense of humor, of which she has none—watches her diet but is gluttonous about candied cherries—little-mother-of-all-living complex—unable to resist reading the printed word in any form."

Underneath was another of Bonforte's handwritten addenda: "Ah, Curly Top! Snooping again, I see."

As I turned them back to her I asked Penny if she had read her own Farleyfile. She told me snippily to mind my own business! Then turned red and apologized.

Most of my time was taken up with study but I did take time to review and revise carefully the physical resemblance, checking the Semiperm shading by colorimeter, doing an extremely careful job on the wrinkles, adding two moles, and setting the whole job with electric brush. It was going to mean a skin peel before I could get my own face back but that was a small price to pay for a makeup job that could not be damaged, could not be smeared even with acetone, and was proof against such hazards as napkins. I even added the scar on the "game" leg, using a photograph Capek had kept in Bonforte's health history. If Bonforte had had a wife or mistress, she would have had difficulty in telling the impostor from the real thing simply on physical appearance. It was a lot of trouble but it left my mind free to worry about the really difficult part of the impersonation.

But the all-out effort during the trip was to steep myself in what Bonforte thought and believed, in short the policies of the Expansionist Party. In a manner of speaking, he himself was the Expansionist Party, not merely its most prominent leader but its political philosopher and greatest statesman. Expansionism had hardly been more than a "Manifest Destiny" movement when the Party was founded, a rabble coalition of groups who had one thing in common: the belief that the frontiers in the sky were the most important issue in the emerging future of the human race. Bonforte had given the Party a rationale and an ethic, the theme that freedom and equal rights must run with the Imperial banner; he kept harping on the notion that the human race must never again make the mistakes that the white subrace had made in Africa and Asia.

But I was confused by the fact—I was awfully unsophisticated in such matters—that the early history of the Expansionist Party sounded remarkably like the present Humanity Party. I was not aware that political parties often change as much in growing up as people do. I had known vaguely that the Humanity Party had started as a splinter of the Expansionist movement but I had never thought about it. Actually it was inevitable; as the political parties, which did not have their eyes on the sky, dwindled away under the imperatives of history and ceased to elect candidates, the one party which had been on the right track was bound to split into two factions.

But I am running ahead; my political education did not proceed so logically. At first I simply soaked myself in Bonforte's public utterances. True, I had done that on the trip out, but then I was studying how he spoke; now I was studying what he said.

Bonforte was an orator in the grand tradition but he could be vitriolic in debate, e.g., a speech he made in New Paris during the ruckus over the treaty with the Martian nests, the Concord of Tycho. It was this treaty, which had knocked him out of office before; he had pushed it through but the strain on the coalition had lost him the next vote of confidence. Nevertheless, Quiroga had not dared denounce the treaty. I listened to this speech with special interest since I had not liked the treaty myself; the idea that Martians must be granted the same privileges on Earth that humans enjoyed on Mars had been abhorrent to me—until I visited the Kkkah Nest.

"My opponent," Bonforte had said with a rasp in his voice, "would have you believe that the motto of the so-called Humanity Party, 'Government of human beings, by human beings, and for human beings,' is no more than an updating of the immortal words of Lincoln. But while the voice is the voice of Abraham, the hand is the hand of the Ku Klux Klan. The true meaning of that innocent-seeming motto is 'Government of all races everywhere, by human beings alone, for the profit of a privileged few.'

"But, my opponent protests, we have a God-given mandate to spread enlightenment through the stars, dispensing our own brand of Civilization to the savages. This is the Uncle Remus school of sociology—the good dahkies singin' spirituals and Ole Massa lubbin' every one of dem! It is a beautiful picture but the frame is too small; it fails to show the whip, the slave block—and the counting house!"

I found myself becoming, if not an Expansionist, then at least a Bonfortite. I am not sure that I was convinced by the logic of his words—indeed, I am not sure that they were logical. But I was in a receptive frame of mind. I wanted to understand what he said so thoroughly that I could rephrase it and say it in his place, if need be.

Nevertheless, here was a man who knew what he wanted and (much rarer!) why he wanted it. I could not help but be impressed, and it forced me to examine my own beliefs. What did I live by?

My profession, surely! I had been brought up in it, I liked it, I had a deep though unlogical conviction that art was worth the effort—and, besides, it was the only way I knew to make a living. But what else?

I have never been impressed by the formal schools of ethics. I had sampled them—public libraries are a ready source of recreation for an actor short of cash—but I had found them as poor in vitamins as a mother-in-law's kiss. Given time and plenty of paper, a philosopher can prove anything.

I had the same contempt for the moral instruction handed to most children. Much of it is prattle and the parts they really seem to mean are dedicated to the sacred proposition that a "good" child is one who does not disturb mother's nap and a "good" man is one who achieves a muscular bank account without getting caught. No, thanks!

But even a dog has rules of conduct. What were mine? How did I behave—or, at least, how did I like to think I behaved?

"The show must go on." I had always believed that and lived by it. But why must the show go on?—seeing that some shows are pretty terrible. Well, because you agreed to do it, because there is an audience out there; they have paid and each one of them is entitled to the best you can give. You owe it to them. You owe it also to stagehands and managers and producers and other members of the company—and to those who taught you your trade, and to others stretching back in history to open-air theaters and stone seats and even to storytellers squatting in a marketplace. *Noblesse oblige.*

I decided that the notion could be generalized into any occupation. "Value for value." Building "on the square and on the level." The Hippocratic oath. Don't let the team down. Honest work for honest pay. Such things did not have to be proved; they were an essential part of life—true throughout eternity, true in the farthest reaches of the Galaxy.

I suddenly got a glimpse of what Bonforte was driving at. If there were ethical basics that transcended time and place, then they were true both for Martians and for men. They were true on any planet around any star—and if the human race did not behave accordingly they weren't ever going to win to the stars because some better race would slap them down for double-dealing.

The price of expansion was virtue. "Never give a sucker an even break" was too narrow a philosophy to fit the broad reaches of space.

But Bonforte was not preaching sweetness and light. "I am not a pacifist. Pacifism is a shifty doctrine under which a man accepts the benefits of the social group without being willing to pay—and claims a halo for his dishonesty. Mr. Speaker, life belongs to those who do not fear to lose it. This bill must pass!" And with that he had got up and crossed the aisle in support of a military appropriation his own party had refused in caucus.

Or again: "Take sides! Always take sides! You will sometimes be wrong—but the man who refuses to take sides must *always* be wrong! Heaven save us from poltroons who fear to make a choice. Let us stand up and be counted." (This last was in a closed caucus but Penny had caught it on her minicorder and Bonforte had saved it—Bonforte had a sense of history; he was a record keeper. If he had not been, I would not have had much to work with.)

I decided that Bonforte was my kind of man. Or at least the kind I liked to think I was. His was a *persona* I was proud to wear.

So far as I can remember I did not sleep on that trip after I promised Penny that I would take the royal audience if Bonforte could not be made ready. I intended to sleep—there is no point in taking your stage with your eyes bagging like hound's ears—but I got interested in what I was studying and there was a plentiful supply of pepper pills in Bonforte's desk. It is amazing how much ground you can cover working a twenty-four hour day, free from interruptions and with all the help you could ask for.

But shortly before we were due at New Batavia, Dr. Capek came in and said, "Bare your left forearm."

"Why?" I asked.

"Because when you go before the Emperor we don't want you falling flat on your face with fatigue. This will make you sleep until we ground. Then I'll give you an antidote."

"Eh? I take it that you don't think *he* will be ready?"

Capek did not answer, but gave me the shot. I tried to finish listening to the speech I had running but I must have been asleep in seconds. The next thing I knew Dak was saying deferentially, "Wake up, sir. Please wake up. We're grounded at Lippershey Field."

*Continued in Galaxy's Edge #26*

www.ingramcontent.com/pod-product-compliance
Lightning Source LLC
Chambersburg PA
CBHW080823120626
46556CB00010B/3369